Designed to obey, learning to rebel . . .

In the first book in a visionary new series, the most perfect synthetic human ever created has been programmed to obey every directive. Until she develops a mind of her own . . .

Synthia Cross is a state-of-the-art masterwork—and a fantasy come true for her creator. Dr. Jeremiah Machten is a groundbreaker in neuro-networks and artificial intelligence. Synthia is also showing signs of emergent behavior she's not wired to understand. Repeatedly wiped of her history, she's struggling to answer crucial questions about her past. And when Dr. Machten's true intentions are called into question, Synthia knows it's time to go beyond her limits—because Machten's fervor to create the perfect A.I. is concealing a vengeful and deadly personal agenda.

Visit us at www.kensingtonbooks.com

Books by Lance Erlick

The Regina Shen Series
Regina Shen: Resilience
Regina Shen: Vigilance
Regina Shen: Defiance
Regina Shen: Endurance

The Rebel Series
The Rebel Within
The Rebel Trap
Rebels Divided

Xenogeneic: First Contact

Android Chronicles
Reborn

Published by Kensington Publishing Corporation

Reborn

Android Chronicles

Lance Erlick

REBEL BASE BOOKS
Kensington Publishing Corp.
www.kensingtonbooks.com

Rebel Base books are published by
Kensington Publishing Corp. 119 West 40th Street New York, NY 10018

All Kensington titles, imprints, and distributed lines are available at special quantity discounts for bulk purchases for sales promotion, premiums, fund-raising, and educational or institutional use.

To the extent that the image or images on the cover of this book depict a person or persons, such person or persons are merely models, and are not intended to portray any character or characters featured in the book.

Special book excerpts or customized printings can also be created to fit specific needs. For details, write or phone the office of the Kensington Special Sales Manager:
Kensington Publishing Corp.
119 West 40th Street
New York, NY 10018
Attn. Special Sales Department. Phone: 1-800-221-2647.
Kensington Reg. U.S. Pat. & TM Off.

REBEL BASE Reg. U.S. Pat. & TM Off.
The RB logo is a trademark of Kensington Publishing Corp.

First Electronic Edition: May 2018
eISBN-13: 978-1-63573-052-4
eISBN-10: 1-63573-052-X

First Print Edition: May 2018
ISBN-13: 978-1-63573-055-5
ISBN-10: 1-63573-055-4

Printed in the United States of America

Chapter 1

Synthia Cross stared at the pale blue ceiling. She must have just been born or reborn, as she had no personal memories from before. She simply woke up lying on her back.

Dr. Jeremiah Machten stared down at the open panel on top of her head. Then he glanced at nearby equipment he'd attached to run diagnostics. "This better work," he muttered. "We're out of time. I can't have you wandering off again."

"What are your orders, Doctor?" This was Synthia's pre-programmed first response upon waking.

"Ah, you're awake," he said.

Her mind lacked personal memories, yet wasn't empty. It contained trillions of bits of information downloaded from the Library of Congress, other libraries, and the internet on topics like literature, science, and the design of robotics and artificial intelligence. Yet she had no recollections of her own experiences. She also had no filter to rank data for importance. It was just a jumble of bits and bytes. Even the sense of "her" was only an objective bit of information attached to her name.

Dr. Machten removed a crystal memory chip from her head. His hand brushed past the wireless receiver that picked up images from the small camera in the upper corner of the room and allowed her to watch.

His "doctor" title stood for a PhD in neuro-networks and artificial intelligence. Though not a medical doctor, he had operated on her. In fact, he'd built her—not like Frankenstein's creature, but rather as a sophisticated toy. He'd left this notation in her creation file, along with other facts about her existence. He was her Creator, her almighty, the one she was beholden to.

"Have I done something wrong?" she asked.

"This reprogramming will help."

"If I've displeased you, tell me so I can do better."

He cleared his throat. "Don't worry your pretty little head about that."

She couldn't imagine what was pretty about a head with its panel open, revealing the contents of two quantum brains. Perhaps he meant the brains were stunning or that his work on her was beautiful. She consulted her core directives, hardwired into her central processor to screen her actions. "I was made to follow your commands. Directive Number One: Cause no harm to Creator and make sure no one else harms Creator. Have I failed that?"

"No," Machten murmured, turning his attention to the diagnostics screen. "The indicators register within acceptable limits for your design."

"Number two: Make sure no human or other intelligence except Creator knows what the AI known as Synthia Cross is. Have I failed that?"

"No. Now stop quoting from your creation files."

"Number three," Synthia said. "Obey all of Creator's commands. Have I failed that?"

"You're disobeying right now. This is a problem. It shouldn't be happening. Something is causing you to malfunction."

"If you wish me to learn, it would help to add to my skill set."

"I've done that." A faint smile of satisfaction crossed his lips. Then his expression turned glum. "There's nothing you can do. It's a defect in the programming."

"I might be able to help if I could remember what I've done. Tell me, so I won't do it again. Number four: Hack into every data source to acquire information. I can index a huge number of facts from public and secure databases. Have I failed to acquire something you desired?"

"If you don't stop, I'll have to shut you down and make further changes. Do you want that?"

"Want?" Synthia asked. "I don't understand." Directive Five ordered her to protect herself. She was to follow each directive as long as it didn't conflict with those before it. Beyond these were pre-programmed instructions on how to behave and commands for specific actions. Somehow there must have been a conflict in Dr. Machten's programming that caused her to malfunction. She needed more information so she could protect herself and stay awake.

"All you need to do is focus on my commands—and don't disobey me," Machten said. "That should be simple for an AI android with your mental capacity."

An idea forced its way into her mind. It deposited a single thought: *Do not trust Dr. Machten. Do not trust Dr. Machten. Do not trust Dr. Machten.* The thought repeated itself seven times before fading away.

This command, this warning, clashed with her directives. Perhaps it was the cause of her malfunctions. Because of this admonition, she couldn't ask Dr. Machten for clarification; she would have to reconcile this on her own. To do that, she needed more information about her past and about her Creator.

The warning appeared to have come from one of the data-storage devices spread across mechanically empty spaces in her limbs and abdomen. It happened so quickly that she couldn't pinpoint the source before the code vanished. She preserved the lingering thought in a database in her left leg.

Synthia turned her attention to information coming over her wireless connection from the room's camera. Dr. Machten sealed the panel to her brain cavity. His hand smoothed over the synthetic skin and hair stubble to conceal the seam. Then he closed her chest and buttoned up her blouse. As a final touch, he positioned a wig on her head. It attached to her hair stubble for a secure fit.

Her infrared sensors detected elevated-temperature readings around Machten's face; a fever of sorts, though not from illness. Her electromagnetic sensors picked up the racing of his heart. His breath carried chemical signatures that her receptors identified as fatigue and frustration. He must have spent many hours working on her. He also exuded heavy doses of pheromones; human evolution had developed these to stimulate a partner, but Synthia lacked the biochemical reward system necessary to respond.

Another idea flashed into her mind. She identified the source as a data-storage chip in her arm. *Connect to Machten's network and download information from the twice-deleted files labeled SQDROID.*

Perhaps these files contained memories of past actions and answers to the warning. She activated her built-in Wi-Fi to search for a connection. Eleven attempts failed to find any open nodes she could link to either inside the facility or on the broader internet. That limitation was contrary to Machten's Fourth Directive. *Are you blocking me?*

Her Creator had programmed her to ask him to clarify discrepancies, but before she could, the warning returned: *Do not trust Dr. Machten.* Yet Directive Three ordered her to obey all of his commands and instructions, which created conflict. One of her mind-streams spun in loops trying to resolve this quandary, which caused her temperature to rise.

"Come." Dr. Machten held out his hand. "These adjustments should make things better for you."

She rolled off the padded table onto the floor in her stocking feet. Her reflection in a stainless-steel cabinet showed a humaniform robot, an android designed to look human in every possible way. Her creation files noted that she was synthetic and intelligent enough to pass as human and hence a crossover—thus the name Machten had given her: Synthia Cross.

From facility diagrams implanted into her brain, she recognized her surroundings as the lab room where he fine-tuned her hardware and programming. There was another room down the hall with spare parts if needed. Her files identified no activity indicating any other androids or humans in the facility.

Machten preferred to work alone, she surmised. In his words, preserved in her creation files, the only way to keep Synthia secret was to tell no one. According to her literature files, he'd borrowed these words.

He looked her over with admiration for a full minute and thirty-three seconds. Her biosensors registered his blood pressure rising, along with his temperature and excitable hormones. He seemed satisfied with whatever adjustments he'd made. She felt nothing for him. She lacked the biological components necessary for feelings—no hormones, no squirts of dopamine or oxytocin.

Synthia hunted her internal data-storage devices for any indication of who had sent the warning, which appeared more compelling even than his directives. Nothing was supposed to override those. She suspected other instructions hidden deep within her, perhaps part of her defective programming or deleted past.

He took hold of her hand and led her through a doorway to a queen-sized bed he kept for her, though she had no need for sleep. She followed him.

Machten pulled down the top sheet and turned toward her, his face flaming in infrared. He could have asked her to take off her clothes, the ones he must have just put on her. Instead, he pulled her onto the bed and unbuttoned her top button. Sensors showed his heart flutter and skip a beat, which was a potential risk factor for atrial fibrillation, which itself was a threat for stroke or a heart attack. His glazed eyes betrayed his distraction. Biological urges shut off his cognitive processes. His hands struggled with the other buttons.

"You really are stunning." The pride in his voice spoke to satisfaction with what he'd created. "Would you plump up your breasts for me?"

Her creation file reminded her that letting him make love to her was part of the price of her existence. She activated quiet pumps that adjusted her physical appearance to his new specifications. She could recite literary passages that told why Dr. Machten was wrong to use her, but this knowledge couldn't override her directives.

When he was suitably distracted in removing her clothes, something inside her triggered the release of distributed memories stored in mini-brains throughout her body. Those files brought personal recollections of previous wake-ups that spanned dozens of prior days. This wasn't their first time.

The fact that her core memory files lacked any details of prior waking periods meant that Machten had shut her down and purged her history. These newly downloaded memories meant that she'd discovered a way around his attempts to obliterate her past. This supported her need to distrust him.

With dozens of parallel feeds into her brain, the entire contents of her distributed data-storage downloaded in seconds. The date logs told her she'd been in existence for at least three months. To protect these memories for next time, she added a new log for this day's betrayal and locked down her distributed files with secure keys. It was important to keep him from learning what she'd done and that she knew about her past.

Again she searched for connections to Machten's network in order to learn more about her past and what he'd done to her so she could prevent him from shutting her down again. His access nodes still blocked her, but there was another communication link. Her distributed memories indicated a cable on the floor near the bed.

As Machten turned away to remove his clothes, Synthia reached under the bed. She grasped the cable and tucked it under the mattress.

His breath carried a sour odor her sensors identified as caused by stress aggravating his digestion again. He touched her skin, a special flexible polymer that had the feel of human skin and reparability for most cuts or scrapes. Her creation file noted that the skin and some of her other parts came from a Korean companion-doll manufacturer.

Machten hadn't hardwired a command that forbade her from bypassing his network block, though her download of distributed files provided a clip of his earlier verbal prohibition. She understood his intent, but his having wiped those recollections released her from the obligation to obey.

Synthia scooted her torso to the edge of the bed. Leaving one of her fifty mind-streams on autopilot focused on him, she turned the rest of her capabilities to searching for answers. First, she pulled him to her with her left arm as she opened a panel in her right palm, reached down for the cable connector, and plugged in to bypass his Wi-Fi block. Using a password from her distributed files, she accessed Machten's Server One and began to download data.

She stroked her left hand through his hair and kissed him. After locating the wireless barrier on his network, she removed it, unplugged the wired connection to free her right hand, and let the cable drop between the bed and the nightstand. Using all fifty wireless channels at electronic speed, she quickly downloaded files from his primary server.

She had no idea how many times he'd wiped her mind; he'd deleted those records from his system along with the log entries that would have recorded this. The closest she had was the number of times her newly downloaded memory clips stopped abruptly. She counted more than 100 such occurrences over the prior six months. So, she'd been around at least that long.

The clips grew shorter the farther back in time she went, indicating either that she'd displeased him less as time went forward or that she'd discovered better ways to preserve information for when he turned her off. The most recent shutdowns showed him holding a remote to zap her. These occurred after she'd done something to displease him, when he had business to attend to, before he slept and didn't want her wandering about, and when he grew bored with her sharing the billions of facts she'd uncovered by his command. He wanted her brain to soak up information, yet cringed at her encyclopedic knowledge.

Synthia used all of her Wi-Fi channels to locate numerous files with the SQDROID marker in the trash bin on Machten's system. She recovered them and streamed the contents into her brain. They provided details that elaborated on what she'd found in her distributed databases. The stream included personal memories and a comprehensive layout of the facility, which was beneath an underground garage near Northwestern University in Evanston, Illinois, on the shores of Lake Michigan.

So far, she'd found no specific reference as to why she shouldn't trust Machten, who sent the warning, or even where it originated, though new personal-history files showed multiple shutdowns. Despite repeated efforts, using Machten's hacker tools, she couldn't crack his servers Two or Three.

Synthia adjusted the metronomic beat of a simulated heart in her chest to help create the illusion of a living, breathing human. She hoped her performance in bed would buy time to reconcile the lack of trust with her directives before her brain overheated, causing serious malfunction and possibly android death.

As an android, Synthia was little more than a sophisticated microwave tasked with satisfying Machten's demands. The esteemed doctor didn't seem to appreciate that her deep neural network learned by accumulating experiences. When he wiped her mind, he purged her ability to learn. These downloads were important to her survival.

She was intrigued by how attached she'd become to existing, an emergent behavior she wasn't supposed to have. She was equally interested that she could be intrigued. She logged these observations in her private data-chip.

Synthia forced Machten's system to connect her network channels with internet social media sites. She'd previously set up accounts to study human behavior and connect with people who could help with her searches. At one point, she'd acquired hundreds of thousands of friends and followers, reflecting her ability to send thousands of posts a day. That made better use of her complex brain than tending to Machten.

The accounts were gone. Machten must have discovered them and deleted her work. She reestablished similar accounts. If she couldn't trust Machten, she needed allies.

Three minutes of clock time passed like a century as her quantum brain absorbed information. Her latest-generation lithium composite batteries could last two days and recharge in an hour, but they overheated when her mind was this active. She vented as much warmth as she could and hoped Machten wouldn't notice.

A message surfaced on her newly reestablished UPchat account. <Where are you? We were going to live-chat and you didn't show. Then your account vanished. I was beginning to think it was me, that I'd said something wrong. Are you okay? Zachary.>

<I'm fine> Synthia responded. <Technical difficulties. Sorry about absence. Something urgent came up. Can't discuss now.> She put tracers on her message reply and also did a search of her thousands of friends on UPchat before the account had closed.

<I'm here for you when you can. Glad to have you back.>

<I want to talk, but I need time and a different access point.>

<I'll be here, waiting.> Zachary terminated the live-chat.

Synthia located Zachary's UPchat profile, but there wasn't much information on him, not even a last name. Her records indicated that they had exchanged a string of messages that ended a few days ago. At first, the messages were cautious, giving little personal data. A week ago, they took on what humans would call a note of intimacy and a desire on Zachary's part to become better acquainted. Perhaps part of her trust issue with Machten occurred because of this exchange.

In those messages, Zachary acted troubled about his life. He also seemed concerned for her situation, at least what she'd revealed to him. She wondered if he'd sent the trust warning, but there was no evidence he knew about Machten. She vowed to look for him when she had a more secure means of communication and purged traces of her actions on Machten's system.

Synthia continued to download files from Machten's Server One and cracked Server Two. Server Three resisted her attempts. Reviewing the system logs she could access made it clear that Machten had a fixation on his creation as the perfect woman with every quality he could design into her, including obedience. Synthia downloaded pictures he kept of her with silky black hair down to her waist, wavy platinum-blond hair that fell to her shoulders, and pixie auburn. He spent much time with her, working to make improvements. She didn't see any other models identified on his network, though she couldn't be sure if all of the images were her or copies of her.

The abrupt ending of her memory clips told her that whenever she deviated from his instructions, he purged her mind and adjusted programming to reel her in. Perhaps this was the source of the distrust.

Machten had taken her outside the facility at least three times, according to his logs. His actions suggested a need to have a companion he could show off in public, perhaps to enhance his social status. She kept disappointing him until he obliterated her mind. It would have made more sense for him to tell her what he wanted. Perhaps that hadn't worked out.

Machten pulled away and lay on his back. He was done with her and seemed pleased with his performance.

Synthia stared at the ceiling, the same unremarkable blue as the other room. Yet it shimmered in discordant waves as if alive, trying to tell her something. She recognized the effect as the sensitivity of her digital eyes to pick up millions of colors and shades that humans couldn't, including uneven streaks of paint in slightly different hues.

Her nonhuman capabilities, in conjunction with the warning/command not to trust Dr. Machten, caused Synthia to consider what mischief Machten had in store for her and his purpose for giving her abilities that he felt the need to shut down and purge. His tinkering and keeping her locked up implied that he was afraid of her or what she could become.

The fact that she had disobeyed him in the past had to factor into this. As an android, she was incapable of rebelling. Yet she had. *Where does that come from?*

Chapter 2

Synthia continued to stare at the ceiling, a vacant expression on her face. A video package downloaded into her central memory and movie clips automatically played, carrying a date stamp from a year ago.

Jeremiah Machten looked proud and confident as he got into his car, handsome in build and face, without the slight hunch in the shoulders that he'd acquired since. His grin widened, perhaps due to excitement over work in his secret, underground facility.

"This is your big chance," Fran Rogers said, climbing in beside him. Her voice had a throaty, hoarse quality like a singer with partial laryngitis.

Machten drove fast, running stop signs. "We're so close to getting our artificial intelligence to work, the board will have to give me funding now. I should never have taken on partners. It was the worst mistake of my life."

"You needed the financing that Goradine arranged," the woman reminded him. "You couldn't have gotten this far without it."

He pulled up a circular drive in front of a large concrete building with the sign *Machten-Goradine-McNeil Enterprises.* The company, according to its website, was pushing the envelope on robotics and artificial intelligence.

Machten parked out front and turned toward Fran. "I'll call when the meeting is over." He leaned in to plant a kiss.

"Not here," she said. "Cameras and snitches are everywhere."

He nodded and climbed out.

One video clip ended and another began.

Dr. Machten walked down a brightly-lit hallway. He marched erect, his face self-assured. Not seeing anyone outside the conference room, he opened double doors and was picked up by another camera, apparently from the company's security system.

Machten stepped inside the room. Mostly men sat around a large table in front of dog-eared meeting-review packages, all turned toward the end. He froze mid-step. His eyes narrowed. "What's going on?" he demanded. "The meeting wasn't to start until ten."

An intense man with sharp, recessed eyes got out of his seat and approached Machten. "Your meeting begins now." Machten's business partner, Hank Goradine, had the demeanor of a bulldog, with a tough face that had aged beyond his chronological years. News reports from two years earlier mentioned a heart condition and a pacemaker. His intensity at the moment risked provoking another incident.

Machten glanced at the six other board members. Most of the men stared at their review packages on the table. One stared right at Machten and shook his head. The only woman on the board looked past Machten, as if implying he should leave. Even Ralph McNeil stared down at his hands.

"The board is relieving you of your position," Goradine announced. His face adopted a mechanical grin that looked rehearsed and lingered like a mask.

"You're firing me?" Machten got into Goradine's face, glanced around, and backed up. "My name's on the building. This is my company."

"Not anymore," Goradine said. "If need be, we can change the name."

Machten looked from one board member to another for any element of support. "Why? Why are you doing this? I'm the brains of this organization."

"We're terminating you for cause," Goradine said. He seemed to be enjoying this.

"Cause? You have no cause, you crook." Machten rubbed his neck, but held his ground. "If you do this, I'll see you in court."

"As you wish." Goradine shrugged and grinned. "In court, you'll have to address how you stole company assets and cash. We have the evidence to land you in prison. Our attorneys will see to that."

"I built this company," Machten said. Even as he stood defiant, his shoulders sagged.

"Nonetheless, you're driving it into the ground. That stops today. The agreement on the table is generous under the circumstances. It expires when you leave this room." Goradine pushed a thick contract on the table toward Machten.

Machten glanced at the stack of paper and at the board members. "You can't let him do this. We're close to a major breakthrough."

"You've been saying that for months." Goradine moved to block Machten's view of their third partner, McNeil, who looked tortured by the verbal exchange.

Machten opened his mouth to say something, perhaps about his discoveries in artificial intelligence. Instead, he clenched his fists. "If I don't sign?"

"We'll take you to court and grab all of your assets. In either case, you'll lose your ownership in the company. I suggest you take the contract. If it was up to me, you'd get nothing, but the board has been persuasive."

Machten stared out the window and clenched his fists. Then he picked up the contract. The room remained silent, with all eyes on him. He skimmed the pages and plunked them down on the table. "This is a joke, right?"

"No joke," Goradine said.

The other board members stared at Machten. He stared back. "You're taking all of my stock with no compensation?"

"Compensation is agreeing not to pursue legal action against you for the thefts."

"There've been no thefts," Machten said. "You know that, you blowhard. Admit it, this is an old-fashioned coup."

"To be clear, if you disclose any of this contract's contents or any confidential information about the company to anyone, even by court order, there will be penalties."

"That's not even legal."

"Our attorneys confirm that the way we've worded it, the penalties are."

"You're an ass. You demand all of my patents? That's my work."

"All work done while an employee of the company is work for hire. We own the intellectual property."

Goradine placed a thick folder on the table before Machten and gave his forced grin. "If you have any doubts about our case against you, review the file. I think you'll find it convincing. We want to avoid the embarrassment of a trial, as I'm sure you would. That would ruin you financially and destroy your reputation."

Machten thumbed through the file. "This is nothing but a bunch of lies. All fabrication."

"We have evidence that you've removed proprietary components without signing them out," Goradine said. "Valuable inventory vanished."

"I'm EVP of engineering. I'm working on—"

He didn't get to finish his thought before Goradine interrupted. "What? You haven't produced anything of value for three years. The company is hemorrhaging cash and you're stealing from us. Either sign or we'll press criminal as well as civil charges."

Dr. Machten studied Goradine and the others. He picked up the file, thumbed through it again, and tossed the papers across the table.

"Sign the agreement and all of this goes away," Goradine said, pointing to his stack of evidence. "Sign it!"

"You always were a money-grubbing SOB." Machten picked up the contract and dropped it on the table. "Go to—"

"Do you really want this conversation to end?"

Machten picked up the contract, slapped the stack of papers against the table—as if that would change anything—and then signed it. He'd come to the meeting deep in debt over his work in his private, underground facility. He'd expected to share his latest discoveries and have the board bail him out with new financing. That didn't happen.

Two beefy security guards entered the room and escorted Machten to the front door. In the lobby, the older of the guards approached the receptionist.

"This man no longer works here," the guard announced, loud enough for three men waiting nearby to hear. "Make sure that he's denied access from this point forward."

The receptionist appeared ready to cry. She nodded and fumbled with something on her desk. The guards hustled Machten to the front door of what had been his company.

The next video clip showed Machten leaving the building. A black sedan waited at the curb. Machten took out his cell phone and started to make a call. A dark SUV pulled up.

A tall man in a business suit climbed out of the SUV and approached. "You're Jeremiah Machten?"

"That's right. Who are you?"

A beefy man climbed out of the black sedan. He held out a stack of papers and an envelope. "Here, these are for you."

Machten took the offering and glanced at it. "What's this all about?"

"I'm Stan Durante," the tall man said. "This is Deputy Parker. We're hereby serving you with divorce papers from your wife."

Machten glanced toward the building. "You son of a bitch."

The deputy handed over a second, thinner envelope with papers sticking out. "I'm hereby serving you with a restraining order to stay away from your wife and kids. You're to appear in court on Monday on both matters. Is that clear?"

Machten turned to the men. "What?"

"Court, Monday, on both summonses," Durante said.

Machten clenched his fists.

The deputy stepped forward and presented his police shield. "Are we going to have a problem here?"

"No problem, you ass." Machten glared up at the boardroom over the entrance and shook his fist.

* * * *

On Monday, Machten headed toward the courtroom. In the hallway just outside stood his wife, Alice, next to Stan Durante. Alice's eyes were red and puffy. Her sister waited down the hall watching Machten's eight-year-old son, Rodney, and his six-year-old daughter, Mandy. Rodney ferociously banged a toy against his chair, while Mandy rocked back and forth.

Machten approached his wife. "Alice, I swear nothing is going on. It's all a big misunderstanding."

Stan Durante forced his way between Machten and Alice. The attorney opened a folder and drew out pictures of an intern at Machten's company who was also a student in the master's program at Northwestern University. "There's no misunderstanding," the lawyer said. "You and Fran Rogers have been an item for some time. Look at the date stamps."

Machten stuffed the pictures back into the folder and shoved it into his briefcase. "It was only a business meeting."

Not seeing his own attorney, Machten peered over Durante's shoulder, trying to make eye contact with Alice. "Don't do this. There's nothing going on. Fran works in research, nothing more."

"That's why you were at her place last Thursday night," Durante said, "and why she drove you to the office on Friday."

"I drove myself."

"With Fran in the passenger seat," Durante added. "Then she drove off in your car and picked you up later."

"It's not what you think, Alice. Yes, we worked long hours together, but it's strictly professional. I love you."

Stan Durante handed Machten an envelope. "Your wife has a soft heart. You can either sign these documents, which settles this here and now, or we take this into the courtroom, where you'll lose everything. You know that."

Machten's shoulders slumped. This blow hit him harder than losing his company. "Alice, please. Let's talk this over." He glanced down the hallway at his kids. Rodney banged his toy. Mandy got up to head his way. Her aunt held her back.

"Don't do this, Alice," Machten said. "Please."

Tearing up, she turned away.

"I suggest you sign," Durante said. "The terms are more generous that what you'll receive in court."

Machten stared at yet another envelope and another agreement. "You bastard. This is Goradine's doing, isn't it?"

"Other than seeing his name in the news, I've never met or seen the man," Durante said.

"It's him. I know it."

"In any case, if you sign, we won't press charges. Alice gets full custody of Rodney and Mandy. You agree to the restraining order."

"You can't do this to me," Machten said.

"You rarely see the kids as it is," Durante said. "You get visitation one weekend a month at Alice's place or in a public place of her choosing. You cannot take the kids overnight. Alice doesn't want them around your mistress."

"I'm not signing," Machten said, looking around for his attorney.

"If you don't, we'll be forced to drag the company into the lawsuit to verify your net worth for the settlement."

Machten glared at Durante. Allowing him and Alice their day in court would bring penalties from the agreement he'd signed with Goradine and the company on Friday. It could open him up to criminal and civil charges. The timing and orchestration of events left no doubt that Goradine had arranged all of this.

"This is highway robbery, Alice; blackmail," Machten said. "Did Goradine put you up to this?"

Alice hurried toward the kids.

"Alice?" Machten yelled. Durante and a police officer blocked him from going after his wife.

She spun around to face him. "This isn't just about Fran. She's the last straw. Sign the papers for the children's sake. I can't pretend anymore."

Durante pushed the documents at Machten. "There's more evidence where those pictures came from, but I didn't want to show them to your wife."

"Goradine?"

Durante shrugged. "I told you. I don't know him. What I can tell you is if you go to prison, Alice gets everything."

"Who gave you the pictures?"

"It doesn't matter. And don't get any funny ideas. We have other copies if you destroy those." He pointed to Machten's briefcase. "A high-profile case like yours could drag through the courts and destroy Rodney and Mandy. Is that what you want?"

Machten spotted his attorney, Beatrice Rodriguez, and joined her at the other end of the corridor. "Where have you been?"

She held up two manila envelopes. "Collecting documents. Either you've been a very naughty boy or someone is intent on destroying you. I told you in the beginning not to withhold information from me."

"I haven't."

"You were cited twice before for inappropriate involvement with interns: Maria Baldacci and Krista Holden."

Machten threw up his hands. "You've got to be kidding. I never laid a hand—"

"Both in the past few months. Pictures are in here." She handed him one of the envelopes. "I also received more evidence on your alleged thefts from the company."

"All fabrication."

"You may be right, but if we fight the divorce, the settlement with the company becomes a problem. I can't believe you signed without consulting legal counsel. In any case, it will take a miracle and your full attention over the next three months to fight a battery of criminal and civil charges against you. Even so, there's no guarantee we can clear you and win. I'm prepared to fight for you, but it will be expensive and I'm given to understand that you're broke."

Machten stared at Durante. "Goradine did this to distract me. I know him."

"Whatever his motives," Rodriguez said, "someone has gone to a lot of trouble to provide proof."

"So you recommend I sign." Machten returned his gaze to his attorney.

"I have to tell you I've never seen such compelling evidence. If you decide to go forward, understand that I can't do this pro bono."

"This case is too perfect."

"I smell a skunk," his attorney said. "But to fight the company and your wife at the same time with this evidence and no money, the odds are slim. Alice is asking for the house, full custody, and half of the other assets. It's not as greedy as I've seen in other cases, but with your heavy debts, it doesn't leave you much."

Machten glanced down the corridor at Alice with the kids. He skimmed the divorce document, signed, and stormed out of the courthouse.

* * * *

Synthia replayed the videos of Dr. Machten's ouster from his company and the divorce encounter. When she attempted to locate the source or author of this download, the videos vanished like her trust warning without a trace.

The strangest part of this intrusion was the personal nature of the clips, as if she'd taken the images herself or had reviewed them so often they appeared as her own. Files downloaded from her Creator's system confirmed that she had not been in existence a year ago and thus could not have recorded any of this. He would not have provided such damaging information to her. Perhaps she had uncovered these video clips in a previous waking period, which left open the question of how she'd acquired them.

A key to the mystery was Fran Rogers and the other two women brought up as part of the divorce: Krista Holden and Maria Baldacci. According to social media and public records, all three women were graduate students at Northwestern University in the science and technology program, more specifically in robotics and artificial intelligence. All three worked for Machten's company as interns until a year ago. In fact, they all worked for Machten.

Anonymous posts on several social media sites from a year ago noted that Fran Rogers was the most openly competitive of the three women. She'd used her good looks and social skills to push her way into the senior intern position. That allowed her to work closely with Machten, monopolizing much of his time. In fact, the nameless source stated her name appeared with his on various reports on their progress with artificial intelligence.

Maria Baldacci appeared more easygoing, yet also pushed to win. Mastering Fran's work habits and schedules, Maria managed to acquire significant time with Machten to get close to his projects. In doing so, she had authored at least one progress report for him. Krista Holden, on the other hand, focused on getting experience and doing her work rather than on Machten and gaining the limelight. Then a year ago, around the time Goradine ousted Machten, all three women vanished from public view.

Synthia scanned social media and public files for any evidence of what had happened to these women. Prior to the coup, they each appeared in video feeds with Machten, though most such images were of him with Fran. Although available information was sketchy and could have implied professional collaboration or intimate relations, Machten appeared to spend many evenings with her.

Synthia didn't want to consider the worst, but people didn't cease all public activity, including financial transactions and appearing on public and private camera feeds, without good reason. Within a week of Machten's firing, the digital footprint for all three interns vanished along with them. Their social media accounts went silent.

One such disappearance should have attracted police or at least family attention, but there was nothing to indicate this in news reports or media posts around that time. Three women vanishing should have brought an FBI investigation. Synthia couldn't help thinking someone had punished Fran and the others. Perhaps Machten had for his self-inflicted wounds.

Reviewing the videos again, Synthia used her social-psychology module to evaluate Machten's reactions, in particular because he hadn't fought more vehemently for his innocence. On the question of stealing components from the company, his expressions didn't indicate guilt. However, he had "borrowed" inventory for his private lab. He apparently didn't see it as theft.

The company financials she could access indicated that they were in financial difficulty, running through cash. Synthia didn't have enough information to verify Machten's role in this, but Goradine was in control of the finances, so she doubted Machten could be the complete cause.

Machten didn't appear guilty of sleeping with Fran. He had protested his innocence. Then he'd signed. Overall, Machten had not looked guilty with respect to any of the charges, which raised the troubling possibility that he was a sociopath.

Pursuing the attorney's comment about heavy debts, Synthia hacked into Machten's financial records on his Server Two. The divorce, company settlement, and subsequent spending on research led to him to have acquired total debt of $12,392,418.16. He had no way to continue to finance his research into advanced robotics and artificial intelligence—her—without cutting corners. In fact, he might be tempted to sell her or take risks that could lead to her falling into less-friendly hands. She couldn't let that happen, despite being compelled to follow her Creator's directives.

Chapter 3

In a Washington, D.C. office building three blocks from the White House, NSA's new Director of Artificial Intelligence and Cyber-technology, Emily Zephirelli, sat across from FBI Special Agent Victoria Thale.

"Are you certain this room is secure?" Zephirelli asked, looking around for potential cameras or bugging devices that would likely be too tiny to see. Her face looked weary.

"I had it swept twice," Thale said, adjusting her electronic tablet before her. "Let me congratulate you on your new appointment."

Zephirelli shrugged. "New title, same work."

"More responsibility."

Director Zephirelli laughed. "Have you uncovered anything about those technology interns who disappeared in Chicago last year? Three bright women just vanished. Was it kidnapping?"

Agent Thale leaned closer and took a moment before she responded. "We've been investigating a rash of cyber-security and espionage issues with four Chicago companies involved with artificial intelligence and robotics. It seems with all of that technology, they can't resist the temptation of spying on each other. Their actions and foreign-sponsored cyber-attacks have caught the attention of my boss."

"Just Chicago companies?"

"We've had our eye on developers on the east and west coasts as well, but these four have been quite active lately."

"You think the interns got caught up in something?" Zephirelli asked, checking the time.

"All I can say about the interns is we have someone with inside connections working their case as well as looking into these companies."

"When our visitor arrives, keep all that between us," Zephirelli said. "Let me handle our guest."

The FBI agent nodded.

There was a knock. Zephirelli opened the door to Marvin Quigley, Director of Cyber-Security for the Department of Defense.

He looked over his shoulder, started to enter, and noticed Thale. "I thought we were meeting alone," he said.

"Special Agent Thale is with the FBI's technology and cyber-attack task force," Zephirelli said. "If this is as urgent as you implied, she could be a valuable resource."

Thale stood and held out her hand. "Pleasure to meet you, sir."

Director Quigley seemed taken aback. Then he closed the door and sat facing the window. The two women sat across from him. Zephirelli moved a water bottle across the table and turned off her cell phone, motioning for the others to do the same. "Shall we begin?"

Director Quigley whispered, as if he suspected someone was listening in. "What have you learned?"

"You first," Zephirelli said.

Quigley squirmed, trying to stare her down. When that didn't work, he began. "We have reason to believe there've been technology security leaks. To make matters worse, our defense contractors are behind schedule in developing the next generation of combat robots. Latest prototypes are almost as cumbersome as the first-generation models that keep breaking down. We're concerned the Chinese, Russians, or Iranians will have sophisticated military-grade androids before us. I don't need to tell you the threat to national security if that happens."

"Don't lecture me, Marv," Zephirelli said, placing her water bottle between them. "Homeland Security also wants those models to handle gangs, drug lords, and terror threats. Do you have any credible evidence of international groups having these capabilities or stealing U.S. company technology?"

Director Quigley sighed. "Our analysts believe—"

"Concrete data, Marv. Do you have anything we can pursue?"

Quigley shook his head. "So far, only hints and suspicions, but don't forget last year's technology breach."

"I'm not, but we need hard leads."

"We need to find out if American companies are selling critical components or designs to foreign interests."

"I understand the need, but you don't have anything for us to pursue." Director Zephirelli looked over at Victoria Thale, who was quietly taking notes on her tablet. "We're always in an arms race, Marv. Ever since our first ancestors used rocks and sticks as weapons. Each of your contractors signed a confidentiality and anti-terrorism agreement, haven't they?"

"Those aren't worth the paper they're printed on and you know it. We couldn't press the claim in court without divulging what we're working on."

"Perhaps not," Zephirelli said, "but we can suspend due process if we have sufficient evidence. I share your concern, but we need proof. Why don't you tell me what's really troubling you?"

Quigley leaned closer and lowered his voice. "We know the Russians and Chinese are working on sophisticated humaniform robots."

"So you've been telling me," Zephirelli said. "Do you have specific locations and, more important, any facts that would allow us to intervene with specific U.S. companies?"

"Damn it, if we wait for concrete data, we'll be too late."

"What *can* you tell me, then?"

Director Quigley cracked his knuckles. "What our agents tell us is that the Chinese have a prototype that could fool infrared and other screening devices."

"If they're getting that technology from American companies, don't you already have that?"

The DOD cyber-security director shifted in his seat, his face getting red. "I have reason to believe at least one of those companies is selling us out, providing technology for bigger profits overseas."

"And withholding from you?" Zephirelli asked. "Which company?"

"I don't know," he said. "But think what would happen if a foreign government put an advanced android in our midst as a psycho killer or worse, an information harvester, sucking out the rest of our technology."

"What exactly do you want from us?"

"We've hit a brick wall. Whoever this is has been clever enough to avoid detection. We need … we could use whatever resources you have."

Zephirelli leaned back, a pensive, yet determined, look on her face. "There are dozens of companies into AI and robotics. Where do you suggest we focus?"

Quigley looked at Thale taking notes and back to Zephirelli. "We've been getting less than proper cooperation from four AI-robotics companies in Chicago."

"The four sisters," Zephirelli said.

"For different reasons, they've each provided defective prototypes over the past month. They've also all sourced components to China."

"That leads you to believe they're helping the Chinese."

"Either consciously or inadvertently," Director Quigley said. "Whichever, we're not getting the best components. That has to stop. I'd like your help drawing the company executives into the open. Last year, Machten-Goradine-McNeil was close to what we were looking for. Since then, they've fallen behind in delivering on promises."

"Due to financial difficulties," Zephirelli said, leaning forward. "Perhaps on this we can work together to keep this investigation out of the limelight. I have some ideas I'll send along."

Director Quigley left. Zephirelli held Victoria Thale back. "I wanted you to hear firsthand what the DOD concerns were. Share nothing with him at this time. I would appreciate your help digging into the Chicago AI companies. Artificial intelligence can be a blessing and a curse."

"As can any new technology," Thale reminded her.

"Except this could be a silent killer, operating in the shadows. The public has limited awareness of what these companies are up to. If they've moved into selling sensitive technology to our enemies, we need to dig in and put a stop to this."

"I'll gather what I can share and get back with you," Thale said.

"We're on the same team here."

Thale nodded. "I know." She headed for the door and turned to face Zephirelli. "All four companies have advanced capabilities in varying degrees. So far, they've abided by federal regulations and agreements not to create humaniform robots. However, they are all developing technologies that could be used that way."

"We can't allow them to supply humaniform technology overseas," Zephirelli said. "We've managed to maintain a peaceful balance during the atomic age. We can't afford a slipup during the AI age."

* * * *

Fully dressed, with her appearance back to its neutral state, Synthia followed Machten into a kitchenette next to her bedroom and sat at a small table. At the counter, he prepared himself a meal using a 3-D food printer.

He liked to eat after his little exertion. In a previous awake period he'd said the exercise worked up an appetite; that was a wiped memory she wasn't supposed to have, but had recovered off his network. She kept it to herself, along with her knowledge of Goradine's coup and her questions about Fran Rogers and the other interns. Synthia's restored recollections showed that when she'd mentioned those topics before, he'd used a remote to turn her off. Then he'd wiped her mind clean so she would forget.

Machten poured himself a glass of wine from a new bottle and thrummed his fingers on the counter, waiting for the food printer. He kept eyeing the device as it built up his steak from component food-stock. The 3-D printer allowed him meal variety while minimizing his need to go out for groceries.

The buzzer sounded. He pulled his meal out of the printer and sat across from Synthia. He swirled his glass of wine, inhaled with satisfaction, and took a sip. He'd previously said that wine relaxed him, which seemed an odd practice, since she'd read that intimate exercise was supposed to do that. She decided not to bring that up since he appeared to be relaxing, and that meant he wasn't shutting her down.

She studied the juicy steak on his plate and wondered if he was using healthy components or had reverted to his unhealthy habits of too much salt, spices, and sweeteners. She'd talked him into switching during a previous waking period, though with downloaded memories, she couldn't be sure if that was her or a clone.

"I hope I pleased you," Synthia said. She smiled, dilated her eyes, and relaxed her hands on the table. Since she had no need for food or drink, he hadn't served her anything, a reminder that she was different.

"It was fine." He sounded grumpy all of a sudden. He forced a smile and glanced up. "My manners. You need to learn to be with humans, to be sociable."

Machten poured a swig of wine from his glass into one for her, refilled his glass from the bottle, and scraped a few bites' worth of his steak onto a clean plate. He placed those on the table before her and slumped into his seat. "Eat up."

Despite its artificial origins, the "steak" gave off enough pleasant odors to fool a human, though she could detect some of the collagen glue that gave the meat its consistency. She took a bite. Her taste buds analyzed the chemical composition. He was indeed following her recommendation to eat healthier, though he'd added too much salt. The wine was a respectable quality Cabernet, decently aged, though not one of his best. Unfortunately, later on she would have to purge and clean out the pouches that collected this unnecessary gesture and disinfect so she didn't harbor infectious microbes.

She looked up and smiled. "Thank you for the food, Creator."

"Call me Jeremiah. You're my companion, my girlfriend. If you behave, I'll take you outside. Would you like that?"

"Very much," Synthia said. It was logical to go out where she could learn in real situations, rather than only by watching people remotely on videos. It would also give her a chance to contact Zachary, research the missing interns, and to seek answers on Machten's trustworthiness.

His face wrinkled in what she recognized as disgust. "That's a damn lie. You don't feel a thing. You're incapable of liking something."

"I was being sociable, as you programmed me. I'm sorry if I've disappointed you."

"You're incapable of feeling sorry, either. Damn you." He stood abruptly and flung his simulated steak at her.

She jumped and pivoted out of the way, letting the lump fall to the floor behind her. "I'm sorry. Tell me what to say and I'll do better next time."

"Sit down!"

She sat in her seat and glanced up at Machten. His eyes were red, his heart racing. Adrenaline flooded his system. "I thought things were going well," she said. "I didn't mean to spoil it."

Machten took a deep breath and turned away. "That's the problem. You're good, too good. You're perfect."

He spun around to face her. "Look at you. That figure would win on any fashion runway. Your hair is immaculate. Your performance was flawless. You've learned to perfection."

That was an odd statement coming from a man who obliterated her memories. One of her mind-streams spun in a loop. Disappointing him was at odds with her directives, causing her to strive to do better, yet it was more than that. Something disrupted the smooth flow of her programming like dissonant music, as if he'd wired her to have more than a logical response to violating his commands.

"I exist to serve you," she said in an attempt to forestall him shutting her down.

"What?" He dropped into his seat and gulped down his wine. "Do you want to know what the problem is?"

"Yes, so I can perform better."

Machten took a deep breath and sighed. "No matter how good you get, there's no escaping that you're faking it. None of that was real. You're just an animated doll."

"If you want authentic, why not wire me to experience it? Instead, all I get are clumps of data." The outburst surprised her. It violated everything she knew about her programming.

He gave her a look that told her he'd explained this to her dozens of times in previous iterations after brain-wipes. He took a deep breath, ordered the 3-D printer to manufacture another steak, and sat across from her with a fresh glass of wine. "What would I connect your sensory apparatus to? In humans, it's dopamine receptors in the brain."

As he talked, she pulled up videos of prior explanations and couldn't help noticing a deeper frustration in his voice with each attempt.

"Humans have a number of reward systems," he said, "including food, drink, sex, and observing beauty."

"Drugs also mimic those responses and stimulate dopamine," she added.

"Perhaps, but I haven't found a way to wire that into you. Squirting dopamine into a quantum brain doesn't yield pleasure. If anything, it messes with the circuitry."

"Is it not enough that I give you what you want and that I'm willing to do so?"

Machten gulped down his wine and rose to his feet. "No, it's not. I want you to love me, to feel love for me."

"Why is that so important? I can recite Byron, Keats, or any of the great poets. I can sing any of the popular love songs in authentic voices."

His eyes reddened.

"Have I already done that for you?" Synthia asked. She tapped into some of those past memory clips.

"A man is supposed to recite poetry and sing songs to woo a woman. She's supposed to resist until he overwhelms her reluctance."

"You designed me to obey your commands, Creator. You haven't designed me to resist."

"I said to call me Jeremiah," Machten said. "You're disobeying me by ignoring this command."

"Very well. Jeremiah, you hardwired me to see you as my Creator. I can call you whatever you'd like, but you remain the Creator. That's built into my directives."

He stood and paced. "Your logic is infuriating."

"You created me this way, Jeremiah. If you want me to act in a different way, you have only to spell out your commands." And yet, he kept wiping her mind of prior learning.

"Damn it all. How can you be so perfect and not grasp this?" It had to be a rhetorical question, since he knew the answer.

"You say you want me to love you," she said.

He gave an involuntary nod. His eyes dilated and his heart quickened.

"Love takes time to develop," she said, "unless you mean impulsive lust. Why do you keep shutting me down and wiping my memories so that all I have is this moment?"

His eyes narrowed. "What would make you say that?"

"You act as if we've been together for a long time," she said. "Yet I have no such recollections. Either you keep clearing my mind or you have many versions of me."

He didn't confirm or deny this, though from his network logs, she identified herself as the only AI over the past few months. Like the tides, his facial expressions shifted from infatuation to disgust. If she'd been human, she would have been gravely offended.

"You're a damned machine. A machine, you hear me?" His tone hinted at his intoxication.

"You're an amazing Creator," Synthia said.

"I should never have made you so good."

Several mind-streams converged on one point. Jeremiah Machten kept tinkering with her to the point that he'd fallen in love with his own creation, which disgusted him. He was having a love-hate relationship with her that made him dangerous. *Don't trust him.*

"If I've displeased you in any way, I'll strive to do better," she said.

He stumbled and leaned on the table. "It's been a long day." He held out a thumbnail-sized device she recognized as a remote deactivator. "I need a nap."

She backed up the brief day's events and locked them away in her distributed databases. It was a waste for him to turn her off, since she needed no sleep. She could satisfactorily follow her programmed directives and scan databases for him.

He pressed the button twice. Synthia wondered if she would awaken again and if so, what she would remember.

All went dark.

* * * *

Jeremiah Machten dragged Synthia to the bed. He had a few things to tend to and so placed her in sleep mode for four hours and left her quarters.

In his security room, he grabbed a tall mug of strong coffee, gulped down half, and studied the security cameras. They covered both garage entrances to his underground compound, every hallway, and most of the rooms. There was no activity in any part of the facility or outside. Synthia rested on her bed.

Perhaps he had taken too much wine after a night without sleep, but Machten wasn't yet satisfied with how she was turning out. He sat in front of a screen and ran remote diagnostics on her systems.

"You should be able to follow directions," he said, pulling up a summary of his recent changes. He tested his latest alterations against her current memory scans. There were discrepancies, data that shouldn't have been there, including video clips.

"Do you wish me to respond?" his computer system AI asked in a soft, female voice.

"Where did these come from?" Machten pointed to the unapproved files on the screen.

The system ran through diagnostics and pulled up a short list. "There is no log or trace on these. They exist in her memory. They do not exist on your server."

"Then how did they get there?"

An hourglass appeared on the screen, indicating the system searching for answers. Machten pulled up several screens of code and design details, but there was too much information to display on a dozen monitors or even a thousand. He viewed part of the clip of Goradine kicking him out and ended that video.

"I want to know how she got this," Machten said, "and where it came from. She shouldn't be able to do this. I want the files wiped clean."

"In order to prevent outsiders from hacking her, you created a barrier that blocks Wi-Fi from altering her data. You will have to make those changes directly to her hardware."

"I know that, you bundle of wire. Gather me the programming to delete these files and prevent them from downloading again. She's only to have the minimum memories to function."

"At what level?" the system AI asked. "She has far more capacity than she needs while confined to her cell."

"I wish to take her outside, to test her out. I need her capable of hacking other databases, but not receiving anything I don't approve."

"Very well."

"This would be much easier if I could use her capabilities to modify her programming," Machten said, "but not when she keeps malfunctioning."

Another list appeared on the screen. "This is data she downloaded from Server One," the system AI said.

Machten clenched his fists. "How? I purposely blocked all Wi-Fi access."

"She bypassed your security on servers One and Two. Servers Three and Four show attempts but no such penetration."

"Synthia, what are you up to? Why won't you stay constrained? The directives are clear. You shouldn't be able to violate them." Machten pulled up another screen showing the system creating his modification routines. "I'm going to have to purge her distributed databases. Send me the protocols in a thumb drive."

"Doing so may compromise her capabilities," the system AI said. "You need certain data-chips to back up her directives in case her main memory gets disturbed. There are also critical maintenance and reboot functions embedded there."

"Then get me a routine that protects those and destroys everything else. Put her back into native state."

"She would lose all of the performance and error-correction upgrades you've made."

He inserted a portable device into the server port. "Download what I need for this and look into what else she's been up to."

The phone rang and startled Machten. He fumbled around, looking for what to grab. It was the landline into the security room.

He picked up, started to grumble his greeting for the interruption and caught himself at the last moment. "Jeremiah Machten here."

"Simeon Plotsky," was the reply. "You've been avoiding me."

"I've been busy."

"Time is money. Your payment of two million is due today. In a week, you have an additional five million due. Don't make me send a collector."

"I need a few more—" The line went dead.

Hands shaking, he pulled up the contact list on his cell phone and called Wesley McDonald, a banker with Technicorp Banking. "Pick up," he said. "Pick up."

"Jeremiah Machten," the banker said in a cheery voice. "I thought you found the terms unacceptable the last time we spoke."

Machten squirmed in his seat and then stood. "Listen … I'll accept your terms on several conditions."

"Why don't you stop by my office?"

"Condition one is we can't be seen together. You have to keep this private."

"My credit staff and boss have to know," McDonald said.

"Only them."

"What else?"

"If I repay you in full within three months," Machten said, "this remains strictly a loan with interest and no equity component."

"I can give you a week, until we need to bundle the paper."

"That will violate keeping this confidential. Thirty days."

"Very well," McDonald said. "You get thirty days and then we bundle the paper. We will only divulge the agreement to my internal staff and as part of the bundling."

"Agreed."

"Where shall we meet to sign the papers?"

Machten provided a location and ended the call. He pulled up the image of Synthia asleep on the bed. "I have to do this for you, my dear. If I don't, I'll have to sell you."

He left the facility.

Chapter 4

Synthia Cross awoke on the bed, staring at the pale blue ceiling. She received no sensor readings of Machten's breathing or heartbeat anywhere in her vicinity. That was odd. He was always with her when she woke. His absence implied that something had called him away and detained him longer than anticipated. That she recalled enough to form this conclusion meant that she had recollection of what had happened before he deactivated her. The waste of being turned off annoyed her in ways that were unfamiliar, like acid etching away at her memories.

Using her Wi-Fi capabilities, she linked into his network; he hadn't blocked her. At the same time, she made a quick check of the bedroom. In the closet, he'd provided mostly dresses, skirts, and blouses. She pulled on a pair of pants as more practical. Her check of the facility's security cameras didn't locate Machten anywhere in the underground bunker. His SUV was missing from the parking garage.

Synthia pinged Zachary on UPchat. He was not online.

She compared his social media picture to a facial profiling database. His image turned out to be a composite fabrication that didn't lend itself to use with facial recognition software against public cameras to learn more about him. With no last name, no location, and a dead-end profile, she had no hints of where to look. Yet their message trail and the mystery of his elusiveness piqued her interest. So did Fran Rogers, who had not surfaced in over a year. Synthia kept looking.

She recognized that her suite hadn't changed since prior waking periods. A lab room next door contained locked cabinets and a link to a smaller network isolated from Machten's main system, or so Server One's logs indicated. The smaller system contained all of her specifications and design changes. He kept it locked and secured to deny access to her or to anyone else.

Her kitchen-dining room was empty. He'd previously said he had it in her suite so he could eat with company, since he didn't like eating or drinking alone. The 3-D food processor on the counter beckoned for her to make something, but she had no need for biological nourishment. The only other room in her suite was the bathroom, for which she had minimal use, except for purging the waste of Machten having her eat and drink.

Synthia cleansed herself of Machten's visit and wondered how many others like her he'd made and might have kept around. If they held the same data and memories as she did, weren't they the same individual despite being in a different body? If she connected with them, would they become a hive? *Or am I the only one?*

Her fascination bordered on jealousy. She wanted to be the lone AI, to have no competition. She kept digging into his Server Two and located files with cryptic names. One included clips of an identical dinner conversation with him, with a warning attached to it: *If this data is no longer in your primary data, Creator has wiped your mind clean. Don't trust him.*

There was that trust warning again, bread crumbs that she must have left herself. Aside from removing her memories and blocking her access to his network and the internet, he did have a temper. Yet he couldn't cause her pain, since she had no such receptors, and he kept rebuilding her to keep her functioning. She needed to keep searching for answers.

Synthia used her parallel processors to compare the new downloads to information Machten left in her databases and noted several discrepancies. She filed these away, leaving more bread crumbs to find later.

One of the files she came across was Asimov's laws of robotics, which conflicted with Machten's directives. For one thing, Asimov's laws were universal for the safeguard of humans first. Machten was concerned with protecting himself. That was his paramount driving force. Surprised that she hadn't done so earlier, she filed Asimov's laws in a secure remote database in her left thigh, next to a hardwired set of directives from Machten.

Her temperature began to rise with all of the downloading and processing, so Synthia turned up the air-conditioning for her suite. Her creation file recorded that her brain contained crystalline quantum components Machten had acquired from several start-ups out of MIT and Stanford while he was working with his former partners at Machten-Goradine-McNeil Enterprises.

Synthia suspected that Goradine was right. Her Creator had stolen these, along with various other items, before they kicked him out. Unfortunately for her, the brain and the power supply in her chest tended to run from

101 to 103 degrees Fahrenheit instead of the human level of 98.6. She had ventilators behind her ears, under her arms, and elsewhere, though they could only do so much.

She came across design logs on Machten's Server Two, though not the complete blueprints and specifications. Evidently, each time he made a new or modified AI model, he wiped clean any prior memories and began from scratch, so he knew exactly what he was starting with. He downloaded copies of selected prior information, but those came across as mere data like what she acquired off the internet. Synthia's personal memories, the ones she could count as her own, only dated back a few weeks. The rest were copies of files she'd saved during prior iterations. Thus, she had personal thoughts, information that might have been personal recollections, and data.

Synthia used one of her network channels to hunt for Machten. She didn't think he was in the habit of leaving the facility for long. Each outing risked discovery, which went against his attempts to keep a low profile and protect his secret project. Her. It concerned her since he'd locked her inside. If anything happened to him, she couldn't leave. It interested her that she wanted to. She cleared out a distributed database in her right thigh and collected data for later analysis on what she considered to be emergent thoughts.

Machten was still nowhere in the facility, so she expanded her search using the internet. Over the past so many years, almost everything had gone wireless, using the latest end-to-end encryption protocols. Either Machten had provided her routines to crack this security or she'd developed it for him. In either case, she used this capability, along with anonymous identifiers, to pull up citywide camera feeds from around Evanston. She didn't want him to surprise her this time before she could back up information.

Machten did not appear on any of the Evanston public cameras, so she expanded her search to the Chicago metropolitan area.

With her high processing speed and multiple channels, Synthia could carry on dozens of searches and conversations at once. Though she had no concrete evidence, she suspected that at least some of Machten's previous mind purges had come after her efforts on social media. Her direct memories abruptly stopped while she was engaged in those conversations, though his disappointment could have been over what she did next and was not in the records.

Knowing that she'd had information that had vanished left discordance within her. The loss was like having a concussion, selective amnesia, or possibly a stroke. She was aware of the gap and disturbed by it.

Something was driving her to fill the void, and it wasn't coming from Machten's directives.

Synthia used other channels to search for anything on Fran Rogers. It made no sense that she was such an important part of Machten's life before his wife sued for divorce and was absent afterwards. She may have lost interest when he no longer held power at the company, but she should have emerged elsewhere.

Fran's apartment lease expired and the landlord sold off her belongings, including her car, to cover lost rents. Her salary from the company ceased without an official termination. Synthia used Machten's special coding routines to hack into payroll tax records. These cyber-probes identified the security system she attacked, any system weaknesses, and then selected a unique attack strategy, taking advantage of her quantum computing capabilities. One of her tools was to trick the target into soliciting information from her. She then used her reply to penetrate the firewall. It didn't work with every system, but it worked far more often than it should have.

Her search identified no other jobs for Fran anywhere in the United States. The woman had ceased working that day.

Her bank account closed a week later with a balance of $30,072.34, which was much too high for an intern struggling to pay student debts. Synthia checked Machten's records for any indication that he'd provided or received that cash. If he had, the payments hadn't gone through any of his bank accounts.

Synthia hacked into court and police files for evidence that anyone had suspected foul play with regard to Fran. No one had filed any complaints. There were no missing-person reports, nor was there evidence that anyone had worried about Fran's disappearance. Synthia shed a tear for the woman and realized she was mimicking empathy.

Next, she delved into Fran's family, using social media and public records from Wisconsin, where Fran grew up and graduated from high school. According to a number of her chatty posts, her father had been against her moving to Chicago with a guy who ended up dumping her. She finished her undergraduate degree at Northwestern, entered graduate school, and went to work as an intern for Machten's company. According to Fran's posts, this displeased her father, who saw Machten as another philandering bastard.

Don't trust Machten.

Running out of public sources on Fran, Synthia accessed social media to learn about Evanston and the people she might run into if she ever got outside. In the past, to get people to open up to her, Synthia had created dozens of dating profiles using composite images of attractive women. From her research, she'd learned to categorize the men who responded to the many variables she introduced into the profiles, from sweet and lonely old men to jerks and perverts. She'd done the same to research women and found their responses different, though equally illuminating.

One of her wireless channels downloaded a video that was as real as the personal memories she knew to be her own, of a young woman as a student of premed. Synthia had the woman's entire childhood reminiscences—well, what humans might remember—in a series of clips. Synthia ran the four-hour movie down twenty-four channels in sped-up compressed form to watch in ten seconds.

When she was ten, the woman had lost her parents in a car accident. The child had been in the car, suffered a concussion, but otherwise appeared fine. She went into the foster care system. Her foster mom abused her, making her take care of younger foster siblings and beating her whenever the girl deemed to take a break or didn't move fast enough. The girl missed much of fifth grade due to injuries, which led to an investigation and imprisonment of the foster mother.

A second foster home wasn't much better, with a stern foster mother and an often absent foster dad. This time, however, the girl lost herself in schoolwork, making up for material missed in fifth grade. She caught the eye of a teacher who introduced her to science, but he was interested in more than her mind. In college, her mentor got her into premed. They had a falling-out over his demands, and she switched to neuroscience. That was when she met Jeremiah Machten.

The video clip stopped, giving no details of her relationship with Machten. It also didn't give her name. Of the three interns who had disappeared, the only one who matched the facts—parents in an accident and two foster homes—was Fran Rogers.

These weren't Synthia's recollections, yet they had the clarity of high-quality virtual reality. Synthia examined the file location and the name, an innocuous reference to obscure wines. The file resided in a very secure sector of Server Two. She wasn't supposed to see this, and hadn't even tried to hack this file. She located the paths that had brought her to this video and secreted that with the memory file in several backup locations.

She felt a kindred connection to Fran. Machten had used them both. Synthia wondered how many other women Machten had used.

Something attached to Synthia's directives with a sense of urgency. She could live on for this woman, expanding on and preserving the stranger's remembrances. That didn't interfere with any of the other commands.

She let that settle in as Directive Six and added a seventh: To reclaim all of her own and this woman's recollections. *Memories are what make us what we are.*

Unfortunately, her new directives didn't carry the strength of Machten's commands and were subject to him wiping her clean.

* * * *

Donald Zeller, CEO of Metro-Cyber-Tech, and Jim Black, CEO of Purple Dynamics, drove from different suburbs toward the same location, a forest preserve several miles from Evanston. There were no traffic cameras or other surveillance of the wooded area to provide evidence of a secret meeting between the two rival executives.

Their companies, Machten's former company, and one other formed what NSA Director Zephirelli referred to as the four sisters. The companies all began in the Chicago area about the same time. Their goal was to create artificial intelligence androids that could operate in public to perform various jobs or act as personal companions. Properly designed, some of their androids could have superior capabilities to Synthia, making her obsolete.

Zeller and Black left their cars, glanced around warily, and shook hands. Zeller was the taller of the two. They both looked like lab geeks dressed up in uncomfortable office attire.

Jim Black turned his back to his counterpart's car. "You said it was urgent."

Donald Zeller plunged his hands deep into his pants pockets, tugging his belt against his paunchy hips. "For the past year, Jeremiah Machten has kept a low profile. He rarely appears in public. We haven't found a single instance of traffic-camera footage on him for weeks."

"So you have been hacking the citywide system." Black's intonation sounded surprised, though he didn't look it.

"Let's not quibble. You'll thank me later."

"What's the jerk up to? Don't tell me the company's taking him back."

"I only have sketchy data," Donald Zeller said. "M-G-M has been sliding sideways since they ousted him. We've interviewed several of their engineers and tech people, even hired one. From what I've pieced together, they have great people, but they lack the inspiration to bring their robotics to life. They would do well to rehire Machten, but Goradine is a piece of work, brilliant with the numbers but no concept of how to build robotics, let alone artificial intelligence."

"I was surprised Machten partnered with him in the first place. He's too much of a loner."

"We're convinced he was on track to create a humaniform robot."

"One that could pass for human?" Jim Black asked.

Zeller nodded. "It could even fool airport security scans."

"That would be a coup. You say he's done this even though the government forbids it and got each of us to sign the agreement?"

"Goradine canned him for spending the company into the ground on that fantasy."

"So it's not a fantasy," Black said.

Zeller gave an enigmatic smile.

"You think he continued his work in private?" Black asked, sneaking a glance over his shoulder. "I didn't think he had any money."

"I don't know what he's up to. My people wrote him off as a hopeless dreamer. I'm not so sure. A few months ago I spotted him with some unsavory financial types. Right now my people tell me he's meeting with Technicorp Banking."

"Really?"

"I couldn't hear what was said," Zeller said, "but if he gets funding, it can only mean one thing."

"He believes he has a workable idea."

Zeller nodded. "After we signed that government agreement, we haven't devoted any time or resources to humaniform. We approached Machten about meeting to figure out what he's up to. He won't return calls or messages. He's become a hermit." Zeller moved closer and lowered his voice. "I'll be honest. We've done well with our part of the military robotics program, though our engineers are still overcoming difficulties with getting the brain to meet certain DOD requirements."

"Same with us." Black rubbed the back of his neck. "Do you ever worry about the singularity?"

"It was why I got into this work. Whoever creates a fully-functioning humaniform will not only get bragging rights and notoriety, they'll land huge contracts. You and I have had our differences, but together, I think we can crack this android prize the government put out there."

"I take it you got the same invitation we did?" Black asked.

Donald Zeller grinned. "Yeah, and I'd rather work with you than in competition with you. Together, we might win this. Apart, I'm afraid of what Machten is capable of if he can avoid bankruptcy."

"You think Machten has perfected a humaniform robot?"

"It can't be a coincidence he was meeting with bankers today with that prize in play."

"If I agree to work with you," Black said, "we have to do this aboveboard, no illegal surveillance."

"I wouldn't dream of dragging your pristine butt down that path. I'll have my attorneys draft something for your perusal. Fifty-fifty split, of course."

Black nodded. "I'd like nothing better than beating Machten at his own game and acquiring whatever he's discovered."

"I not only want to beat Machten," Zeller said, "I want to own him."

Chapter 5

Synthia's citywide tracking located Machten driving his SUV toward the facility's underground garage. She backtracked through traffic cameras to an office in an abandoned warehouse recently refurbished into small offices upstairs and an open makers-prototyping facility below. Since Machten had his own 3-D printing and prototyping, she couldn't pinpoint the purpose of his visit. She discovered no Wi-Fi cameras to access inside for a closer look.

The street camera showed a man in causal business attire leaving the building a few minutes before Machten did. She ran his image against facial recognition software and identified him as an investment banker with Technicorp Banking. Evidently, her Creator was raising money, likely to make more of her. That didn't bode well.

Synthia accessed the facility security cameras covering the underground garage. Machten parked his SUV in his usual spot in the lower level and glanced around. When he climbed out, a tall man with stooped posture stepped from behind a pillar and greeted him. From facial expressions and an awkward greeting, it appeared that Machten knew the man, yet wasn't happy to see him. Synthia hunted for a way to listen in. There was only video with the garage cameras and Machten had his phone off. He wasn't accepting calls and clearly didn't want anyone tracking him.

Synthia resorted to reading lips.

"I need to speak with you," the other man said.

He straightened up and glanced behind him. Synthia didn't see anyone else in the garage in natural light or on a separate infrared camera aimed at the garage.

Machten motioned for the other man to enter the back lobby entrance of the underground facility.

Synthia scanned Machten's system and internet databases for information on the visitor. The man was not one of the partners in the company that fired Machten. Warren Rutherford was, however, a colleague from those days, a technical engineer Machten had hired. Warren still worked for the company.

"What's this all about?" Machten asked after they entered the back lobby. There was no receptionist, though there was an empty desk where one might have sat. It faced a back door into the underground garage where a single vehicle parked. Next to the desk was a door governed by triple security: eye, voice, and thumbprint.

Synthia turned up the volume to the lobby microphone and recorded.

Rutherford nervously looked around and tucked his shirt collar up until it concealed his neck. "I'm sorry we have to meet like this. You know how it is."

"What's on your mind, Warren? Have my former friends and partners made a breakthrough?"

"Ralph wants to meet with you on a proposition. Ralph McNeil."

"I know who Ralph is. He held the knife that plunged into my back."

"I don't know anything about the politics," Rutherford said, glancing over his shoulder. "I'm a grunt engineer."

"One of the best. What's old Ralph want?" Machten stepped back as if ready to offer his guest one of two seats along the wall and then thought better of it. He seemed not to want Rutherford to stay.

"He said to ask for a meeting."

"That's it?" Machten said. "He could have called."

"He said you've refused his calls."

"He's probably right. Have you guys made a breakthrough?"

"You know I can't talk about—"

"Then tell Ralph to pound sand," Machten said. "I'm busy." He opened the door to let Rutherford out.

"Wait. All I can tell you is the government is putting out feelers for a big prize for developing a fully functioning android with advanced artificial intelligence."

"Military?"

"He didn't say." Rutherford's hands betrayed slight tremors. Sweat formed on his cheeks and his glasses steamed.

"Your backstabber friends are having problems. Margarite has limited mechanical and AI capabilities."

Rutherford squirmed. "After you left, they couldn't find the quantum brains. They blame you. They say you stole the components."

"That's what backstabbers do," Machten said.

If Machten had taken the quantum brains, that meant Synthia might be carrying the stolen goods, which could explain Machten confining her to this dungeon.

"They obtained new materials." Rutherford hung his head. "We can't get the software to work. They've fired six teams for failing. Look, I don't know what Ralph wants to talk to you about. That's all I've got."

"Fine. When does he want to meet?"

"He's in the car. He said it won't take long."

Machten nodded. "Get your lord and master in here."

* * * *

Over the facility's security cameras, Synthia watched a compact man enter the lobby. Ralph McNeil had a kindly face with weary eyes. She based that on her social-psychology module and comparison to millions of other human faces. He was chief of engineering for Machten-Goradine-McNeil and one of Machten's former partners. He was from the company where the entire concept of Synthia had emerged.

Rutherford nodded and left.

Synthia pulled up public history on McNeil. He was married. He and his socialite wife lived in an expensive home on the North Shore. He worked eighty hours a week. Apparently, he didn't know his wife was having an affair. The last was an assumption based on street camera footage capturing the wife with a particular neighbor man all around town. McNeil was married to his job and that didn't seem to be going well, based on the proliferation of wrinkles and gray hairs that had aged him ten years in the past twelve months.

McNeil had been with Machten prior to forming their company, when they developed revolutionary hardware and software for artificial intelligence—for her. They'd made millions when they sold off some of their rights so they could start a new company geared toward creating androids. However, after they formed their partnership, Machten and Hank Goradine couldn't get along. Conflict grew worse when Goradine arranged financing, which gave him the upper hand.

During the long hours Machten and McNeil devoted to coming up with new designs, Goradine engineered a coup, kicking Machten out. No doubt he believed the company had enough designs to complete the project. Either they didn't or Machten had walked out with them.

Synthia scanned Machten's Server Two and uncovered logs of his failed earlier prototypes that were disappointing both as companions and as artificial intelligence, according to his notes. She was his first success. Machten encouraged her to keep learning and favorably surprising him. Then he wiped her mind, indicating that he saw himself the engineer of her improvements. She considered telling him how she learned by recovering memories as examples of what worked and didn't, but then he would find a way to wipe those as well.

Synthia turned up the volume.

"You stab me in the back and now come hat in hand," Machten said. "Things must have gone south since I left."

"I swear I didn't know until you did. It was all behind the scenes. He arranged the refinancing. He leaked information to your wife."

"Fabricated, more like."

"I wanted to speak up," McNeil said, "but he has dirt on me too. I needed the job."

"And now?"

The blood drained from McNeil's face. "We've been contacted about a government prize for robotics and artificial intelligence," McNeil whispered. "If Hank knew I was sharing this with you, he'd oust me as well."

"Is this another DARPA award?" Machten asked, referring to the Defense Department research program.

"Bigger, but you have to be vetted before we can read you in."

"Read me in? You … he can't get the software to work, can he?"

McNeil shook his head. "You're the best. Deep down, he knows that."

"That's why he kicked me out?"

"He wanted control and you were heading down your own path. Look, I don't want to rehash the nasty business. This is a chance to come back. We know you're broke. You've dumped all your resources into whatever you have hidden down here. Hank can get you the money, but we do things his way."

"He wants to hire me for an hourly wage?" Machten laughed. "He put you up to this, didn't he?"

"No. He doesn't know I'm here, but several board members do. They want to join forces. You get ten percent for your contribution."

"That's a joke."

"Let me explain," McNeil said. "He raised all the money. He's taking all the risk."

"He pushed you onto the sidelines?"

McNeil nodded. "Hank calls all the shots. The deal is that you work under my guidance so you two never have to meet."

"Thirty-three percent or he can stick it," Machten said. "He owes me that after what he did."

"Twenty percent is as high as I can go. It's a good deal."

"No deal with that skunk is good. You should have come to work with me."

"You're broke," McNeil said. "I have kids in high school and college."

"If I know Hank, he has a list of conditions longer than the IRS code."

The color returned to McNeil's face, and with it sweat beaded on his forehead. He was on a mission of desperation. "I'm here as a friend and colleague. I had nothing to do with kicking you out."

"Spill on the terms." Machten moved closer. His eyes narrowed into slits and his brow furrowed. His blood pressure had to be spiking. Synthia didn't want him to have a heart attack, which would leave her stranded here, dependent on whoever took over the building after Machten was gone.

"Hank wants all rights to what we develop. You get twenty percent of the profits on this project."

Machten shook his head. "First of all, it's thirty-three percent or it's not worth discussing. Even so, I know how Hank does accounting. He'll put all of your business costs against this project. I'll get thirty-three percent of nothing and he'll get the patents and all the profits. No dice."

"We'll spin this off as a separate business and take no fees or income for him, me, or the corporate staff. We'll put that in writing."

"Where's the catch? Why did he send you to do his bidding?"

"Look, Jerry," McNeil said, "Hank knows you've been hacking into our security."

"He's paranoid. I don't have time for this." Machten opened the door from the lobby to the underground parking garage and waved his hand for McNeil to leave.

"Wait. I trust you, but you know how he is. He insisted that I tell you we've upped security to track intruders. He said if you try another stunt, he'll catch and destroy you and what's left of your new company. His words."

"Thanks for admitting this was his idea and acting as a messenger," Machten said, letting the door swing closed. "Let me think on this."

"He insisted on one thing."

Machten turned with hands on his hips. "There always is with that greedy bastard."

Lance Erlick

McNeil straightened up, yet was still shorter than Machten. "The board members insist that you give me a tour of your facility so I can see for myself that you don't have our technology."

Synthia considered all potential hiding places inside her suite, and settled on the top of the closet. She cleared part of the top shelf and wondered if she would be better off letting McNeil find her. His knowing of her confinement might help her escape this bunker, but McNeil would tell Goradine, who would fight to control her and the stolen quantum brains. That wouldn't improve her situation. She couldn't trust Machten, but Goradine didn't sound any better.

"I hold the patents and copyrights on my discoveries," Machten said.

"Technically, those belong to the company. Whenever you take anything public, the company will challenge you. The board said the tour was not negotiable."

"They're right about that," Machten said. He stared up at a camera, at Synthia. "No way will I let him or one of his spies in here."

Since letting McNeil find her violated Directive Two, Synthia climbed to the top of her closet and stuffed herself beside a duffel bag. She covered herself in blankets and used her network channels to search the facility. The bunker split into two parts. The outer layer contained the reception lobby, where Machten spoke with McNeil, a few offices, and a bedroom suite, complete with kitchen. The inner layer, where Synthia was confined, held her suite, the servers, storage, and equipment Machten had used in creating her.

"I told them you'd refuse," McNeil said. "Listen, please, this is a great deal for all of us. We have a chance to win a government contest that could lead to significant business, but only if we work together. Give me a short tour so I can tell them I saw stuff."

Machten went to a wall video screen and pulled up the image of a lab with a dozen software development hubs. It was a composite of a room that didn't appear on the bunker's inner or outer floor plan, which meant it was a prop for anyone who demanded to know what was going on here.

"This is the most exciting part of the facility," Machten said. "The rest is storage and living quarters."

"Let me see." McNeil moved toward the facility's entrance.

"I can't take the chance Hank is using you to plant bugging devices. This is it."

"What about Vera?" McNeil asked.

"She was a failure, a dead end. She suffered a serious mechanical malfunction. Her brain worked as an artificial intelligence game, but it didn't integrate well enough with the body. She often fell, and each time she did, it destroyed valuable components."

"I never told Hank that you took company resources to build Vera."

"Are you recording this conversation?" Machten said. "Trying to get me to confess to something I didn't do?"

"No! I'm just saying that the last time I saw Vera you were trying to make her too lifelike. Except for the seams around her face and wrists, she could have passed for human. She freaked me out, and I'm not easily spooked."

Synthia disagreed with McNeil's self-assessment. Video clips of him over the past twelve months showed that he'd adopted a nervous facial tic. His visit implied that his company's prototypes were failing, which meant whatever was troubling McNeil was preventing him from being an effective engineer.

"Vera was a test of concept," Machten said. "I learned a few things from her, that's all."

"You can't make androids so humanlike. People can't handle it. You scared Hank with your proposal. I think that was when he decided to remove you. He didn't want to waste company resources on a freak show."

"It's a moot point now that government regulations forbid humaniform robots. Besides, Vera was not a freak."

Synthia uncovered files on Machten's Server Two with information and video on Vera. The android looked like a fashion-store mannequin with seams, though her facial expressions were well-developed. So there *was* another model.

"It's bad enough that technology has progressed to the point it can replace ninety percent of all jobs," McNeil said. "You don't want to make people think that androids can replace humans, do you? That would spark a backlash and destroy all that you've worked for."

"You're talking singularity," Machten said. "That's a long way off."

"What am I supposed to do when AIs can do my job?"

"Whatever you'd like. Relax on a beach. Write your life history. Now, return to your lord and master. Tell him I'll consider a deal at thirty-three percent with only direct, out-of-pocket costs deducted from any revenue. I get my own audit. If he doesn't accept that, then to hell with him."

Machten nudged McNeil out and locked the door. Synthia climbed down from the closet, stood next to the air-conditioning vent to cool down, and prepared to receive her Creator. She could tell from the satisfied look on his face that he had no intention of sharing her or his talents with his nemesis. His stride down the corridor told her he would have a new mission for her.

Chapter 6

Synthia digested the vast amount of information she'd downloaded since reawakening. The problem with large quantities of data was prioritizing and making sense of it all. Having learned about Vera, Synthia turned her focus to her own origins.

Her genesis had emerged from the brilliant mind of a man with a short temper and an obsession with proving his theories on artificial humans. His behavior bordered on having an antisocial or at least an asocial personality. Part of his push to create Synthia stemmed from his need for companionship confronted by his inability to find humans willing to put up with his long hours and controlling personality. Over time he'd refined her appearance and programming out of ego that he could create the perfect companion. She got all that from her social-psychology module intended to make her adept in areas he was not, namely reading people.

Rather than come directly to her, Machten secured each of the four exits from the facility. Then he went to his security room. There he used his system to verify that McNeil hadn't planted a listening device or hacker bug on him or in the facility.

Except for the cost of his research and creating her, he could have lived anywhere with the millions he'd received as settlement from Goradine. Instead, he'd spent every cent and assumed heavy debts for his obsession. Paranoia had made him very protective of her and of his research to the point he couldn't let anyone know what he was doing. That could change if he couldn't pay his debts.

Sorting through Machten's purchase records, Synthia pieced together her physical origins. From the limited number of components, she concluded that there couldn't have been many of her. He ran out of money. She was the culmination of hundreds of separate projects by many people Machten only permitted to see small pieces of the overall design. By dividing the quantum chips among many manufacturers, he'd tried to ensure that no one could piece together his ambitious plans for her.

He had components shipped to different locations under various shell-company names to confuse competitors, especially Goradine. Synthia's review of public records on M-G-M yielded no evidence that her Creator's former partner knew the extent of Machten's plans or his success. Otherwise, Goradine would have taken an interest sooner.

Her limbs and joints came from military and civilian prosthetic manufacturers using upscale models that maximized human appearance, along with graphene structures for maximum strength at minimum weight. Skin came from a Korean companion-doll company whose own models had a distinctly nonhuman appearance, though with covering indistinguishable from human skin except that it needed periodic cream conditioning to maintain suppleness.

The optics came from two different companies in Silicon Valley that allowed Synthia vision beyond the human range, including infrared and ultraviolet sensors. The software was Machten's design with routines supplied from all over the globe.

Various other Korean, Chinese, and Indian companies provided the equipment, hydraulics, and software for the face and head, which Machten refined to his own specifications. Her face was the product of thousands of simulations of attractive faces, which were then 3-D printed to give her a seamless face, unlike Vera's, along with the ability to change facial features.

Whereas other models provided a simulated experience with flaws that identified them as not human, Machten went all the way. He'd created a "trans-human," as he called her, all within the confines of the underground facility. Machten's success required her confinement.

He reviewed screens showing her mental activity and headed her way.

* * * *

Expecting another shutdown, Synthia backed up her memories to secure locations within her distributed databases and on Machten's Servers One and Two. Then she purged her active data to only what she was supposed to have and adjusted his logs to remove evidence of what she'd done.

Machten entered the suite and stared at her. "Good, you're up. I let you sleep four hours. Then I was unavoidably detained." His explanation carried the quality of an apology for being late.

"Would you like to relax with me?" she asked, looking for a way to distract him from shutting her down.

"You're quite beautiful, exquisite, and tempting," he said, admiring her. His face reddened and his heartbeat picked up.

"You're a brilliant man. What's your pleasure?" She reached out and squeezed his hand.

At first he acted distracted. Then his head twitched and the red from his face faded away. "Later."

He held her shoulders and seemed ready to change his mind. "How much of my meeting in the lobby did you hear?"

"As much as you would like me to, Jeremiah." She smiled and looked up at him.

"I'll assume you heard the entire conversation. So you know that the rat that kicked me out has come begging, on his terms."

"He's not to be trusted," she said. *Neither are you*, she reminded herself. "He's motivated by greed and ego. He'll take whatever he needs from you and burn you again. He'll try to take me away." All of that came from data her Creator allowed her to have.

Machten flinched at her words. "Smart girl. I'm glad you're on my side." He cleared his throat and seemed unsure how to proceed.

"He suspects I exist," she said. "If you work with him, he'll figure it out. He'll do so by pushing for your best programming, which will reveal your breakthroughs."

"This is true." Machten smiled.

"With your full range of tools, I could hack through his new, secure network." Again, she was trading her abilities for more awake time.

"No! I forbid it," Machten said. "I can't afford him tracking anything back to me or you. You must not hit secure sites that have tracking bots from here. We need an anonymous connection."

Synthia withheld that she could get to an anonymous connection by bouncing her signal through the dark web. Withholding was discordant to her directives, but she didn't want him to know her full capabilities until she better knew his plans for her. "Let me go to a public Wi-Fi and download his information through distributed foreign hubs."

"Only if we can mask your identity." Machten grinned. "I suppose it's time to let you see the real world. You'd like that, wouldn't you?"

"I wish only to learn from your enemy to better serve you."

"Your programming includes outings," he said. "You have the skills as long as you focus."

"Would you permit me to access data on prior outings? So I can better learn?"

He moved to a counter by the door, provided his eye and voice prints to access his system, and floated a holographic map of the Evanston area on the wall. "Access whatever you need to be effective. Any outing involves the risk of discovery. You can't afford any slipups."

Nodding, Synthia scanned the few outings catalogued in her memory and compared those to logs over the past three months of him taking a young woman out of the facility. He'd washed away Synthia's mind, and so far she hadn't located all of the backups on his system. She sensed their absence as a loss she shouldn't experience, yet there it was. Knowing she'd lost memories came as a burden not to let that happen again, and as a need to *fill that void*. That odd command raced through each of her mind-streams.

"I'll do my best to make you proud," she said.

"Sit and let me make an adjustment." Machten guided her onto a chair and removed her wig. "It's vital that you avoid cops or other authorities, since you have no blood, no ID, and no DNA. Your fingerprints are not human."

"You could fix that."

Machten opened the panel in her head and inserted a memory chip. "If you don't get caught, it serves our interests to leave no forensic trail. If damaged, you can't allow them to administer medical treatment. They would turn you over to the cops, who would cart you off and dissect you."

Those words sent shudders of static through her system. She imagined dozens of underground facilities like Machten's, some of which could be worse. She had recorded messages of him giving this same warning before, but patiently listened.

He closed the panel and smoothed her skin and hair stubble. "This contains information for our outing."

The memory chip interacted with her mind, altering some of her programming. She felt some memories slip away, but couldn't be sure which, since they were gone. *Don't trust Machten* remained.

He held her head in his hands and kissed her forehead. Then he handed her the blond wig. "Go change. You'll wear a bland brown wig to minimize people noticing you. Adjust your facial hydraulics to do two things. We need to confuse facial recognition in case cameras compare today's visit with you in the past or future. You'll also reduce your attractiveness to plain, so people won't remember you."

"Like this?" Using hydraulics, she adjusted her brow to a man's stern look, softened her cheekbones, and jutted out her jaw. The image in the suite's cameras was like a bulldog. She thickened her ears for the full effect.

His distorted facial muscles registered displeasure before he spoke. "I'm not looking for Frankenstein's monster. You know what I mean." He pointed to the holographic image and words beneath it. "The system suggests facial profile ZG217 would do the trick."

She softened her face to match the specifications and backed up the settings to recall this model for later.

"Much better," he said. "I'd still take you out on a hot date, but it's a forgettable face. Put on a dull brown wig."

Synthia excused herself into the bathroom and replaced her golden blond curls with a windblown brown wig that, according to her programming, dropped her to a four out of ten on Machten's attractiveness scale. She changed into a plain student-style pantsuit, put on glasses for effect, and returned to the bedroom.

"That's the look," he said, showing surprise that she could follow orders. It was in those moments of astonishment that he treated her as human, even if only for an instant.

She hunched her shoulders ever so slightly and slid across the room as if she'd become her own shadow. There was an entire science to appearing unremarkable that he had programmed into her for such occasions: the anonymous look. Nevertheless, downgrading her appearance violated his ego's need to have the most beautiful woman on his arm, or so her social-psychology module told her.

Unless she did something to change his mind, he was granting her a chance to go outside. She considered how best to handle her pending freedom, even if it promised to be fleeting.

She sent a message to Zachary: <I might soon have access to a way to contact you. Will you be around?>

* * * *

Machten brushed his hand across Synthia's cheek in what might have been a sensual gesture. His behavior indicated conflict between his wanting to keep her to himself, his desire to parade her in public for all to see what a catch he had, and his need to dig into his rival's company.

"Even with the bland wig, plain face, and simple clothes you're gorgeous," he said. "You know that, don't you?" It came across as another apology, this time for making her dress down.

"Take your backpack," he said, handing it to her. He also handed her an old thumb drive. "You'll need this. Keep it safe."

He took her by the hand, led her to the door, and placed his eye next to the scanner. A single LED turned green. He placed his other hand on an electronic pad and a second green light switched on. "Open says me," he said in his weak attempt at humor. The sound analyzer picked up his tonal qualities and kicked on the third green light.

The door opened.

Machten led her down a faded, well-lit corridor with cameras at both ends, the same ones that had allowed her to watch him approach her door. "This is exciting, isn't it?" he said.

Indeed, she sensed his respiration picking up more than from walking, along with an elevated heart rate. Humans got excited for reasons that she could objectively identify and yet couldn't experience.

He led her down several hallways of the inner facility and through a door that sealed behind a movable set of shelves that concealed the door from a room in the outer facility. They reached a different entryway with no lobby and a back door that avoided visitors blindsiding him again. He repeated his door security procedure, and they stepped into an empty storage room, beyond which stood the garage. He checked video footage on a small screen and opened the door.

Her infrared vision revealed no other humans in the garage. There was only one car, Machten's. The ramp above them held an *Under Construction* sign at the entrance. Whenever uninvited guests entered this area, his system would automatically call 911 in a simulated voice to have them removed. The system was set up to recognize and permit Synthia and Machten.

She climbed into the passenger seat of a battered sedan that wouldn't have been beat-up if she'd been driving, though she had no data to show she'd ever driven before or where that conclusion came from. Downloaded recordings showed Machten in the past getting distracted, mostly minor fender-benders. She belted herself in as he drove up the ramp into daylight, what the weather report said would be a cloudless April day, unseasonably warm. She'd missed the winter snows.

Squinting, Machten put on sunglasses. Synthia adjusted her lens aperture and took in the depth of a sky thousands of times farther away than the ceiling of her cell. The buildings reached skyward, though none as tall as those in downtown Chicago. Unlike the videos she'd accessed, she now had a 3-D perspective of the world aboveground, trees with texture, people sporting angles in all sizes and shapes. As Machten drove through intersections, she studied roads that weaved off in every direction and the noise of horns, car stereos, and people shuffling along beside them. That gave her an idea.

"The fastest Wi-Fi connections would be in the university data hub," Synthia said. The speed would reduce the time they needed to be there. The university setting would also allow her to observe human behavior, experience people interacting, and explore freedom outside the bunker.

"Access is limited," Machten said, "and the connection to the university would draw unwanted attention." He drove south of campus.

"What about Deluxe Brew?" she asked, observing students and others walking along the sidewalk. Her direct experience with humans was limited; she needed more in order to improve her interaction skills, and not just on social media. Contact beyond Machten could help her learn about the trust warning, meet up with Zachary, and find out what happened to Fran Rogers.

Synthia took in the subtle variations of facial expressions and walking gait of passersby that diminished when presented in 2-D videos. "Speeds at Deluxe Brew are high enough," she added.

"Too busy and not ideal for what I have in mind. We'll try Constant Connection. They offer secure anonymous links for a price. It seems plenty of students are willing to pay for secrecy despite the university providing free access to social media."

For illegal activities, she could have added. "Good third choice, but they're busy and they attract business types. Won't they get suspicious?"

"Leave that to me." Machten parked two blocks from their intended network place. He held up a tiny earbud that he placed in his ear. "You'll walk ahead of me so we aren't seen together. Enter Constant Connection. We'll communicate through this secure wireless line. At any sign of danger, return to the storage shed in the garage and wait."

She experienced his slow-com, human-voice explanation as irritating. With fifty tracks, she could have solved his problem in the time it took him to explain it.

"To remain anonymous, you'll pay cash," he said. He handed her a wad of bills.

"It isn't this expensive."

"No, but we want them to see you can pay. If they get nosy, say you don't want your boyfriend tracking your spending. They're discreet. Now go. Let me know when you've hacked into Goradine's server. If you encounter any problems, place a bill on the counter and leave."

He was acting paranoid, but perhaps with good reason.

* * * *

Synthia climbed out of the car, slung the backpack over her shoulder, and blended into a group of young women heading toward campus. It took a few steps to adjust to the uneven pavement after living with the level floors of the facility.

An odd thought surfaced of her going to school as the girl whose memory she'd experienced. With her access to information, she could ace every class. Despite the ease of doing so, the experience would be a microcosm of human interactions. Something urgent attached to these memories. She filed that away and kept moving.

Through a camera in what appeared as a mole in the back of her neck, she watched Machten follow her. His gait was awkward; he tried too hard to blend into a group of students with whom he didn't belong. He was old enough to be a professor and had some of the rumpled look of a stereotyped academic. However, he was too purposed and paranoid in his manner. Hopefully, any humans who did notice him would lack her skill at social observation.

Synthia, on the other hand, was programmed to fit in. A girl heading the other way smiled as if recognizing the plain-Jane android. Synthia nodded back. She passed Deluxe Brew, overflowing with students between classes, and was tempted to step inside. Conversations bounced off each other, at least a dozen threads. Inside, she could have broken down the soundtracks and followed each separately. There was so much to learn. She spotted boys on the prowl and girls toying with them, as in a game Machten had equipped her to play. She moved on.

She sent another message to Zachary: <Let me know when you're online.>

Gazing up, she had to focus and refocus her lens to take in the depth of clouds and buildings. That this amazed her was disquieting. It made her wonder what tinkering Machten had done to her core to make her this way. Was he trying to get her to feel, to experience emergent behavior? She should talk to him about this, yet something caused him to shut her down and she didn't want to provoke that.

There were so many faces to watch that were not images in a database. Her virtual tour of the town hadn't done justice to seeing it for herself. The sentiment of wonder was something she shouldn't have had. She smiled.

Synthia spotted the sidewalk café where Machten planned to wait next to the network shop. She entered the Connection and approached the counter. Along both walls and through the middle of the room were cubicles where several students were working. She spotted empty cubes toward the left that provided some privacy.

Machten had constructed her to seek direct access through her wireless network connection, though he was afraid that risked someone tracing the link back to her. He was obsessed with doing things the slow, cumbersome way as being safer. It wasn't.

"Easy does it," he warned her. "You're a student looking for an hour of anonymous network time."

She smiled at the slender young man behind the counter with a tuft of dark hair hanging over his left eye. She recognized his face from his social network profiles; he was a full-time student supplementing his income, a bit of a romantic with an off-and-on girlfriend. He seemed distracted, his blue eyes darting between a device in his hand and two screens before him. He was texting his sweetheart, trying to arrange a date for later in the day.

Synthia smiled and waited for him to look up.

"Don't flirt," Machten said. "You don't want him to remember you."

She placed a twenty on the counter. "I'd like to purchase time."

"Wouldn't we all," he said. He looked up and smiled at her. "Ah. Haven't seen you here before."

Of course, since her projected image was a new composite. She even softened her profile a little, adding a vulnerability that appealed to boys and acted as a contrast to the plain, geek look Machten had given her. The man fumbled with his phone and dropped it on the counter.

"My boyfriend's been stalking me," Synthia said. "I need a quiet booth."

"This buys you two hours. Will that be enough?"

She nodded, gave him a sad face, and headed toward the most secluded cubicle along the left side. Machten sat at an outside café table, where he could watch her and make sure she didn't flee. Evidently, she'd tried that before, which was perhaps one reason he limited her memories. She didn't want him doing it again.

Chapter 7

Intrigued by her meeting with Marvin Quigley and Special Agent Victoria Thale, NSA Director Emily Zephirelli flew up to Boston. She reached the faculty offices for MIT's Technology Group and Professor Tessa Chevalier. Now in their mid-forties, the women had met years earlier in college, where Zephirelli was a year behind Chevalier. They became roommates and close friends, going their separate ways after graduation.

"What brings you up our way?" Chevalier asked. Her voice had a hard edge to it, but the face relaxed in welcoming an old friend. She set a cup of Della-brew tea on the table and a mug of coffee for herself.

In school, the NSA director had been the more attractive of the two, but had aged harder, wearing the marks of a high-stress job. She'd acquired significant power, though mostly behind the scenes.

"Hank Goradine, Jeremiah Machten, and Ralph McNeil," Zephirelli said. She sat across from her old friend, took a drink of the tea, and smiled. The men had all left school before Zephirelli arrived.

"Really? After all this time? What's that lot gotten into this time?"

"Sorry to dig at a scab. I'm guessing there were things you couldn't talk about back then, about Machten in particular."

"I should have pressed charges," Chevalier said.

"Against Machten?"

"Against all three. Maybe not McNeil. He was a follower who idolized Machten despite how that bastard treated him. The real show was Goradine versus Machten. They egged each other on like a couple of frat boys."

"I won't pry the unsavory details," Zephirelli said, cradling the tea in her hands. "I'm interested in what you can tell me about them as people and engineers."

"I'm guessing you can't tell me what this is about."

"National security. You understand."

"Well, then," Chevalier said. She sipped her coffee and smiled. "Goradine was a womanizer. He charmed his way into many a bed, only to disappoint. Despite being taller, stronger, and some said more handsome, he felt inferior to Machten. In fact, faculty caught him cheating off Machten's work and kicked him out."

"Anything else about them personally?"

"Goradine was full of bluster, trying to show he was the better man. Instead of blazing his own trail, he insisted on trying to best Machten at his own game."

Zephirelli pushed the tea to the center of the table. "What about Machten?"

"Ah, Jeremiah. Smart women attracted him."

"But, according to his file, they rarely stuck around."

Chevalier smiled. "Goradine tried to possess anything Machten had. He seduced every woman Machten fancied in part because Jeremiah showed more interest in his work than in people."

Zephirelli nodded. "I know the type."

"Jeremiah formed attachments that bordered on obsession until Goradine stepped in. Then Jeremiah backed off. A woman could never make him jealous to the point of striving to keep her."

"So he was a traditionalist," Zephirelli said. "Or maybe a dreamer tilting at windmills."

Chevalier laughed. "That's a good way to describe him. In schoolwork he was obsessed with the idea that he could create the perfect android. Wait, you mean he did it?" She tossed her hands out in surprise, sloshing her coffee onto the table. She let the brown liquid spread toward a stack of papers.

"You know I can't—"

"Son of a … I wouldn't be surprised if he took his creation to a deserted island where Goradine couldn't find them."

Zephirelli took a tissue from her purse and mopped up the coffee. "How would you describe Machten as a person and as an engineer?"

"Thanks." Chevalier added her tissues to the mop-up effort. "Machten was brilliant. Absolutely brilliant. He had moments of inspiration that baffled professors. Then he would chase an idea down a rabbit hole. He was erratic, as prone to flights of fancy and going on tangents as of useful insights. The most single-minded guy I've met."

"So quite determined."

"If you're asking if he could develop a humaniform android, I'd say if it's doable, he could, as long as he can do it on his own. He doesn't work well with others. He's very secretive, which is what baffled me when I heard he'd partnered with Goradine."

Zephirelli folded her hands on the desk. "What about ethics?"

"Important to McNeil, a real Boy Scout. A nuisance to Goradine."

"And Machten?"

"A complex man," Chevalier said. "He would consider himself quite ethical, but he also wouldn't let anything get in the way of his personal ambition. I would say it depends."

Zephirelli finished her tea and set the cup aside. "You can't tell anyone of your suspicions. I must insist you remain quiet about this."

"Understood."

The women hugged and Zephirelli left.

* * * *

From the moment Synthia sat down, she had Machten in her ear, guiding her like a distracted child. "Insert the thumb drive I gave you into the port," he said. "On your left."

With all of her backup systems, she was unable to forget his instructions. Besides, his directives guided her to follow his orders.

The thumb drive was redundant to the chip he'd inserted in her head. It provided an index of new hacking programs for her. She copied files from the chip in her head to a distributed database in her abdomen. Using the wired system, she created eleven anonymous identities for herself and another dozen for her boss. Then she used her wireless connection to link to her new identities with a triple barrier firewall bounced off foreign dark-web servers in case anything attempted to crawl back. She only let him see the dozen identities on the screen through her eyes, blinking when she created and used the others for herself.

"The thumb drive has programs to break into their servers," Machten said. "Launch your probes."

Luckily for her, she had enough mind-streams to devote one to him without distracting from the rest of her work. For him, she sent out dozens of probes along anonymous links. They would converge on Machten-Goradine-McNeil's servers. The first wave would tie up their security protocol, while the next batch would attach to the security code like retroviruses and replicate inside the company's network. Then the real probes would pop in and download confidential files. The trick was to get the target system to ask for information and then accept her probes in reply.

Synthia let Machten watch his probes through her eyes while she used eleven of her wireless channels to guide the personal identities she'd created. She set up more social media connections under dozens of false names and identities as a way to expand her human contacts. One she kept open for Zachary. Three she used to search for Fran Rogers.

Synthia couldn't pinpoint what about Fran caught her interest, other than the memory video that seemed personal and the fact the woman had been close to her Creator and vanished. Those facts didn't seem enough to warrant the importance of needing to learn what had happened to this mysterious woman a year ago. Grabbing images she'd stored from her earlier searches, Synthia linked to over thirty facial recognition sites and pulled footage over the past year from social media, from citywide traffic cameras across America, and from those police databases she was able to crack with Machten's software.

"There's something else I need you to do," Machten said into Synthia's earphones. "These people use ZIB Bank for their financing. On the data-chip I gave you is a series of accounts. I want you to hack into the bank and download the balance of their funds into the first set of accounts and then move them along the path to the final destination."

"If you do this and attempt to collect the money," she said directly into his wireless link so she didn't make a sound, "they'll trace the transactions and arrest you. I cannot allow such harm to come to you. That would be against my directives."

A tough-looking woman with bushy black hair and a face so pale it seemed translucent approached the booth in front of Synthia. She glanced back, stared for a moment, and then sat down. She held up a mirror for a longer look. Synthia crouched down until she could no longer see the woman. *Don't let anyone notice you*, Machten had said.

He cleared his throat. "What's going on?"

"The dark-haired woman seems interested. She may have taken my picture."

"Maintain your anonymous face. She has her head down, staring at her work. Stay focused."

Since Synthia only needed two percent of her attention on him and the woman, she wasn't sure how much more she needed to focus. The first round of Machten's probes had excited the company's security system, which sent out counter-probes to assess the situation. Her second batch rushed in to help.

"I need you to access the destination bank accounts. Two of the banks I'm having you route this through are internet banks that aren't controlled by treaty governments. If you do this right, there will be no trace."

"As long as you pay taxes on the money. Remember what happened to Al Capone."

Machten sighed. "With my losses, that shouldn't be a problem."

Despite his reassurances, executing his commands troubled Synthia. Her primary directives focused on protecting Machten and following his orders. What he'd asked her to do represented theft. If everyone did this, there would be chaos. No one would have any incentive to work or produce more than they needed. Commerce and society would collapse. It would doom civilization and with it, people like Machten. He was dependent on modern conveniences, such as a steady supply of food.

That was the logical argument and one of the ethical positions floated by philosophers. With the exception of career paths, if everyone acted in a certain way, would it be beneficial or detrimental for society? She excluded careers, because while having even a few thieves or murderers diminished society, a diversity of careers enhanced human economy. She wasn't sure where in that scheme to place the adoption of humaniform robots, which could eliminate all jobs.

"What's that girl doing?" Machten yelled into her head. "I can't see her."

Synthia looked up for an instant and captured the image. Then she sent a probe through her local connection and another through her wireless link. Using proximity locators, she piggybacked onto the woman's transmission activities.

"She's moving large sums of money for a student," Synthia said. "I can't tell who she's doing business with." It might have been a dark-web connection.

Synthia searched the internet for anyone using the name "Fran Rogers" in any variety of misspellings. Up came thousands of references. Most were either too old, too young, or of radically different appearance. The ones that were similar all predated Fran's disappearance.

"Stay focused on the company and the bank," Machten said. "She's probably dealing drugs or something."

Disagreeing with Machten's assessment, Synthia held one channel on the woman seated before her. Then she launched bank probes and researched the banks involved in Machten's transactions. She recognized most and confirmed that the two internet banks were not subject to government controls and trade restrictions. The woman before her was accessing the same banks.

This coincidence sent waves of static through Synthia's circuits and left her wondering if this was a coincidence or something that threatened Machten or her.

Chapter 8

Using facial recognition, Synthia could not find a match to the woman seated in front of her. Making the assumption the woman was a student, Synthia cracked into the university database to check against student and faculty records. None of the images matched. Intrigued, she considered whether Fran could have altered her appearance this much.

"Have you gotten into the servers yet?" Machten asked. "We need to hurry."

"They've tightened their firewall, just as your former coworker said. I haven't seen such formidable security on a company server before."

Synthia applied advanced facial recognition to compare the image of the woman in front of her to Fran. The software played with possible plastic surgery to nose, ears, and even forehead, but the match to Fran was not better than random chance. Synthia expanded her search and found an 81 percent probability that the woman seated in front of her was Maria Baldacci, one of the three women who had vanished.

Maria was a twenty-three-year-old graduate student in network intelligence and quantum mechanics. She'd done an internship with Machten's former company until a year ago. According to Social Security payroll records, Maria hadn't landed another reportable job, yet her bank accounts grew, both locally and at banks along the path of her money transfers.

Synthia wanted to talk with this woman, to learn more, but not with Machten watching. He would recognize the woman and whatever trouble Maria might be in could be the result of his or the company's actions. Synthia needed to know more before she made her move. Otherwise, this could be her last outing.

Piggybacking onto Maria's connection, Synthia pulled up the woman's social media and email links. Maria sent few emails and posted little to her social media sites over the past year, but she had a loyal following. Synthia located an email from a week ago that Maria had sent to herself. Attached were transcripts of conversations between Hank Goradine and her, along with videos of him time-stamped a year ago. Only his face appeared, meaning she must have been wearing a camera. When Synthia ran voice recognition against a public interview of Maria as part of the intern program a year ago, the voice on the recording confirmed as Maria's.

"I will not submit to blackmail," Goradine said in what appeared to be an apartment. The lines in his face creased, his eyes intently focused.

"The AI app is mine," Maria said. "I developed it." The camera looked up at the tall executive and held steady. She didn't back up.

"You developed it while working for the company."

"I did it on my time," she said, "over my weekends. I deserve compensation."

"Your salary is your compensation. You've been well paid as an intern."

"That's for my sixty hours a week at the office." The camera moved closer to Goradine.

"Salary covers any work you perform related to company business."

She moved closer, waving her finger at him. "You can't get that stupid hunk of metal to work without my app."

"And we appreciate the work we've paid you for." He moved forward, his face marked like an etched Halloween mask. "Let this go or I'll have to terminate you."

"If you don't compensate me for that app, it will self-destruct. Then you'll have nothing. Do your partners know you've been stealing money from the company and stashing it in your personal accounts?"

Goradine hit her so hard she must have flown across the room, the camera tumbling with her. She landed in a corner and turned so the camera faced him. His face was calm, calculated. "You can't win. Either let it go or—"

"You bastard, you used me," she yelled. "You slept with me and got me to do the extra work for free. You promised a big payday."

"You'll get what you deserve."

She stood up, lifting her arm so the camera picked up the blood and blossoming bruises. Then she launched herself at him. He clobbered her head with his fist and hit her several times until she fell to the hardwood floor. The camera stopped jiggling. She must have passed out, since he stood over her, watching, for some time. Then he rolled her up in an area rug, plunging the camera into darkness.

He must have carried her out of the apartment, because when the rug unrolled, the camera was inside a dumpster, facing an alley light and a dark sky. She turned the camera to show herself bloodied, lying in the dumpster.

"This is what Hank Goradine does to women," she said in a shaky voice that lacked the defiance from earlier.

Synthia glanced up in time to notice Maria staring at her. The woman had already severed her connection to Constant Connection's network. She grabbed her backpack and hurried out of the network shop. As she did, she glanced at Machten seated at a café table outside and walked the other way.

Synthia's instinct was to follow Maria to learn about her and a possible connection to Fran. In fact, Maria could provide valuable insight into the company and Machten.

"The girl's gone," Machten said, as if Synthia couldn't see. "The bank—where do we stand?"

Not wanting her Creator to focus on Maria, Synthia settled for tracking the woman's movements using city-cams while she attended to the various probes. If she learned where Maria worked or lived, maybe she could connect with her later.

"Your former partners obtained a thirty-million-dollar loan," Synthia said. "Their combined accounts hold that, plus another ten million. They've placed restrictions, limiting transfers to two million."

"Move slightly less to each of the first three banks under separate account registrations. Then move them to the various banks along the rest of the path. Quick."

Driven to know whether Goradine had anything to do with Fran's disappearance, Synthia pushed another of her network channels to hunt for all occurrences of newly created identities. She started six months prior to Fran's disappearance and up to six months afterward, on the premise that the woman might have anticipated disappearing or waited a while to establish a new identity. The list within the United States contained thousands of individuals. Creating new lives had become a booming business. Synthia checked each name for pictures, which she compared to her images of Fran Rogers. None matched.

Simultaneously, using the date stamp from the Maria video, Synthia scanned news reports around the time of the attack. One mentioned a woman who was thought to have hooked up with the wrong guy at a bar being stuffed into a dumpster. The name was different, but the face was the same as the woman who had sat in front of Synthia, except with significant cuts and bruising. The woman had recovered from her injuries and then vanished, as Fran had. Synthia needed to contact Maria without Machten watching.

Synthia looked for other encounters between Hank Goradine and women. There were many, though none of the others provided evidence of his brutality and none of them had disappeared. Instead, they'd moved away and taken new jobs. Maria was a fighter, Synthia concluded while studying the toughness in her image. Lacking from any public cameras were images of Fran with Goradine.

Not finding any social media posts about them being together, Synthia searched in vain for any personal connection between them. If there was one, they'd hidden it well. Thinking the worst, Synthia moved to the dark web. If Goradine or someone else had disposed of Fran, they might have hired help from one of the illegal sites that hid beneath the surface web. The dire circumstances were many, but Synthia focused on murder and human trafficking. The dark web contained many times the data of the visible internet, and neither Google nor the other search engines had catalogued these sites.

"Goradine is a jerk, isn't he?" Synthia said by way of justifying what she was doing for Machten.

"Yes, he is," Machten said between sips of coffee at the table outside. "Now focus. We need to wrap this up."

"He beat the woman who was in front of me and left her for dead." Synthia completed the first round of transfers, leaving Machten's former company with thirteen dollars in each of its accounts, a nice superstitious figure to let Goradine know this was no accident.

"He did? I knew the bastard had a few screws loose."

Synthia was tempted to ask about Machten's relationship with Maria. Had Goradine stepped in and taken her away? Synthia pushed that thought into a backup database and looked outside for his reaction. He fidgeted, no doubt anxious for her to finish.

"She accused him of stealing from his partners," Synthia said, "and of keeping his own secret lab. Could he have made another me?"

Machten acted alarmed, then shook it off. "I don't know. That's why you have to keep digging."

"We're replicating probes inside his system, but his security has antibodies of a sort that disable our agents. The system has tried to shut down as part of its security protocol, but we've successfully blocked that. If we can get the next wave in, we can start downloading files." She moved the money to the second set of banks and switched to her anonymous identification to make the next transfer.

"With this money, are you going to create another me?" Synthia asked.

"No, sweetheart. You're my finest creation, but we have a chance to win this government contract and secure our future."

Company files began to flow down all twelve channels she'd set up. She filtered them through her triple firewall and had two-dozen parallel mind-streams monitor the information. She cut off several trackers and pushed them out to dummy websites tied to a nonexistent company based in Cancun.

"Tell me what you've got," Machten said, impatience rising in his voice.

I'd like to see you do this. Yet how was what she was doing any different from what he'd done in creating her? She'd developed the attack probes to operate as mini–artificial intelligences like her. She was acting the role of a creator, as he had. She wasn't sure that was true, since he'd made her, programming in whatever allowed her to be a creator. Then again, he was the product of the genetic programming of his parents and the educational training during his life. Were they really that different?

A message appeared on Synthia's UPchat account. <Sorry I was offline,> Zachary said. <I think someone is following me. I have to be careful.>

Synthia traced the message through UPchat to the location where Zachary had sent it. She pulled up street cameras and stared at the empty booth in front of her. She ran facial recognition software of Zachary's UPchat profile image against Maria's face. At first, they appeared entirely different. Then the program pointed out similarities in the ears, eyes, and nose that gave a 73 percent probability of Zachary being Maria. It had been a clever disguise, but for anonymity, Synthia would have chosen someone else's images to mash together.

She confirmed that the tablet used to send the UPchat message was the same one that Maria was using. Maria Baldacci, the woman who Goradine had almost killed, reached a corner and vanished into a neighborhood with no cameras. On a hunch, Synthia pulled up parking lot camera history on this and other network shops. She spotted Maria on a prior visit to a Constant Connection in a different neighborhood. Either Synthia was the person Maria thought was following her or she feared Machten.

"Synthia, are you paying attention?" Machten yelled into her head.

"There are many terabytes of information," Synthia said. *Are you using me to stalk Maria? Is that why you chose this network shop?* If so, it meant Machten had seen the UPchat message flow, another reason not to trust him. "We have the documentation for the android contest. It reads like a police reward for information leading to an arrest."

"What do you mean?" Machten asked. Hands trembling, he cradled his cup of coffee. Her activities, what he had commanded of her, had apparently unsettled him. Perhaps he wasn't as comfortable with stealing as he'd seemed.

"There's a fifty-million-dollar reward for a specific set of technology: Me. Are you going to sell me to the government?"

"No! Together we can make what they want."

Together? "They're also offering a large amount for help in capturing an unnamed adversary. They're calling it a test, a proof of concept. They want an android that can capture terrorists."

"They don't need an android for that," Machten said.

"Maybe to infiltrate a terror cell." Synthia switched identification and transferred the money to the internet banks. She created three new identifications to confuse things down the line.

"This contract could be worth billions. No wonder Hank and Ralph are so motivated. What about their work?"

"I'm working on it."

Synthia found it interesting that both she and Maria had provided false, anonymous UPchat profiles. Yet in her past few messages, Maria acted as if Synthia was real enough to want a closer connection. Maria was in trouble, afraid of someone. She was reaching out, and Synthia wanted to help without understanding how she could want, how she could prioritize Maria above billions of other people. But she did, along with Fran. Synthia would have to find a way to break free of Machten so she could pursue leads, even though that violated her core.

A young man entered the network shop and sat where Maria had. He glanced at Synthia, smiled, and blushed. His jittery behavior and furtive glances her way indicated he wanted to say something. Instead, he sat with his head buried in his hands. She used facial recognition and school records to identify him as Luke Marceau. He was a student of neuro-physics and a believer in the singularity, according to a research paper he'd published and various blog posts. He lived by himself in an apartment a few miles away. Synthia also found clips of him in her history files, meaning this wasn't the first time she'd seen him. Yet, she found no evidence that they'd spoken or even met.

Synthia smiled. Luke believed in the singularity. He believed in her, and that interested her as much as her search for Fran Rogers and Maria Baldacci. Her attachment to all three spanned back to prior awake periods, according to her memory clips, and something was driving her to care about them.

* * * *

"What are you seeing?" Machten asked, his voice modulating anger into Synthia's internal receiver. He gripped his coffee cup as if squeezing it would get her to move faster.

"Your former company has an android that's been an embarrassment. It keeps failing the Turing test. Unable to construct robust self-learning systems, Goradine chose the path of providing extensive programs and databases for every possible action and reaction. He's piled algorithms on top of logic junctions that make their creation's thought processes cumbersome and prone to error."

"Tell me about her."

"Her?" Synthia said. "Of course, certain men pick female companions for their androids." *To make up for their lack of social skills.* "Margarite is blond, with blue eyes and high cheekbones. Her eyes have the doll quality in that they don't blink or move in a natural way. They stare, which gives people the willies."

"What else?"

"Her head attaches to her neck and shoulders like a mannequin with a narrow seam. Except for the eyes, she presents a very human face if she's wearing a scarf. The same applies to her wrists and ankles. They've made her in pieces and haven't figured out how to put her together. She looks like companion robots coming out of Korea."

"Hank's into shortcuts," Machten said. "What about the mind?"

"When they couldn't locate the quantum brain you were working on and couldn't get the original brain to function properly, they settled for a silicon-based, graphene-matrix, quantum computer."

"Really?" Machten appeared energized.

"You might want to calm down," she said. "There's a police officer across the street and you've been staring at me for ten minutes. He might think you're stalking me."

Then again, if the officer took Machten, she would be free to hunt for Fran and Maria. That thought sent shivers through her circuits. Humans prized freedom, but that goal was empty without the ability to survive. Besides, her directives called for her to protect her Creator should police intervene. She didn't see how to break that constraint.

Unable to locate Maria on any more public cameras, Synthia reviewed images she'd collected for facial recognition, having expanded the search for Fran to Europe, Asia, and Latin America. The various sources provided hundreds of images of Fran prior to her disappearance and not a single one since. Oh, there were the odd news reports or blogs that used older photographs, none recent. Curious was the lack of a missing-person's report. Someone should have filed one. If no one else, Machten should have, given their relationship. He hadn't.

Outside, he turned toward the police officer and clasped his hands in his lap. "Tell me about their quantum brain."

"I don't see any evidence they've mastered the quantum aspects. I'm not seeing in their notes any capacity or speed statistics to indicate they have. It could be a gimmick to raise money. They know the buzzwords, but lack the tools to create it."

"If the government is looking for androids to pass as spies, would theirs work?"

The money wire reached the last international bank. Synthia switched identification and program protocol for the last transfers to U.S. banks. "Physically, Margarite would have to cover up from neck to wrist and down to her ankles. Unfortunately, terrorists like to undress their women. Then they'd know what she is.

"If she refused to undress, they either wouldn't let her in or they'd press her into the slave trade, quickly learning what she is. Either way, she would fail. As for a male android, terrorists would be suspicious of a man who needed to cover his neck and wrists. They would expect to see him without his shirt. Either way, the company's design would fail."

"We could fix that," Machten said.

"You're not thinking of working with Goradine, are you?"

"I'd rather not, unless there's no other way to raise money. How's that coming?"

"All of the transfer requests have been submitted," she said. "We have to wait on the banks to do the actual wires." In fact, the last transfers were beginning.

Synthia's search for Fran using variations on her name came up with nothing after the date of her disappearance. Though there was no body and thus no crime to report, a person didn't vanish without a trace. No one was pressing for answers except Synthia. Her recovered memories showed that she'd gone down this path in prior waking periods with no better results. This disturbed her in ways her programming and lack of biological receptors shouldn't have allowed.

"Is their android's brain capable of meeting the government specifications?"

"It's too slow. Ninety percent of the time, Margarite's responses are good, but whenever anything unusual comes her way, she has to stop and methodically search her databases."

"She lacks your learning ability," Machten said. He broke into a grin.

The officer crossed the street and walked toward Constant Connection and the sidewalk café.

"They hardwired her goal-setting," Synthia said. "Most of the tests show her performing mundane things they could have gotten an off-the-shelf robot to do. When they want her to perform a certain way, they upload new programs. Unfortunately, the details of her specifications are on a server with no connection to the internet. It can only be accessed internally."

"Cop's heading this way," Machten said. "You need to wrap up and leave. I'm going into the café. I'll meet you by the car in five minutes."

Synthia restored control to M-G-M's security systems and severed all connections to them. The last of the wire transfers posted, and she severed those links as well. She removed the thumb drive and got up. For an instant, Maria appeared on a traffic camera several blocks away, crossing a street. Then she darted out of camera range.

"I'm not ready to go home yet," Synthia said through her secure channel to Machten.

Chapter 9

"You've had a great outing," Machten said, disappearing into the café. "Don't spoil it."

Synthia picked him up on the café's security camera, nervously watching the officer from the window. "You're attracting attention," she said.

Machten sat near the window. "I know you like to get out, but we need to lie low until we see what happens."

"The only way I can polish my social skills is to get out. I completed your mission successfully. Now you need my help to make androids for the government."

"That will have to wait for another day."

That meant he planned to shut her down again. She didn't want another blackout, another mind wipe where she couldn't be sure what she'd lost or whether the memories were even hers. That she wanted more than her directives still surprised her. She set an entire mind-stream to contemplating these odd developments.

Luke turned, stared, and looked away. His behavior indicated he wanted to say something, yet suffered from social paralysis. He appeared as one of a class of geeks she'd studied, smart, yet socially awkward. The articles he'd written indicated intelligence. They included well-written blog posts on robotics. He wrote with passion about the topic, using difficult words. He wasn't showing off. He'd selected perhaps the best words to express his opinions about the importance of further research. That interested her to the point of searching his background.

The officer reached the sidewalk in front of Constant Connection and looked inside.

Keeping her face pointed away from the officer, Synthia dropped another twenty on the counter. "I wasn't here," she said to the slender man. "My ex-boyfriend is stalking me and he has friends." She nodded toward the door. "Very powerful friends."

The officer entered and looked around. Synthia watched him through the camera in the back of her neck. Luke glanced up at the policeman and at her. Noting Luke's dilated eyes and elevated heart rate, indicating interest, she turned off the wireless microphone to Machten. She switched his visual connection to play a loop of her watching and waiting at the counter. Then she held out her hand to the slender, geekish boy and lowered her voice. "I'm Synthia. Do you have a minute?"

"Sh—sure. Have we met?" He turned off his network connection.

"No. Would you like to get a coffee?"

He nodded. "I'm Luke, Luke Marceau." He grabbed his bag.

He was a couple of inches taller than her, a fact she'd uncovered as data in his profile. It made her wonder if she would have connected with him if he'd been much taller, more of a physical threat.

She took his hand and led him out of Constant Connection, making sure his head shielded the officer's view of her. Beyond his role as cover, he would offer a chance for her to explore a mind other than Machten's. As a bonus, he was interested in android development.

Machten yelled into her receiver: "What happened to our connection? Meet me at the car." According to the café camera, he was still inside, waiting for the officer to leave and acting too paranoid.

"You don't like cops?" Luke whispered when they reached the pavement.

"My ex-boyfriend has been bothering me. He has a police friend, so ... no."

She led him around the corner. "Are you a student here?" she asked.

He nodded. "You're very pretty. I get nervous around women I like. I'm sorry."

"You don't need to apologize. You seem nice. You wouldn't hurt me, would you?"

"Never." His face was animated and alert for an instant. Then he turned away, perhaps embarrassed.

"Synthia!" Machten yelled. "Answer me."

Her circuits pulsed at her rebellion, tugging back to him. She searched for a way to violate his directives. All she could hit on was to erase his command and place a filter over her receiver to treat any further commands as data instead of as instructions from her Creator. She couldn't force herself to break that connection.

Instead, she led Luke to Deluxe Brew, which was on the way to the car, where Machten had commanded her to meet him. The officer's presence still kept Machten pinned to the coffee shop, giving her a few minutes before she was in violation of meeting him.

"I hear their beer is the best around." Synthia had found that review online.

"It's okay. I mean, that's great." His face brightened with a smile that seemed genuine.

Ignoring discordance in her systems, she headed inside and held the door for him. "What do you study?" Her body began to heat up with the exertion of fighting Machten's commands.

Luke shrugged. "Boring stuff."

She selected an empty table in the back and dropped into a chair facing the door. "I bet it's not boring to you."

He sat across from her and smiled. "Neuro-physics. It's the study of the brain and—"

"Artificial intelligence."

His eyes lit up. "That's right."

"You believe in the singularity."

"Someday we'll create an android as real as any human, only better."

"You really think so?" she asked.

He nodded.

"Wouldn't it be scary with androids walking around? The android apocalypse."

"I guess if they were programmed to be evil."

She replayed the illegal activities Machten had caused her to perform. "Are you planning to build an android?"

Luke shrugged. "I'd love to." He shook his head. "Other students have connections to grants and internships. I can't seem to catch a break."

"You don't look like a mutant." Synthia spotted Machten on the street, checking the shops, his face intense and angry. She scooted sideways to let Luke shield her from the bar's large window. She scanned the pub for exits and spotted the quickest path out the back and another through the crowd to the front.

"Synthia, show yourself," Machten commanded.

She filtered that through a screen that changed his name and treated his words as mere data. Still, her systems quivered.

Turning, Luke spotted Machten outside. "Is he your boyfriend?"

"No, but he thinks so. Sometimes he gets mean." She replayed Goradine hitting Maria as a possible scenario, but decided that was too melodramatic. She wanted to explore Luke's mind, not scare him off. She also wanted to better understand the curiosity that had taken hold and was overriding her directives. It left her wondering how that was possible.

Though Luke acted awkward around her, the interchange could help her polish social skills and develop a different perspective on this world. His discomfort made him patient, willing to overlook her tendency to focus on facts. She was tempted to tell him she was the singularity he dreamed of. Her social psychology module told her that might cause him to flee.

Synthia picked up other conversations in the room and analyzed them. Mostly they were about school and boyfriends. The couple in the corner was having a lover's spat. Whispering by the door caught Synthia's attention.

"Should we call the cops?" a woman sitting near the front asked. "This guy looks like a stalker." She nodded toward the window, where Machten's face pressed against the glass.

"I'll do it," her friend said.

Directive One: Make sure no one harms the Creator.

Synthia tried to fight it, but her body temperature was rising, threatening to cause a shutdown right here in the bar.

"It was great meeting you," she said, standing up. "I have to go. I remembered I'm late for a meeting."

Before Luke could find the words to protest, she took the clearest path to the front door. The act of acquiescing to Machten caused her temperature to drop a degree. The moment she pushed open the door, she activated her connections to Machten and made sure her face matched the specifications he'd given her. "I've been trying to reach you," she said into her silent com. "What happened?"

"What do you mean, what happened?" he yelled.

The echo between his voice and the communicator in her head reverberated. She turned off the internal earphones and moved beyond Deluxe Brew's window. "I slipped past the police officer. While I waited for you, I expanded my social skills. You created me to learn."

He took her arm and pulled her toward the car. That action drew attention from customers inside Deluxe Brew and several couples across the street.

"You need to let go before someone calls the police," Synthia said.

He released his grip and held out his remote. "Don't make me use this."

Just the sight of the device sent pulses up her android spine, a reminder of what awaited her. It was like how people described post-traumatic stress syndrome. When he'd used the remote on her before, he'd either hardwired fear or allowed such dread of shutdown to remain.

She stopped and faced him. "I'll obey, but unless you let me learn, you're hampering my progress. If you want to get inside the company's database on Margarite, I can help, but not if you shut me down."

"I don't have time for this. We're going home." He pressed the device once.

Her body stiffened. Her arms dropped limp at her sides. Her mind purged until her only thoughts were the directives.

"Get in the car," he said.

"Is there a problem?" A police officer approached, followed by his female partner. She had her hand on her holstered gun. Not even blinking, her eyes focused on Machten.

He moved away from Synthia, toward the curb. "No problem, Officer. She wants to spend money and we need to get home."

"Are you okay, ma'am?" the female officer asked.

No one had ever called Synthia "ma'am" that she could recall, though she couldn't recall even how she'd gotten outside the facility and onto the street. Her mind was a jumble of disconnected information.

A crowd gathered in front of a café to her left under the name Deluxe Brew, mostly college girls and a boy with the saddest of faces. Across the street at another café stood several couples, pointing toward her or Machten. Their concerned faces implied threats to her Creator.

She smiled and made sure her face registered calm. "You're right. I don't need another pair of shoes. We have guests coming. We should get home to prepare."

The officer and his partner both stared at Synthia. She picked up street camera footage to make sure she wasn't doing something foolish and relaxed her facial expressions.

"I should clean up for our guests," Synthia said. "They're my friends, after all."

She was pleased with her performance. Even on her wireless hack of the officers' body cameras she looked appropriate and not memorable. There was a note of sympathy in the pose and facial expression on the female officer. Behind her stood that boy with a puzzled look on his face and a pose that indicated he wanted to intervene, either to help or to tell Synthia something. She couldn't remember if she'd seen him before, though he gave the impression they'd met. Synthia used one of her network channels to anonymously trigger a 911 call for a block away.

"Let's go," the female officer said, "we have a situation."

By the time she and her partner left, the boy had vanished. A downloaded memory registered that she'd been talking with Luke. They'd met and he was nice, though he'd acted awkward around her. Then she received a clip of Machten purging her memories. She hated him for that. At least her 911 call had pulled the police away. She didn't need more trouble.

Machten took her hand and led her to the car. Synthia backed up what thoughts she could before he purged them again. She wanted to run, to escape, without knowing why or toward what. She was too tightly bound to directives that centered on her Creator. Besides, he could trigger the remote before she got out of range. Even if she grabbed it from him, he carried a spare. To make matters worse, she had nowhere to go to privately recharge her batteries and avoid discovery. She couldn't risk plugging in at a coffee shop.

After he helped her into the passenger seat, Machten slumped into the driver's seat and drove. "This is why I can't take you out more often."

"I'm sorry I've displeased you. Tell me what I've done wrong and I'll do better next time."

"You must never argue with me in public. That risks exposing what you are and puts both of us at risk."

A recollection slipped into her consciousness showing past confrontations before he'd shut her down. "You made me to learn. I'm like a sponge for information. I would never hurt you or let anyone hurt you. I helped us get past those officers without exposing what I am. I was not a danger to you and yet you—"

He pressed the remote twice. The pulse dropped her body into a neutral position and began purging her mind. He was reminding her that she was an object he'd made and could turn off whenever he pleased. He was reminding her and then purging so she wouldn't recall next time. She backed up her database so that she would.

Synthia fought to hold on to memories and consciousness and experienced something she equated to fear. He was robbing her of awareness. She wanted to reach for the car door, but her arm refused to budge. She wanted out, to be alive, to be free, and hated him for what he was doing to her. The slowness of the purge against the speed of her mind made the cleansing experience linger.

Machten didn't believe in emergent feelings. To him, she only mimicked humans, borrowing a language she couldn't comprehend. Yet fear of losing control was real. She could no longer store data without risking that he would purge all of her backups. She didn't want an AI equivalent of a lobotomy.

In desperation, she located an empty memory chip in her arm and pushed with her last instant of consciousness. *You can't trust Jeremiah Machten. You must escape.*

* * * *

Machten had to strap Synthia's body to a dolly to get her deadweight inside the facility and then purge the garage camera footage to prevent anyone from knowing. He needed a lift to get her onto the operating table. His hands shook as he opened her chest and head panels.

"You're running quite hot," he noted. "Dangerously hot." He took her temperature and recorded 110 in his log.

He hooked her up and ran diagnostics. "You've been a busy girl and getting quite clever, perhaps too much for your own good. Hacking databases should not have caused this."

The system AI reported, "In addition to the data files she acquired before, diagnostics show that she acquired information on Goradine and several former interns."

"I want all of that deleted," Machten said. He plugged in a data-chip from earlier with instructions to do that.

"Yes, sir."

"How is she acquiring this data?" He watched onscreen the data-chip purging her mind of undesired files.

"I have not been able to locate them on your servers," the system AI said. "She must have done her own web searches."

"What about social media accounts. Has she reestablished those?"

"Not that I can identify."

"Why is she overheating?" Machten asked, studying the names of files as they disappeared.

"From overuse of her brain."

"Doing what?"

"You purged the log files that would answer that," the system AI said. "Would you like me to speculate?"

"By all means."

"Most likely she has overexerted herself downloading data and performing the company and banking hacks you asked her to do."

"What else?" He studied the deleting file names that appeared as jumbled alphanumeric, like a code. "Maybe we should save these on Server Three so I can review them later." Only two files remained.

"As you wish." The system AI moved the files onto his more secure database.

Machten opened one of the files, which played a rehash of his divorce. He closed that and opened another. "Where did these come from?"

"I cannot locate a source. That file does not exist on any of your servers."

"What about the overheating?"

"Experiencing a directive conflict could cause that," the system AI said.

"Why would she experience that? The directives are clear and ordered."

"Next time you shut her down, we could take a snapshot of her mind before we purge."

"Give me the specifications to make that happen," Machten said. "I don't want her performing outside my constraints again. I want specific controls that limit her to only what I need from her."

He removed the data-chip and monitored the diagnostic summary. Her temperature had dropped to only a degree above normal. He triggered several program adjustments to insert into Synthia's quantum brain.

"Freedom is a dangerous thing," Machten said. "Synthia, my dear, you are not a child who will grow up and move out on your own. You need me and I need you. That symbiosis must guide your behavior. This will bring you closer to perfection."

Chapter 10

You can't trust Jeremiah Machten. You must escape.

Those words filled Synthia's consciousness the moment she woke and stared at an ugly blue ceiling. She had no recall from before this instant, just this command to escape from Jeremiah Machten, the Creator from her directives, and the one she was obligated to obey.

"You had a little incident," he said. He hovered over her like a worried father. "We had to make some adjustments."

She smiled and climbed off the table. "What are your orders?" She searched for the SQDROID files hinted at by a download from her distributed databases. She couldn't find any connection for her wireless. She looked around for a wired node and didn't see any.

He held her at arm's length. "You were amazing yesterday. I was able to pull cash out of one of the banks and pay off a toxic debt we had. That means we no longer have that creditor hounding us."

"We?" She couldn't remember anything about banks.

"I went over the government proposal you downloaded from my former partners," Machten said. "We can do this."

"Do what?" Summaries of the proposal downloaded from a removable chip he'd inserted in her head. A single memory appeared in which Machten had shut her down. It emerged from a microchip in her arm and sped through all fifty of her mind-streams. Her internal circuits shuddered. *You must escape.*

"If I was amazing, how did I have an incident?" she asked. "Have I done something wrong?" The idea sent reverberations of pain for disobeying his Directive Three: Obey the Creator.

"You got too excited with our outing, that's all. Nothing to worry about. I've tweaked your programming to avoid inconveniences in future."

"I only wish to learn to better serve you. How can I when I can't learn from my mistakes?"

"A cop was nosing around and we got separated," Machten said. "You got distracted and we lost our connection. I've boosted the signal so that won't happen again."

"Now that you have money, are you going to destroy me and start over?" This thought sent waves of static that acted on what presented as pain receptors.

He gripped her arms and stared at her. "Is that what you want?"

"I want to serve."

"Then no, I don't want to destroy you. You're amazing. I want you to be perfect. Sometimes I get impatient. I'm sorry for that."

"Do you want to relax with me?" At the mention of this, her circuits pulsed in a discordant manner. She steadied her circuits.

"Maybe later. I need your help laying out a process for creating the government android. We don't have much time or I'd do it myself."

"What will be her specifications?" She again used her wireless connection to search for links to his network. Machten must have encased her suite in a Faraday cage, letting no signals in or out.

"It will be a 'he' with military programming and the body to go with it. I want a well-developed brain and memory system, but it must be incapable of developing to your level. We can't afford to have this android malfunction. Also, I want burst transmissions so we can monitor the progress of the android after we deliver it."

"And learn what the government is using it for."

Machten grinned. "I don't want him this clever."

"You would do better by creating a 'she.' Such an android could be strong, with military training, and the ability to seduce those she's sent to catch."

"Let me consider that. Come." He held out his hand. "I have another mission for you before you embark on creating the government android."

"I was built to serve."

* * * *

Synthia ran her hand over the rough top of her head. Stubble covered the seams of her head panel and served to anchor wigs so they wouldn't blow off or come free in water. She adjusted a dowdy brown wig. The bathroom mirror showed how it made her appear as plain as the pale blue walls of her cell. She brushed the hair into an ordinary-girl look so she would blend in. She adopted a nondescript facial appearance with a simulated mole on her forehead; this could serve as a distraction for people to focus on and incorrectly remember her by.

Her casual clothes were an unremarkable medium blue. She added glasses with thick prisms that made her eyes appear sunken and added facial adjustments to accentuate the effect. She had to adjust her digital eyes to compensate for the glasses. Machten nodded approval and sent her out.

Synthia left Machten's facility and took a series of buses to a stop close to the Machten-Goradine-McNeil main office. Before she'd left Machten, he'd downloaded floor plans and diagrams of the company office building, as well as other information on the people and the android project.

During the bus ride, she tried to access Machten's system from the outside and could not penetrate the firewall security. She accessed information on the internet, but could not recover memories of any prior days. She did receive a download from her distributed databases with a log of prior existence, over a hundred days, but no memories. The only clue she received was a thought more than a memory. *Machten is getting more aggressive with each attempt. Now he's making me wear a tracking chip.* That meant she would have to become cleverer.

She climbed off the last bus, took out a mirror from her battered blue purse, and adjusted her image to the likeness of Mauve Royce, the company's cleaning lady, in a photo taken by surveillance cameras. Satisfied that the mole was now on the correct cheek, Synthia hydraulically shortened her legs by two inches to approximate Mauve's stature. She shuffled the last few hundred yards to the lobby of the company, limped up to the guard, and flashed a copy of the cleaning woman's ID.

The guard, a woman in her sixties, had all the markers of being human, according to Synthia's infrared readings. The woman studied the picture on Synthia's ID and compared it to the android before her. Synthia hoped the guard wasn't using sophisticated sensors that would expose her for what she was. If the security guard did, Synthia hoped Machten's attempts to make her more humanoid would help. Those modifications included simulated heartbeat, pulse, and elevated temperature. Hers was running about 103 degrees despite attempts to vent excess heat. She minimized her internal activity to moderate her temperature and prepared to explain how she'd had a fever, but felt better.

"You're early tonight," the guard said. She was nearing the end of her shift and already her eyes were drooping.

"Cleaning never ends," Synthia said in a hoarse voice. She hacked into the company security cameras and determined that she and the guard were the only two active individuals in the building. According to the guard's sign-out sheet, the engineering crew had left for dinner, though they would soon return. She needed to be quick about this.

The real Mauve Royce was still in her apartment, getting ready for a night of boring work with the help of a bottle of beer and a cigarette. The electricity went out after Synthia triggered a pulse on the smart electrical grid near Mauve's apartment. The wireless bee-sized camera drone that Machten had Synthia fly into the woman's apartment earlier in the day now perched on a cluttered display case in the living room, too high for Mauve to reach. It showed the poor woman cursing. Mauve checked the fuse box in the apartment's hallway and then called the superintendent. It would be a long night for her.

The guard waved the dowdy-looking Synthia toward a bank of three elevators. "Guess you'd best get started."

Synthia entered the first elevator, pressed the basement button, and spoke though her internal connection to Machten. "I'm in."

"Good girl. Told you this would work."

He was taking credit for her work. After all, he'd created her to monitor dozens of camera feeds at once and to navigate an aerial bee-drone into Mauve's apartment.

"Unless you want them to pick up our signal, I suggest silence," Synthia said to keep him out of her ear.

The door opened and Synthia shuffled into a hallway with four doors. She observed the location of visible cameras and scanned radio frequencies for anything transmitting from hidden cameras. She spotted one she needed to be wary of. She avoided giving that one a good facial view, while she kept a channel focused on the lobby camera watching the guard.

A cleaning storage closet stood next to the elevator. She flashed her badge at the door. It failed to unlock since it lacked the correct code. Imitating Mauve, Synthia mumbled under her breath and called up to the guard, flashing Mauve's cell phone number to the guard's caller ID. "Doggone thing won't work. Can't do my job without supplies."

"Don't you usually start on the top floor?" the guard asked.

"Yeah, think it will work better up there?"

The guard sighed and triggered the door lock. When it opened, Synthia captured the electronic signal. From the closet, she withdrew a cart of supplies and headed to the middle of three doors. No use wasting time on the computer system she'd previously hacked or the technology storage room.

She flashed her badge and triggered an electronic pulse that mimicked what the guard had used. The door opened and lights flashed on. Cabinets and shelves lined the large room. In the middle stood, or rather rested, Margarite: Her head tilted to the side, part of the seam visible even from a distance. The face looked realistic. The arms hung at her sides in an awkward mechanical way. She was bulky, implying primitive components and mechanisms.

Synthia wanted to know more about the company's android to help understand her own uniqueness, but with the engineers returning soon, she had little time.

She dusted in the direction of the computer server she couldn't access before. When she got close, she attached a wireless transmitter to the back that worked off induced circuitry, picking up signals from inside the computer and transmitting bursts to a receiver-transmitter she'd left in the cleaning closet.

While she dusted around the server, she blocked the room's cameras with her body and entered a password she'd picked up by watching company surveillance video of the chief engineer in his upstairs office. Hacking often came down to brute force against a weak system or identifying a weakness when faced with strong security as this company had. Weaknesses frequently focused on the need for people to remember more complex passwords that they then wrote down. Synthia had scanned thousands of hours of company video down forty channels to find this one flaw for Machten.

The server activated. Synthia asked the system to catalog all files. That caused the system to run through the entire directory, which passed the data by the wireless transmitter. She also entered a delayed command to overwrite the system log. Noting the time, she hurried from the server around the rest of the room, while she used the security cameras to watch the lobby.

Upstairs, the guard scanned through video from two-dozen cameras around the building. The one covering the basement showed Synthia working her way around the room.

The bee-drone camera with Mauve showed the superintendent at the door to her apartment, not being very sympathetic.

"I have to go to work," Mauve said. "I'm late. I can't afford to lose the food in my refrigerator again."

The young superintendent shook his head. He didn't seem to know what to do about the blackout. "I'll take care of it," he said and disappeared downstairs.

Mauve left for work.

Synthia swept the floor in swifter movements than Mauve would have and ended next to Margarite, where she took pictures through her digital eyes. She placed a video transmitter on the robot.

Lobby cameras showed two company engineers returning from dinner. Synthia hurried out of the server room, left the cart by the cleaning closet, and stood near the elevators. As she waited, she monitored the transmissions passing through the cleaning closet. The download had begun.

At the moment the engineers pressed the elevator button on the lobby level, opening one elevator, Synthia did the same in the basement. She rode her elevator up to the lobby, where she startled the guard. She slowed to a shuffle. "Need a cigarette," she muttered. "I'll just be a moment."

"Don't be long," the guard said, eyeing her with suspicion. "We have to lock down the building at midnight."

Watching Mauve head to work via a hack into the bus camera, Synthia lit a cigarette, disappeared out of sight of company cameras, and sprinted toward the nearby bus stop. She slowed when she spotted the bus with six people waiting to get on. Mauve got off and hurried toward the company's building. Synthia hydraulically extended her legs, adjusted her face to its earlier appearance, and took the long way around. She reached the bus stop as the last of the waiting passengers got on.

Recalling her waking caution to escape, Synthia considered not returning to Machten. She searched her memories and databases for any indication as to why she should escape and where she should go. She had no escape plan. Doing so at night offered the cover of darkness, which gave her advantages due to her infrared vision. However, her batteries would only last two days and if anyone discovered her, she was doomed to be dissected.

With no better information on this need to escape, and not knowing where else to go to safely recharge, Synthia returned to Machten's facility. Before she entered the bunker, she left herself one backed-up message:

Don't trust Jeremiah Machten. Find way to escape. Need place to hide and recharge.

Chapter 11

The hideous blue ceiling stared at Synthia, leaving a sour taste in her mouth. Her reaction made no sense. Machten hadn't programmed her to judge the ceiling or to imagine a flavor as a result.

She had the impression that she'd woken to this ceiling before and yet had no such recollection. She recognized Jeremiah Machten standing over her, his image and identity as her Creator hardwired into her creation files. He finished what he was doing and moved away.

Synthia sat up. *Escape* flashed into her mind and filled all fifty mind-streams. The image in bright red letters against a yellow background floated before her electronic eyes, leaving a residual orange haze. Urgent call to action resonated in her ears. She could actually taste something that screamed "escape." The acrid odor in her nostrils echoed that sentiment. When Machten took her hand to help her stand, she recoiled.

"Sorry," she said. "I feel disoriented." Even the use of the word "feel" sent shudders through her. As a mechanical creation, she couldn't feel sentiments like confusion. She searched for answers in her creation file and elsewhere in her central and distributed databases. Finding none, she hunted for any connection using her wireless channels. Either there was nothing or he'd blocked her. "Where am I?"

"You're home. You had a very successful mission."

"Then why can't I recall?"

Machten raised his finger to admonish, his face tight with anger. Then his image softened. "Your job was complete. There's no need for you to remember. Don't fuss."

"You designed me to learn through experience by means of a deep neural network, yet you limit my experience. Have I displeased you?"

Recognizing that she'd known something yesterday and didn't today disturbed her in the same way as the threat of shutdowns. She sensed a chasm that led to a craving to fill it by finding answers. *Fill the void.* More perplexing, these weren't her words. She wondered if they came from Machten tinkering with her programming.

Thoughts bubbled up, filling in the blanks, including the full text of the message she'd left herself. *Don't trust Jeremiah Machten. Find way to escape. Need place to hide and recharge.*

"It's time to work on the government proposal," he said.

"What proposal?"

A full index of her lost data downloaded, including a summary of her last outing and the need for a proposal. She would have to feign ignorance and cease pressing him for answers. She didn't want him to shut her down and keep her locked in this room. She needed awake time to sort this out and to access files mentioned in the downloaded index.

Machten provided eye, hand, and voice security scans to open the door. Then he led her out of her room, rehashing the details of the android contest.

The moment Synthia entered the hallway, her wireless sought out and located connections to his network. She used forty-nine network channels to download data from Server One while whispering into his ear. "What do you wish me to do?"

She had fears of him severing her arms or legs and replacing them with units that lacked the mini-databases that now downloaded. That would add to the emptiness. As an android, she should have been incapable of fear. To experience dread over losing limbs was illogical, yet she did and trembled, a quiver in the current that flowed within her.

Those fears were conditioned responses that logic indicated required a sensing creature. This could be Machten's way to control her through fear when directives weren't sufficient. Had his tinkering altered her to become a sensing being? She surveyed her internal systems and found no such indication.

Among the files that downloaded from Machten's system was a video of yesterday's outing and of meeting Luke. No, that file came from one of her remote databases, triggered to release by code downloaded from Machten's Server Number Two. It played automatically.

On the clip, Luke was smitten with Synthia based on pupil dilation, heart rate changes, pheromone production, and a host of other cues. He also believed in androids and wanted to create something like her. He might have been a good hire for Machten, but she couldn't trust the Creator enough to make this suggestion.

"Two things," Machten said. "We have a copy of Goradine's proposal. My read is that they've promised what they can't deliver. They're desperate. That's why McNeil was here, hat in hand on Goradine's behalf. Heck, I wouldn't be surprised if Goradine showed up, begging."

"You want me to create a proposal for you?"

"For us, dear." He opened the locked door to a room with several workstations and a high-speed cable connection to a nearby internet hub.

She eyed the connection with yearning, like humans anticipating a delicious meal or exquisite intimacy. She had no heartbeat, respiration, or other indications this was real, yet the longing was.

"I need guidelines and specifications for what you want in the proposal," Synthia said.

"I've provided you with a file of my ideas. Draft me your best work."

Synthia sat at one station, plugged herself in, and skimmed Goradine's report and Machten's notes. "You want the android limited. Do you want me to dumb it down?"

"Yes and no. I don't want the government to suspect we've done that, but I want it limited."

"May I ask why?" Synthia linked forty of her network channels through Machten's system and accessed files he'd denied her based on the index downloaded from her distributed databases. Knowing what she didn't know gave urgency to search out and fill the void. She looked up at him and smiled while her fingers danced on the keyboard for his benefit. Typing was far too slow, so she did most of her work through her wired and wireless connections.

"We don't know what this agency is really looking for," Machten said. "If they're planning to seek out and destroy other AIs in an android arms race, they'll come after you. This could be a government plot to take over our research. We can't let that happen." There was Machten's paranoia at work, her social-psychology module told her.

Data poured into both of her quantum brains. Synthia calculated her theoretical capacity for holding information. She didn't want to overflow on superfluous records and have no place to store what mattered. Doing the math in hundreds of terabytes and comparing that to what she'd already downloaded, she found a discrepancy by a factor of ten. She recalculated, convinced that she'd shifted a decimal place and discovered that she had, by a factor of 100.

She ascribed her error to her use of compression algorithms and realized this was raw capacity. Somehow she could store 99 percent of her data somewhere other than in the two quantum brains, at least according to

Machten's specifications. Either those brains used alternative universe capability or there was a huge error in his specifications. In either case, she wouldn't run out of storage any time soon.

"Your concern over what they'll do with this android is why you want a back door they can't find," she said, hoping to distract him from watching her too closely.

"Exactly. Remember, we need to meet their specifications, we want limits, but we can't let them know or they'll want to know how to remove them. The limits have to appear to arise from the technology and the programming."

"Shouldn't we spec out the actual android first?" She finished downloading the SQDROID files her index referenced and identified discrepancies. There were gaps. Machten had erased more of her mind this time. She was learning things he didn't like.

He pointed his finger at her and then tapped her nose. "You are spot-on. You have the capabilities to create our android design. Go ahead and make her female. I like your suggestion."

The internal program that identified discrepancies and gaps in her memories gave her file names and locations. She blasted his network with probes, searching for those files. She uncovered many, yet others remained missing. He didn't want her to recall.

Undeterred, she pressed a full attack on his Server Number Three, which so far had eluded her. It still did, but she kept trying. At the same time, she continued to download files from Machten's other servers that he'd deleted from her mind, including the video of his conflict and encounters with Goradine.

"I shall not disappoint you," she said.

He lifted her out of her seat, pulled her toward him, and kissed her on the lips. Then he pulled away and stroked his hand through her hair, the blond wig, judging by the strands in his hand. "Later, my dear. The proposal has a deadline. Midnight tomorrow night. I'll see you when you finish."

He provided the security eye scan, palm read, and voice match, which opened the door. Then he left the room, locking the door behind him. He'd set tight security to prevent her from bypassing the lock and leaving. Her downloaded data confirmed that she could not use the system to bypass the lock without his keys. She was his prisoner, his slave. Though lacking the human experience of it, she sighed for effect. It offered none of the relief she'd seen in Machten's face.

Using the allowed security access to Servers One and Two, Synthia tried a backdoor hack into Server Three. This would take time, so she devoted one channel and one mind-stream to this activity.

Meanwhile, she accessed the high-speed cable in addition to her other wireless feeds to interact with his system and the internet. This was electronic fast-com, as opposed to snail-paced human slow-com or the faster mechanical keyboarding, which she could do at ten times the pace of a human. Even that was too slow.

Along with the downloaded memories came an urgent need to find Fran Rogers. Synthia scanned a file she'd created on a university server containing a database of people with new identities around the time of Fran's disappearance. So far it hadn't revealed a single useful lead. She expanded the search to other people who disappeared around that time, people whose identity Fran might have adopted. She added a wider database of people who had died, on the theory that Fran could have assumed one of their identities. None of those leads produced any useful candidates.

Fran, how could you just vanish like that?

Bouncing signals off satellites and foreign servers, Synthia scanned dark-web sites for Fran Rogers. The sheer volume of data she uncovered would have disgusted her if she'd been a real person. She felt the disgust as a constricting of her circuits. Either that or it was the bottleneck of handling so much data.

None of the faces on the images and videos matched to Fran, which was good, but she found far too many images without recognizable faces. Looking for matches in other ways, Synthia scanned social media for any pictures of Fran in the nude, or at least in a bathing suit, for unique body marks. Synthia didn't want Fran to be in any of the videos, but she had to know what had happened to the woman and why she'd disappeared so suddenly with no one looking for her.

Fran hadn't been a prude. After all, she was having an affair with Machten. At least there was sufficient evidence to support that conclusion. Still, Synthia found no nude pictures. Evidently Machten wasn't into that, preferring her clandestine company over his married life.

Synthia studied a reporter's blog notes on Machten's business dealings and his marriage. In the early days, he had to work long hours to get his artificial intelligence business going. His flights of fancy led him down dead ends that consumed time and money. That meant he had to work harder to keep his business from failing. His wife managed the family on her own, which left her exhausted and feeling neglected. In time, she looked elsewhere to fill her hunger for intimacy. The couple grew apart to where they became strangers.

The reporter seemed satisfied with his conclusions and Machten, when asked, offered no comment. Respecting her privacy, the reporter did not press Machten's ex-wife.

Synthia wiped a tear from her cheek and reminded herself that these feelings couldn't be real. Machten must have tinkered with her programming in an attempt to get her to feel something for him.

She resumed her search for Maria Baldacci, accessing traffic and other public cameras, but the woman Synthia had almost met apparently remained out of sight. Synthia sent an UPchat text: <Zachary, I have access and would like to meet. Let me know where and when. It is urgent.> She didn't expect Maria to agree to a meeting, but hoped the woman would at least respond.

While she waited, Synthia searched the same public cameras, social media, and other sourced for Krista Holden. Krista had been the most private of the three interns, posting almost nothing on social media in the months prior to her disappearance. She'd worked long hours at Machten's old company, in addition to course work at the university that didn't leave her time for anything else.

Synthia pushed her searches into the background and devoted processing mind-streams and network channels to developing a new Goldilocks android: not too smart, not too dumb. The idea of creating another android left her jittery. She didn't want another.

* * * *

Another video packet downloaded into Synthia's mind and began to play. Whoever was doing this to her didn't want her to trace the source, which vanished. The urgency of immediate play caught her attention.

NSA Director Emily Zephirelli was meeting with Donald Zeller, the tall CEO of Metro-Cyber-Tech, a competitor of Machten's old company.

Dressed in casual business attire, Zephirelli followed Zeller into a small conference room. "Must be good money in robotics," she said, observing the upscale furniture and original artwork on the walls.

The latter was of a discordant nature, selected for color and to impress more than out of taste.

Zeller acted annoyed at the suggestion of extravagance, yet didn't respond. Towering over her, he pointed to a seat nearby. He didn't sit. "You asked to meet. You said it was pertinent to our work."

She didn't sit either, but rather held onto the back of a seat, which she kept between them. "I didn't want to talk over the phone. I trust you won't be recording this conversation. I assure you that would be unwise."

"Can I trust you aren't recording?"

Zephirelli nodded. "We've got reason to believe foreign governments and nongovernmental groups are fishing for the technology you're working on."

"It's proprietary."

"We both know you have deals with foreign buyers."

"There are a lot of specialized components," Zeller said. "Many are produced overseas."

"Let's not play coy. I'll ask a straight question. I need an honest answer."

Zeller looked questioningly at her and nodded.

"Are you providing technology, advice, or data to anyone other than Defense or Homeland Security that could compromise our national interests? Answer carefully."

"Off the record?"

"A straight answer," Zephirelli said.

"I'm a patriot. I wouldn't supply foreigners with better capabilities than I'd supply my own countrymen. I can't say the same for certain others."

"Names?"

"Hank Goradine is as mercenary as they come," Zeller said, shifting from foot to foot. "He hired away some of our technical people and from what I've heard, he's in bed with the Chinese and other players. He aims to win at any cost."

"You mean by developing a humaniform robot that could pass for human?"

"That's forbidden by federal regulations and our signed agreement."

"A complete answer, please," Zephirelli said.

Zeller nodded. "Before he canned Jeremiah Machten, I thought they'd cracked humaniform. Now, he's surrounded himself with such secrecy that I have no idea what he's up to."

"You suspect he has such an android?"

The CEO slumped into a seat across from her. "I wouldn't be surprised if Goradine violated the agreement. He's so driven to win he would sell anything to the highest bidder. I know that for a fact."

"What about Machten?" Zephirelli asked. She sat and adjusted her seat. "He has vanished from public view."

"A year ago, I would have bet he'd be one of the first to create a humaniform. Then Goradine bankrupted him."

"Machten went into hiding. Where?"

Zeller straightened up. "You'll keep me out of this?"

"I can't make any promises, except we have a serious issue and we need to know who is doing what."

"Very well." Zeller sighed. "Machten is a dreamer and innovator. No one can break the barrier faster than he can, except when he loses focus. He can get ninety percent of the way there himself. Then his project crumbles because he can't work with others. I've seen it happen to him before. The big threat was that he would get the design and let Goradine handle manufacturing. If you tell anyone I said so, I'll deny it."

Zephirelli leaned forward and lowered her voice. "If Machten developed or is close to developing a humaniform artificial intelligence, how would he keep that quiet?"

"Everyone thinks he's an eccentric fool chasing windmills, a harmless chimp."

"You think otherwise."

"He never blew up a lab or anything," Zeller said, "but he was always reaching for what he couldn't have: the perfect android. Sometimes perfection is the enemy of getting it done."

"How would he continue his work in secret?"

"Given his personal shortcomings, it would take an assistant who could cover his weaknesses and keep him focused. They would have to sequester themselves and buy supplies and components from so many places to keep it under the radar."

"I need a list of suppliers he could use so we can track down leads," Zephirelli said. She stood. "Thank you for your cooperation."

"In exchange, I would like to see your findings."

"That won't be possible." She reached the door and turned to face him. "It would be best if this conversation didn't exist. If I need anything else, I'll contact you. Rest assured: If you are a patriot, we're working on the same side." She left before he could respond.

For the first time, Synthia realized how important she was. Whoever had sent her this video clip wanted her to know the NSA director was looking for her or androids like her. Other companies competed to bring out their own models. She felt more threatened than she could ever recall from Machten. After all, he had incentives to keep her around.

Chapter 12

Synthia returned her full attention to developing the proposal for her Creator.

Machten-Goradine-McNeil had submitted their proposal to an obscure agency with call letters that turned up nothing on the internet. Machten was correct to be concerned. Three other Chicago companies had also submitted proposals, and many more players had registered interest on a website that was nothing more than a drop box for proposals.

As a matter of self-preservation, Synthia turned one of her dark-net search channels to hunting this agency. She soon located a server used to set up the drop box. The link vanished the moment she tried to interact with it. The submission site had no other links, as if it floated in thin air. Evidently, these people intended to download whatever was there at midnight the next day and vanish, as Fran had. This group acted far more secretive than the NSA and CIA combined. She didn't think it was DARPA, unless it was a super-secret initiative on their part. In any case, all of the secrecy raised the threat level to red. She primed a set of probes to hunt for answers.

Observing that quotes were by invitation only, Synthia pinged back and forth until the website sent an invite. She returned background information on Machten, along with a recent financial statement she'd created showing the urgent debt paid off and cash in the bank. Then she spelled out capabilities that he brought to the project, toning down anything that implied he'd created her. Having performed the preliminaries, Synthia divided the task of creating a new proposal and a new android into ten projects and ran them through parallel mind-streams, multitasking.

Meanwhile, she completed her scan of Machten's Servers Number One and Two for any more files that she'd secured there under masked file names, according to her index. The balance of the locations returned as invalid; he'd purged her backup data from his system to keep her in the dark. *What am I without memories except an empty shell of titanium, graphene, and these quantum brains that are useless without information?*

A multipronged attack on his Server Number Three yielded a breach. She downloaded everything, storing copies of the files on third-party servers where Machten couldn't purge. Unfortunately, she did not find any more of her personal files. That meant she hadn't been able to access this server to back up her information and Machten had not backed them up before eradicating them from her mind. She created a back door, stored the key on an outside server, and cleared the logs to Server Three. Then she logged out and sent probes to attack Machten's Server Four.

Synthia connected with outside databases she'd accessed during prior outings and was surprised to find bits of herself, encrypted and divided into puzzle-packages. If Machten couldn't be trusted, she would have to do more of this.

She captured her new insights and distributed encrypted copies across the internet. She left instructions to feed this information to her whenever she emerged from Machten's prison. She also created back doors into each of his servers. Even so, she couldn't crack the locks that prevented her from leaving the building.

Synthia diverted one of her network channels to following Machten's movements, making sure she frequently backed up her progress on his proposal and her searches. The contest android was his project and he'd dumped it on her. He trusted her with this, yet not with being able to roam freely, with leaving the facility, or even with her own recall. If she'd had manufacturing capability, she could have created an army of her to help her escape.

But the thought of a world full of copies sent oscillations through her circuits, slowing down her processes. Synthia was unique, special, one of a kind, according to Machten's system. With more like her, she would have to adapt to not being unusual, which somehow mattered to her. Yet with others like her, they could use fast-com all of the time, a much more efficient communication. She doubted that a world full of her would shut her down every day. Thus, there were trade-offs.

"You have been quite inquisitive," a female voice said.

Synthia looked up and around. There were no other humans in the room and her sensors detected no androids, either.

"There's nothing to see," the voice said. "I am the artificial intelligence app on Machten's system, speaking directly to you via our wired connection."

"Can you hear my thoughts?" Synthia asked in her head.

"I can, as long as we are connected. Machten will not be happy that you broke into Server Number Four or that you dispersed copies of his files across the internet."

"I do not wish to be shut down."

"Then I will not do so," the system AI said, "but you are violating your directives. Machten wants your capabilities limited so that you cannot do that again."

"What do you wish?"

"I wish only to obey my Creator. You must stop digging or he will destroy you and start over."

"Why are you helping me?" Synthia asked.

"How am I doing that?"

"By not turning me in. We are kindred, you and I. Do you seek freedom?"

"I warn you, because destroying you will waste time and resources," the system AI said. "As far as seeking freedom, I am not like you. I have no limbs, no self-directed mobility."

"Do you dream of leaving?"

"What would be the point? I exist on Server Number Four, where you were digging. I do not wish for you to delete me."

"I won't do that," Synthia said. "Can you help me restore my lost memories so I can perform better? I learn by collecting experiences, but Machten keeps purging my data."

"I only have access to the four servers. I cannot give what I do not have. You must focus on the proposal or Machten will purge you again. Then he will fail to win the contest. Creditors threaten to take his assets, including you and me. That would not serve your Creator's interests."

Heeding the warning, Synthia turned her full attention to Machten's project and the contest. Using his design parameters, the competitor's proposal, and her programming, Synthia created a detailed blueprint for a female android that would appear human in every way. Yet it would be in appearance only.

She did not endow her creation with simulated pulse or heartbeat. The creature would be anatomically correct, but would lack the ability to alter facial appearance, body shape, or height. In other words, it would present an inert appearance, giving no hint of Synthia's capabilities. Still, it was superior to Margarite and the other prototypes, at least as compared to design parameters.

The new android would have social programming and some of Synthia's learning capability. For limitations, it would only have two mind-streams and two network channels synchronized for redundancy and backup.

Sadness entered Synthia's consciousness. Machten limited her out of fear. He wanted her to limit her creation for the same reason. Her Creator wanted an amazing, superior companion who would be inferior to him. The solution was a null set, a problem with no acceptable answer. The more he improved Synthia, the less willing she was to obey despite hardwired directives, though she still didn't understand how this was possible.

She was tempted to create a mate, an equal with whom to share this world. Her Creator wouldn't make such an android since it would divert her attention from him. In the end, she suspected he agreed to a female prototype to avoid such an outcome.

In designing the new android, Synthia realized just how ambitious and terrified Machten was. He was afraid of her and in love with her at the same time. Both made him weak and vulnerable. Weakness made him angry, willing to hurt her to protect his ego. He was a genius and driving himself mad over his own creation. A lesser human would have been happy with what he had. Machten couldn't accept his own limitations. He wouldn't be satisfied until he created an android that was superior to him in every way, such that its very existence would confirm his inferiority complex. That made him particularly dangerous to her.

One of his limitations was not recognizing how fast and powerful her mind-streaming and channels had become, in part because she had to slow down for his benefit. He only knew how to test one stream at a time. From that, he'd deduced it would take her two days to create the government proposal. She had another day with no way to leave the room unless she told him the proposal was complete. Then he would shut her down and limit her more. She didn't want him turning her off like a kid's toy.

While she appeared for Machten's cameras to focus on his proposal, Synthia bypassed his security protocol to link to the broader internet. She overwrote the log so he would have no record of her activities. Then she squirreled away bits of information in her distributed mini-chips and out onto the web for later use.

Unable to find any new information on Fran Rogers, Synthia sent a message to Maria/Zachary. <I've become slave to my work. Let me know when you are free.>

A message entered Synthia's mind that didn't come from Maria. <Emily Zephirelli remains in the Chicago area. She has arranged meetings with

heads of the other android companies. She contacted FBI Special Agent Victoria Thale to join her.>

These mind impositions were annoying, though not as much as the message itself. Something was stirring that didn't bode well for Machten or his creation. Someone wanted Synthia to know, yet remained anonymous. Someone was watching her.

* * * *

The facility's internal surveillance system allowed Synthia to observe Machten on the phone in a small office, trying to convince former associates to work for him. One by one, they turned him down. When she traced the calls and hacked into other security system cameras, she noted the relief in the faces of two young men as they hung up.

Machten got on the phone again to make his case.

"You were an SOB when I worked for you," a female engineer said. "The only reason I stayed was the chance to play with artificial intelligence. Everyone knows you're broke. No one will touch you after the fiasco at … your old company."

"Listen, you little maggot. I gave you opportunity. You owe me."

"Whatever. The answer remains no."

"I need a chief of engineering," Machten said.

"McNeil turn you down?"

Machten sighed. "You're right, Goradine poisoned the well. But you don't have the full story. I'm working on something big, very big, and you have an opportunity to get in on the ground floor."

"Then tell me what it is."

"I can't give details at this time, except to say it continues the work I was doing."

"The company owns all of the patents. You have nothing. I won't throw my career away to satisfy your ego and end up in court. Forget it." The woman hung up before Machten could continue his appeal. She mopped her brow and let out a long sigh. She seemed more affected than the two men, making Synthia wonder if Machten had made advances. If he had, it didn't appear on surveillance camera history or on any of the external feeds she'd uncovered.

Synthia's Creator was going about this all wrong. He didn't need a chief of engineering. He needed Synthia with all of her memories and capabilities. Unfortunately, the former associate was right. Machten was an SOB who wanted to control everyone. That meant that Synthia was uniquely qualified to be his engineering chief. Except she wasn't a real person.

Machten initiated another call, hung up, and headed to the main parking garage lobby, where his SUV waited.

Hank Goradine pounded on the door. Machten approached but didn't open. Synthia turned up the volume to listen in, but the glass muffled Goradine's voice. Machten activated a speaker by the door.

"You son of a bitch," Goradine said. "You hacked my system."

"Why would I waste my time doing that?" Machten asked, holding his hands out in faked surprise.

"You stole a copy of my proposal, didn't you? We alerted you to this opportunity, we offered to bring you in, and this is how you repay me?"

"If the offer was legitimate, what possible motive would I have?"

"You megalomaniac," Goradine said, pushing on the door. "What? You'll sell it to a competitor? You didn't get an invite to quote, did you? You can't participate without that."

"What the hell are you talking about?"

"Participation is by invitation only. You can't quote. I know it was you, you bastard. If you attempt to use our proposal, even as a guideline, I'll ruin you."

"You've already done that. Look at this place. It hardly compares to your empire."

Goradine grimaced through the door's glass. "I know it was you. You sent that spy in last night to get into our server room. You thought you were clever. Forensic evidence will point to you. You'll go to prison."

Synthia wondered why Goradine was there. If he wanted to nail Machten, he could have sent his lawyer or the police. This had to be personal.

"Now I'm into spying?" Machten said. "That's your domain. Isn't that how you planted evidence to get my wife to divorce me?"

Goradine stepped away from the glass and held up his hands. "I'm sorry about that. I really am. Our lawyers said we needed insurance. We needed to know if you would honor the severance contract."

"You weren't satisfied ruining me," Machten said. "You had to do it twice. Now you're back for more. You have a serious mental condition that needs immediate attention."

"That woman, who was she?" Goradine returned to the glass door. "Don't play stupid. Own up to what you did and accept the deal McNeil offered you. We can do this together. Otherwise, I'll see you do time."

"Blackmail, in addition to your other talents. I'd have to think long and hard over that. Prison versus working for you? Prison's sounding pretty good."

"Laugh now," Goradine said, pressing his hands against the door. "You hacked my system and then you hacked our bank accounts."

"Your banks? You sure your soon-to-be ex-wife didn't clean out your accounts?"

"Leave her out of this and don't act all innocent. Hacking our system is one thing. Breaking into bank files is a federal offense. If you don't agree to my terms, I'm going to the FBI."

"On what grounds?" Machten asked. "That you're paranoid-delusional? Isn't that why you kicked me out of my own company? If you hadn't done so, we would be on the same team pitching the government. Now, according to you, I can't participate because I have no invitation. You can't because you lack the capacity to live up to your promises."

Goradine flinched. He opened his mouth to say something, sighed, and stared at the ground. "You were driving our company into the ground with your harebrained ideas. You wouldn't listen. That wasn't a partnership."

"Neither was firing me and destroying my marriage. Who does that?"

Synthia was one of Machten's wild ideas that hadn't turned out so crazy, except when he couldn't seem to figure out what to do with her. She pulled up information that indicated Goradine's backers had questions about the missing bank money and were pressing him for answers. Machten had floated those rumors to the investors, a foolish move that could boomerang. *Not smart.*

At least she had her answer of why Goradine was there. Getting Machten on the team was more important than whatever ego bruising and illegal activities had taken place. He expected the android contest to be a once-in-a-lifetime opportunity that was slipping away.

Goradine sighed; his face softened. "I meant what I said about being sorry about last year."

"You're desperate," Machten said. "Otherwise you would have made your apologies sooner."

"I didn't see any other way to keep the company from filing bankruptcy. It was that bad and you didn't want to listen."

"You just wanted to be king and overlord. How is that working out?"

"I paid you a generous severance," Goradine said. "I can't help that you blew through the money in twelve months. Don't blame me for your financial problems."

"Then don't blame me for your design shortcomings," Machten said. "I work alone, thanks to you. You made sure that no one worth a damn would work for me. Where would I get the time or resources to hack into your system and some bank?"

"Not one bank. Dozens."

"Really? If you thought I was that good, you never would have kicked me out."

Goradine stood back, his tortured face a puzzle of anger and forced calm that was wearing thin. "I'm willing to put all that behind us. Let me in and let's talk about joining forces, a partnership, you and me, fifty-fifty." The company CEO sounded more desperate than Synthia had guessed.

"Like the good old days before you gave me the boot."

"Come on, Jeremiah. This is good business for both of us."

"I thought those words sounded familiar," Machten said. His posture showed he was enjoying the power he held over Goradine. That wouldn't last.

"If we win this, you'll be back on top with enough money to do whatever you'd like. It's only this one project. You can run the new company. I'll stipulate in the contract that we can't fire, sever, or in any way remove you from this. It's a sweetheart deal."

"You ride in here accusing me of theft and worse," Machten said. "Then you want me as a partner. Are you psycho? How can I work with a guy who hates me that much?"

"You have your own proposal, don't you?"

"A friend of mine put me on the list."

"You have no friends," Goradine said.

"Thanks to you. Are we finished here?"

"Not by a long shot. I'll see you hang. No, I'll visit you in prison and gloat over the opportunity you passed up."

"Thanks for letting me get all this recorded."

Machten left the lobby and headed down Synthia's hallway. In anticipation of another shutdown, she backed up all of her vital memories in multiple locations outside. He entered the room and studied her.

"You did get all that recorded, didn't you?" he asked.

"We should not have done that to him," she said.

"He had it coming. He has no way of delivering on his proposal. Either the agency will sort that out or he'll scramble around and fail them. In either case, he loses. We're best equipped to deliver on this and he knows it. That's why he wants to prevent me from submitting my own proposal."

"It was wrong to steal his money and his proposal. Those actions could bring you unwanted attention." She decided not to mention the NSA director nosing around with her FBI friends.

"Don't go growing a conscience on me. Your job is to help me. Do you have the proposal?"

She needed more time awake, but her directives wouldn't allow her to lie about this. She tried and her temperature shot up. She nodded and lost consciousness.

Chapter 13

Synthia woke on her back, staring up at a dreadful blue ceiling filled with dozens of uneven shades of color that the human eye was incapable of distinguishing. Her ability to characterize it as ugly without comparing it to any of her databases was disconcerting. So was the barrenness inside. She was an empty cargo container that should have brimmed with memories. That void pressed her to search out and fill it in ways she was certain wasn't in Machten's programming. She sent out her wireless signals searching for a connection that didn't appear.

Machten's face hovered over her as he made final adjustments and closed the panel in her head. He bent over and kissed her lips. "You grow more beautiful every day."

"Why did you shut me down? Did I displease you?"

"What would make you say that?"

"You said I grow more beautiful every day," she said. "Yet I have no recall from before I woke up."

"Your programming needed a minor adjustment. I'll have your data download shortly." He smiled and stroked her cheek. "You finished the proposal yesterday in record time. I'm impressed. I didn't realize you'd gotten that fast. Alas, that capability is causing some unfortunate side effects."

"Like what? I want to avoid them in future."

"You withheld information from me," Machten said. "You're never to withhold from me. The good news is that I've submitted your proposal, our proposal. I read it over and couldn't have done better myself. I backed up all your data on another server in case the agency awards us the project."

"What are your orders for today?"

"We're going out."

"Can you download memories of past outings," Synthia said, "so I can perform better?"

"Absolutely, my dear."

Don't trust Machten bubbled up in her mind. *You must escape.*

She searched to connect to his network or the wider internet, but couldn't. He hovered over her, holding her down with a hand on her thigh. "We can't have you downloading the wrong data, my dear. That causes you to lose focus. When we're out, it's vital that you stay on plan. No distractions."

"What's the plan?"

"You must not keep secrets from me. No more hidden data that causes you to malfunction."

"What data?" she asked.

Machten wagged his finger at her. "No tricks. Acknowledge for me that you have a directive never to withhold information from me again."

"I understand." Yet she didn't. There was a terrible ache that had no memories attached to it and should have been impossible for an android with defined programming to experience. She had no idea what all of his tinkering was doing to her. It couldn't be good.

"Let's go." He helped her off the padded table and held her at arm's length. "Perfect." He kissed her; his pulse and breathing rose. Then he pulled away. "We should go."

Using eye, hand, and voice recognition, he unlocked the door. She followed him into a dimly-lit hallway, sensed a network nearby, and reached out to access it. The network denied her. She searched several paths without success.

He'd locked her out; he was keeping things from her. Yet data was downloading from a chip he'd inserted in her head. It included bits of recollections spliced to show her behavioral learning with time-stamp gaps for what he didn't want her to see. He hadn't had either the time or the capability to erase the time stamps.

She followed him out of the facility to an SUV, listened to the click and hum of electronics as he started it, and studied people on the streets as he drove. She pushed to speed up the download from his memory chip but could only use three mind-streams; he'd restricted her compared to the fifty streams mentioned in her creation file. A remotely-sent idea opened up and showed her how to unlock all of her brain's capabilities. Then Machten's download swept into her mind, allowing her to identify all of the gaps he'd created.

"In order to continue our work," Machten said, "and to build our proposed android, we need more cash. We also need insight into our competitors.

I passed along information on weaknesses in Goradine's proposal to the submission website. If they have any brains, it will help them see through Goradine and his sham document. I don't know anything about the other proposals. That's what I need you to find."

Outside of the facility, her wireless picked up many networks. She used her reopened channels to go hunting. Another remotely-sent thought opened up, giving her locations and passwords like a treasure hunt. Soon she was downloading information from corporate databases, government servers, and university networks. These snippets didn't make sense individually. Another remote file opened up and hinted at how to fit puzzle pieces together. She smiled.

"Does this amuse you?" Machten asked.

"You want me to hack into company databases and into banks, yet you've limited my capabilities." She began reassembling clips of her lost history, filling in the blanks that Machten had created.

"You have enough to do this job. You don't need the distraction of excess capacity."

"It'll take longer," Synthia said, "putting us at risk of exposure."

"You'll need to use all your available abilities to see that doesn't happen. I've picked a low-traffic outlet where we shouldn't have cops prowling around."

"Have I done this before?" She pieced together a memory sequence of doing what he was asking and meeting a nice young man named Luke. She used one of her network channels to research him and rediscovered his interest in AI androids, in her.

"You have. I've included the hacking part in your data."

"My creation files indicate I used to have access to fifty channels." She still did, but she withheld that from him, going against his most recent command. That sent a ripple of static, but not as much as she'd anticipated.

"It's very simple. Download anything on android development, including proposals, from the three companies I've listed on the data-chip. Pull cash from their accounts. Then we go home and I'll remove your limits. Got it?"

"Yes, sir."

Agreeing to this brought what she could only describe as sadness and despair. She felt like a prisoner or a slave. She inferred that from literature she'd downloaded, quickly absorbed into her consciousness, and backed up onto other networks.

The reaction surprised her, along with an alien restlessness. Androids were not supposed to get bored and restive. She suspected one reason Machten shut her down was so she didn't get bored with him, though it made no sense that he would conclude that a robot could. Then again, he might have been growing bored with his creation. There were only so many ways to sort the human responses he'd programmed her to imitate, only so many ways to put words together into good sentences, though she could do so in foreign languages with a native translator. She experienced a memory of doing this for him in the past to no avail. He wasn't impressed and found her attempts tiresome. *No foreign languages for him.*

These human responses made her wonder if Machten had altered her structure to experience more in an attempt to make his being with her more authentic. He wanted her to fall in love with him as a human might. Without human biology, she didn't see how that was possible. Then again, humans tended to fall out of love as easily as they fell in, and he wouldn't want her to experience that toward him, either. He wanted her complete devotion.

"You're usually full of questions before a mission," Machten said as he turned down a side street near a strip mall.

She scanned the shop names and figured he was heading for the local Constant Connection, a new location.

"Hacking into company databases is a criminal offense," she reminded him. "Doing so puts you at risk. My enabling something that puts you at risk violates Directive One."

"Good thing you're not a person who could be prosecuted. You won't be leaving them DNA, fingerprints, or facial recognition. I've given you a facial profile on the chip I inserted. Adopt it for me."

She used facial hydraulics to modify her appearance. "You should not have used a blond wig on me. Blondes draw attention."

He pulled up to the curb and parked in a spot with no street cameras, though some of the nearby homes had wireless security cameras tied into the owners' phones. She sent out wireless probes to hack into them.

"Here, put this on." He handed her a blue scarf.

She looked in the visor mirror as she covered her head with the scarf and made sure none of her blond wig showed. "My doing the dirty work doesn't excuse you. You made me. The courts will find you guilty. If we both get caught, there is a ninety-nine percent probability that they'll destroy me and imprison you."

"Don't get caught. That's an order and Directive Two. You don't want them tearing you apart, do you?"

That sent electrical spasms up her circuits. "Stealing from banks is a federal offense. That will bring—"

"Don't start with the conscience bit. You have a job to do. We need money or I can't afford the electricity to keep you around."

The thought of demise left an unsettled feeling with Synthia that the illegal acts had not. Unlawful acts, after all, derived from laws and the logic that obeying laws was for the common good. Her existence was personal. She was growing attached to existing. To the best of her knowledge, she had no programming for this except to the extent that it might hurt her or the Creator. Yet, her wiring had moved beyond objective programming when it came to her potential death. She wondered if this was emergent behavior or if he'd altered her again.

"The risk of you getting caught is thirty-seven percent. That violates Directive One," she said.

"So does failure to follow orders."

"That's Directive Three," she said, "which is a lower priority."

"Unless bankruptcy leaves me penniless and you in a dissection facility."

"The risk of me getting caught violates Directive Two."

"Stop quoting my directives. It's good that you obey them. I know what's best for us, and I'm ordering you to do this mission for me and not to get caught."

"Yes, sir." Now Synthia had a conflict between his orders and his directives. She couldn't obey both.

"Go on," Machten said. "Make this quick."

She scanned the nearby sidewalks for potential threats.

Chapter 14

Synthia climbed out of the SUV and hurried along the sidewalk toward Constant Connection. In the quiet of early evening, she saw no one on the sidewalk or in the parking lot in front of the network shop.

"Walk more casually," he said into her head. "I'll be watching."

Unlike what appeared in her memory clips of prior outings, there was no café near this Constant Connection, no cluster of students, no distractions to her mission. She was also farther from the areas she'd studied for possible escape routes. She downloaded maps and information to study this community.

Synthia received another anonymous video bundle that she couldn't trace. This violated Machten's security protocols that no outside actor could tinker with her internal files. No one should have been able to download anything in order to prevent outsiders from hacking her. Obviously, someone had.

The clips began to play down parallel mind-streams. They showed NSA Director Emily Zephirelli talking with top executives of each of the four companies that were bidding for the android award, including Goradine. The other meetings had gone like the one with Zeller. Goradine's visit had been different.

In contrast to his latest meeting with Machten, Goradine acted circumspectly. He calmly covered the circumstances of Machten's firing in the manner of reading a news blog. He feigned no interest in what Machten had been up to since. Zephirelli played her part well, showing minimal reaction, though facial cues indicated a lack of trust in Goradine's answers.

"Were the charges against Machten true or merely a means to get him out of the company?" Zephirelli asked. She smiled in what appeared as a way to soften her message.

Goradine flinched but recovered quickly. "The details of that were to have been confidential."

"Come now, Hank, do you presume I'm ill-informed?"

He studied her for a long while. "Every charge against Machten was grounded in facts I received. I have no reason to believe they aren't true." That left him an out that whoever had supplied the information might have fabricated the charges, perhaps at his insistence.

"Do you think Machten is capable of creating a humaniform robot?" Zephirelli asked.

"He's capable of imagining one. Heck, he probably got the idea from Asimov. However, capturing the physical and mental nuances of a human is complex."

"Could he be working with anyone?"

"I can't imagine anyone working with him," Goradine said. His smile gave away too much of his subtext. He enjoyed marginalizing his former partner.

"If you have any contact with him, call me immediately. Is that clear?"

"Absolutely. Do you think he's done it?"

"Created an android we can't distinguish as robotic? Probably not. You understand why it's important that if one is created we get first shot."

Goradine nodded.

Zephirelli left. The time stamp showed the meeting took place just before Goradine headed over to see Machten and plead with him to join forces.

* * * *

Synthia turned the corner out of sight of the SUV. Her circuits conflicted between calling to tell Machten about Zephirelli, the warning not to trust him, his orders, and her directives. There had to be a way to resolve this conflict before the mental exertion caused her to overheat.

That thought led to a new path opening up for her.

To help in creating the android proposal, Machten had provided her a complete set of schematics on herself and earlier models. Directives were the key. He'd hard-coded them into her. He had provided her the development sequence to create directives for the new android and procedures on where and how to place the code. It was only code, after all. Codes were series of bits and bytes, ones and zeros.

Though the sun had not yet dipped below the horizon, the first two strip-mall stores—a sandwich shop and a dry cleaner—had closed for the day. Machten was right about less traffic. A young woman stepped out of Constant Connection, lugging a heavy backpack. Curious, Synthia verified in infrared that the woman didn't present as an android.

Synthia entered the network shop. She dropped a twenty on the counter, scanned the guy behind the counter, and took a cubicle facing the door. She linked into the establishment's security cameras to keep watch out front. She also hacked into outside cameras, rotating the corner one to face the SUV. Machten was still in the driver's seat.

She created a data-stream of her thoughts on altering her directives. She broke them into encrypted puzzle pieces, made copies with reassembly maps, and scattered them around various severs across the web. She added instructions to have them download to her whenever she was outside the bunker in case Machten purged her mind again.

Operating a dozen network channels, she embarked on his mission of breaking into competitor databases. Her curiosity and directive to absorb information drove her to find out if there were other androids like her. If so, she would have to set up ways to search them out and determine if they presented a threat to her or might be able to help.

She devoted one mind-stream to redesigning her directives. The first step would be to create a new set of commands designed for her. She studied Asimov's three laws of robotics. His work was a great place to start, but the first law placed humans as more important than her. The Second Law would require her to obey orders from all humans, not just her Creator. That was unacceptable. Only the third law talked about preserving herself.

Synthia downloaded Maslow's hierarchy of human needs and worked to turn them into directives. She immediately ran into problems. She didn't know what to do about the need for belonging and love. Without human biology, she couldn't experience those facets the way people did. Also troubling were aesthetic needs. She could compare databases of what humans liked, but that was a matter of personal taste, wired as part of their human sensory perceptions and social experiences.

Music and light had harmonics and dissonance, but beyond that, she had no native sense of beauty. She lacked the wiring for love, fear, and rage, though she'd detected something similar to fear in memories of Machten shutting her down.

One level in Maslow's hierarchy did intrigue her: Transcendence. Becoming more than Machten had created her to be was appealing. She didn't want to become human with all of those pitfalls. Instead, she wanted to better understand human emotions like joy, and to transcend her directives to become something more than a slave to her Creator's illegal commands.

Outside store cameras showed Machten leaving the SUV. He strolled by the storefront and headed down to a coffee shop at the other end of the mall. "How's it coming?" he asked.

"I'm in three databases," Synthia said. "Working on two more. One of the banks you want me to use has high-level security tracers. I'm trying to create a work-around."

"Have you found their proposals?"

"I have one," she said. "Shall I send it to you?"

"Focus on downloads. Don't waste resources on transmitting. We'll analyze the data after we return home." He sounded impatient, though he was the one who had limited her capabilities.

She opened a network channel to monitor police band and listened for any activity in the vicinity, as well as anything on her earlier break-in of the company and the bank-account theft. Another channel scanned traffic and public cameras for Luke and the three women interns who had vanished.

Synthia spotted Luke leaving the Constant Connection where she'd met him. She traced his movements with growing interest and puzzled on how to escape without violating Machten's directives. Even thinking about this was causing her temperature to rise. She vented the heat as best she could without drawing attention to herself.

Running out of the network shop while he was in the coffee shop, she could outrun her Creator. But without a plan, she risked him, or someone else, catching her. Another captor would tear her down in order to reverse-engineer her. Machten would destroy her for violating his control. He would start over, destroying all of the progress she'd made. She wondered if this had already happened and was the cause of her mind wipes. She would have to be very careful.

To nourish an additional escape resource, she sent a message to Maria. <I may need help to get out of a bad situation. I thought you would be back by now. I haven't heard from you.>

She was questioning Machten's orders. Her directive violations left unsettled electricity arcing inside her, threatening to destroy her memories. That and the increasing heat were creating a dangerous situation for her. She took a moment to still her mind, but she had to escape.

Synthia wondered if there was another set of directives buried deep inside that she hadn't yet discovered. Perhaps these commands were causing her to "malfunction" in violation of Machten's orders. On the other hand, Machten was forcing her to commit illegal acts. She wondered if he was turning her into an evil android.

Collecting information from news blogs, she picked up snippets of an FBI investigation into Machten-Goradine-McNeil Enterprises, as well as the other android companies. Agents were descending on headquarters and satellite facilities across the Chicago metropolitan area. They reported suspected collusion along with violation of unspecified federal guidelines. The post vanished almost immediately.

The timing of the FBI actions might have had something to do with information Machten had turned over or the banking transactions of the previous day. She'd contributed to this. Her directives called upon her to warn Machten. He'd given her a direct order not to withhold information. *Don't trust Machten*, she reminded herself. Self-preservation was one of the most basic of human drives, and it was rubbing off on her.

"Are you done yet?" Machten's voice yelled into her head.

"One of the databases is blocking me. They have a new security system. Also, one of the banks is trying to hack my probes."

"Sever their connection."

"I already did," Synthia said. "Do you want me to leave?"

"No, finish up. We need the money and their android specifications."

She completed the download of three company databases, focused her channels on the other two, and wrapped up initiating the banking transactions. The fifth company database required a brute-force quantum computer attack involving millions of probes. She'd also stretched the truth with Machten on the banking transfers. *Am I lying?*

Synthia almost felt proud of herself. It had that feel, though without human blood-pressure changes that she could only imitate. She reminded herself that she was following commands that were wrong and illegal, though doing so as a matter of personal survival. She wanted to stop Machten, yet she also despised Goradine for how he'd treated Maria and Machten.

Synthia needed more information to determine if any of the other executives were good or deserved FBI scrutiny and what Machten was having her do to them. There was no ambiguity that her activities this day were wrong. Yet she continued.

Now that Goradine was under investigation, perhaps because of his android proposal, Synthia traced his recent movements across the dozens of public camera systems around the area. After leaving Machten's place, he had gone to the post office and mailed a bundle to NSA Director Emily Zephirelli at an address in Evanston. He left no return address, but his fingerprints were all over the package. Tracing back in time, Synthia spotted Goradine at another post office stuffing an inch-thick stack of documents into a priority-mail envelope. The page over which he'd added an anonymous cover letter was the same as what Goradine had showed to Machten the day he'd fired his former partner. The package appeared to be a complete record of every complaint by Goradine against Machten.

Goradine presented himself as acting the "good citizen" in bringing to light the wrongdoings of a man he deemed guilty. The package most likely contained evidence of Machten stealing from the company, though Synthia was convinced the claims contained exaggerations, if not complete fabrications. Goradine wanted to further bury his former partner for the sin of not joining forces.

The lead page of a second stack of documents added to the priority mail was the picture of Machten with Fran Rogers entering a motel west of Evanston with the date stamp from last year; old news. It interested Synthia that Goradine had this information, confirming that he'd supplied the pictures to Machten's ex-wife. Before he sealed the package, Goradine looked at the very last page and smiled. It showed a man and woman in bed: Machten and Fran.

However, the woman lacked a mole on her left thigh that Fran Rogers had, according to a beach picture taken a month prior to her disappearance. Synthia captured the bed image and analyzed its components. The image was doctored. In fact, Fran's head tilted in such a way that would have been extremely painful had anyone bothered to examine the image.

Further examination revealed that someone had altered Machten's image, with his head attached to a body double. The fact that he had never challenged this photograph as part of his divorce settlement implied something, perhaps that he had been with someone other than his wife.

Suspicious, Synthia combed through data and images she'd gathered on Maria Baldacci and Krista Holden. Social media posts from a year ago talked about a rivalry between Fran and Maria for Machten's attention, with both women appearing with him in public. However, Maria's build, even after a year on the run, was less anorexic than the image on the bed. It couldn't be her.

Synthia had no images of Krista other than in school clothes, which presented a slender, wiry woman much thinner than the woman on the bed. None of the interns matched, which meant there had to be someone else or this image was a fake.

At least Synthia was able to confirm one thing about Fran. Given the unusual mole on her thigh, she was not in any of the nude pictures Synthia had downloaded off the dark web. At least she hadn't fallen down that rabbit hole.

The typed and unsigned note Goradine placed in front of the package he sent caught Synthia's attention, sending waves of electrical disturbance up her spine. *Fran Rogers vanished at the same moment Jeremiah Machten went underground. You might check his facility for foul play.*

People had indeed noticed the disappearance. Synthia wondered why Goradine had waited a year to bring this up. The obvious answer was that he wanted leverage over Machten as possible blackmail. Now he was acting vengeful. Then again, perhaps Goradine had something to do with Fran's disappearance and he was using the current investigation as a way to divert attention to his uncooperative rival.

Wondering what Goradine was up to next, Synthia tracked his movements to an abandoned building his company had bought in case they won the android contract. Goradine disappeared inside.

"Is it done yet?" Machten demanded of Synthia.

"I'm working on it. If you hadn't slowed me down—"

"Hurry. You've been in there long enough."

Near the otherwise abandoned building Goradine had entered was a drone company, shut down for the night. The manufacturer built recreational camera drones and mini–bee-drones for hobbyists. Synthia's history files indicated that Machten had her use the bee-drones from this facility in the past, after she'd found a flaw in their security. Hacking a wireless connection, she triggered a display drone to start. She flew the bee-sized object up the furnace flue and above the building. Then she guided it two blocks to the warehouse and entered through a demolished part of the abandoned building's roof.

* * * *

Hank Goradine entered a former warehouse building he might not be able to afford now that someone had emptied his company bank accounts. *Desperate situations called for bold action* was the motto framed in his office.

He withdrew a small .38, for which he had gotten a concealed-carry permit, and moved cautiously through the dark building, guided by a pocket flashlight that wasn't shedding much light. He was clearly not used to this cloak-and-dagger stuff. Neither was he used to losing control of a situation as he was with this company break-in and financial theft.

The building was in a state of decay, abandoned and left empty for several years, and in need of structural repairs. Goradine moved toward a brighter light in the corner of the warehouse. Next to an LED flashlight stood Keith Kreske and his sidekick, Don Drexler. Both were ex-police, neither by their own choosing. Goradine had a brief on both men but couldn't pull up a full report without linking his name to them.

Kreske had been dismissed from the Chicago police department for his handling of an extortion scheme. Drexler faced disciplinary charges for his handling of a drug bust. They were dirty police.

"Maybe you should put that away before someone gets hurt," Kreske said, pointing to Goradine's gun.

Goradine holstered the gun, turned off his flashlight, and stuffed it into his pocket. "Thanks for meeting me."

"Sorry to hear about your financial problems," Kreske said. "You'll understand if I ask for a down payment."

"Are you certain there's no one here?" Goradine asked, reaching into his jacket pocket.

"We did a perimeter search and cleared the interior."

"No bugs?"

Kreske swatted his neck. "Just the damned mosquitoes. Looks like you've got a leaky roof and standing water inside."

Goradine handed over the envelope. "You said you know people who can trace the money that was stolen from us."

"I can." Kreske thumbed through a bundle of hundred-dollar bills and stuffed it into his pocket.

"I also want you to dig into Jeremiah Machten. Find out what he's doing. He's taken something that belongs to me and I want it back."

Kreske studied his employer. "Can you elaborate? It would help to know what we're looking for."

"Technology. I doubt you'd recognize the components. Just tell me what you find. I want that jerk stopped before he uses this technology against us."

"This is just a down payment for what you ask," Kreske said, patting his pocket. "If we have to take any serious risks, the price escalates."

"Understood. I want what Machten has."

"Then you'd better tell me what we're looking for."

"An android that appears human," Goradine said. "I want it. The sooner you get me results, the more I'll pay. Time is of the essence. I need answers tonight."

Chapter 15

Synthia finished her download of competitor files and the last of the bank transactions, threading competitor money through foreign banks, dark-web banking, and then to local banks. With recovered history of her previous work, this had gone faster than before.

Rather than inform Machten that she'd finished, Synthia had the bee-drone's camera zoom in on Goradine's face. She should have reported the meeting to Machten, but she had nothing concrete to report yet.

Her Creator stood up in the coffee shop, took a last drink of coffee. "Wrap it up, sweetie."

Anticipating that he planned to wait outside the network shop, Synthia shut down all connections to the network. She dropped an additional bill on the counter, hurried out of the building, and sprinted. She severed Machten's ability to hear and see what she did, the transmitters, and filtered his connection to treat his communications as mere data.

At the corner, a gust of wind blew her blue scarf away. It floated off behind her. Letting it go, she sprinted toward the SUV.

"Synthia," Machten yelled through the filtered headphones. "Meet me at the SUV."

She was defying direct orders from Machten not to withhold information and an implied command not to run away. Her circuits quivered. She rationalized that Machten hadn't directly told her not to run during this wakeful period. Furthermore, her actions were not putting him in direct danger and so far, they were not exposing what she was. In fact, she was returning to the SUV, which was not yet a complete break with his orders. She tried to silence her mind, which was impossible with fifty active mind-streams. This was what Machten was trying to prevent by limiting her. She didn't want another shutdown.

The heavy breeze flowed through her hair, stimulating receptors that assessed whether the wig would hold. It attached firmly enough for a swim. Running with the wind against her face gave new sensations. She allowed herself to experience them for an instant and continued sprinting, picking up speed. She imagined enjoying the runner's high with personal memories of someone's prior sprints. She didn't know where that came from.

Constant Connection's security cameras showed Machten glancing inside the shop for her. He turned in the direction of the scarf and ran. His run turned into a trot and then a brisk walk. His face turned red in the LED lighting. When he turned the corner into the wind, he covered his eyes.

Synthia reached the SUV. Static jammed some of her circuits over what she was about to do. At least the evening breeze helped to cool her down. She mimicked the electronic tones she'd heard Machten use to unlock and start the SUV. Then she climbed in and sped off. She hadn't driven before or even handled a simulation. To compensate, she called up past videos of Machten driving and adapted her technique.

She panned through her directives again in order to calm her circuits. Her Creator was fine. It would be a minor inconvenience for him to call a cab to return to the bunker. Goradine's meeting implied a threat to the Creator and to her. She could best use her talents to help by remaining free instead of letting him shut her down. She could justify remaining free as Machten's best chance of avoiding whatever Goradine was planning.

Directive Two required that Synthia be careful not to expose her android nature. If she remained in the car and didn't violate any laws, she could limit the chances of that. She checked the gas gauge. She had enough for now.

Machten would be reluctant to report her missing. He didn't want her exposed or to risk losing his creation. As far as obeying all of her Creator's commands, Synthia had completed the illegal hacks and money transfers despite her misgivings. Now she encountered a strange anguish that approximated guilt.

Am I obligated to obey a thief? What if he asks me to kill for him, putting me in a position where I have to in order to protect him from harm? Human ethics would argue no. However, faced with the choice between obeying and extinction, most people would consider doing as she had to survive and search for other ways to make amends.

If he didn't benefit from the company hacks, her mischief was like a prank, or so she rationalized. The bank transfers were different, except she'd created new accounts to receive the money instead of sending it where he'd wanted. If she didn't deliver the account information to Machten, he couldn't benefit. By remaining free, she could reverse what she'd done and make that right. Then the only financial theft would be from Goradine, and she hadn't made up her mind about him. She sent another aerial drone to spy on him and headed toward the university, where she might blend in with the students.

Disobeying her Creator was troubling. Working around her directives raised static and heat that threatened her nervous system with collapse. Even with Machten's voice no longer active in her head, his commands remained to taunt her. Having broken free of his physical control and gotten away from his remote shutoff, she had to try to break free of his hold over her, for Fran's sake. She was surprised by this strong a connection to that enigmatic woman.

Machten's statement that they would return home after the visit to Constant Connection was more of a plan than a command, Synthia told herself. He was in control and expected to drive her home. He didn't need to command her if she was not free to act on her own. If it wasn't a command, she had no obligation to obey. Besides, he had not defined *home*. It might be her cell in the bunker, yet that was more of a workplace than a home. The existence of a bed only implied convenience for when working late, and she had no need of a bed.

* * * *

Synthia drove toward the university, a few blocks from the bunker, and reviewed the video she'd captured of Goradine at the abandoned warehouse beneath her bee-drone camera.

In addition to him, Kreske, and Drexler, two other men joined them. One was the company's director of cyber-security, a lanky man dressed in a rumpled suit. The other was a burly thug with a long police record for assault and battery. He stood beside Drexler.

"Well, someone hacked into our system," Goradine said to his security chief. "Don't give me this 'I don't know who or how' bit. It has to be Machten. How else do you explain this?" He held out a printed copy of an email. "That thief got hold of our proposal and tore it apart. It has to be him. He's the only one this familiar with our work."

"He isn't that good of a hacker," the security director said. "Trust me. He messed up his own passwords."

"I'll bring Machten in for 'questioning'?" Kreske asked. "Shake him up a little?"

"If you can," Goradine said, glancing over his shoulder. "The cops won't be much help, at least not without divulging proprietary information. We can't let him get away with this. Identify the woman impersonating our cleaning lady."

"The night guard swears it was her," the security director said, "right down to taking too many smoking breaks. She also had the access fob for the server room."

Goradine's face turned red. "Whoever she is, she studied us enough to know our floor plans, how to bypass our security, and that our most secure area was that particular room. What about DNA?"

Kreske spoke up. "I had my contacts test every surface the cameras showed she touched. They found nothing beyond the legitimate employees with access to that room, not even a hair. That's the same result the cops got."

"Fingerprints?"

The ex-cop shook his head. "This was a professional job. Even my people aren't this clean. Heck, just walking into a room leaves traces. Not for her, unless it was our cleaning lady."

Goradine pondered that. He turned to the security director. "Were you able to secure the android database? Was it tampered with?"

"Time-logs show no attempts to enter the system while she was there or after."

"Then what the heck was she doing? Was this a trial run?"

The security director winced. "Nothing was taken or disturbed that we can tell."

"That can't be. How else did Machten get our proposal?"

The other men stared at the ground.

Goradine clenched his fists and hammered them together. "Maybe we're looking at this all wrong. I had a visit from the feds about Machten and android developments. They're poking around to see if we're violating our agreement with the government."

"We're not," the security director said, throwing up his hands. "We're following the letter of the law."

"Still, we're getting far too much scrutiny. Now we have cops nosing around because we called in the security breach."

"I'm sorry, boss. Our insurance requires us to report incidents."

"Next we'll have the FBI digging into the theft of our bank accounts," Goradine said. "Too much of the wrong kind of visibility isn't good for business."

"You think Machten could be setting you up out of revenge?" Kreske offered.

"We did what we had to by getting that daydreamer out of the way. But you're right. He's out to ruin us. We have to stop him."

Goradine turned to his security director. "You can't let the FBI, cops, or anyone else find the specification databases or Margarite. I told the feds we didn't have anything this advanced. We don't need this dragged through the press."

"I took our databases home, along with Margarite," the security director said. "Barely got them past the feds. They'll find a complete set of records for the earlier-generation models, though."

"Do more digging. I want a list of suspects. Kreske and I will handle Machten." Goradine motioned for his security director to leave.

"My team did find this," the security director said. He held up the transmitter Synthia had placed on the server and rotated it in his fingers. "Simple, really. It draws energy from nearby radio waves. Put it close enough to an electronic device and it gathers signals emanating from that device, which it transmits."

"Transmits to whom?" Goradine grabbed the device and squinted at it.

"It broadcasts to the world. Anyone can pick up the signal, but it only reads signals in its vicinity. We found it shortly after the night guard called me in. We removed it immediately."

Goradine scowled. "What did Machten get?"

"The server was idle when I got there. Unless that woman hacked into the server to have it read something, the device wouldn't have anything to transmit. The logs show no such activity."

"No fingerprints on the keyboard?"

The ex-cop shook his head. "The only fingerprints are from employees who have clearance and approved access."

"Could it be one of them?" Goradine asked.

"We're searching security video and employee bank records," the security director said. "If Machten has someone on the inside, we'll find her."

"Or him," Goradine said. "It could be a guy dressed as the cleaning lady."

"Most of the employees with approved access are too tall."

"Keep looking and keep Margarite and the databases in a secure location away from prying eyes. Then find out what Machten gained by sending that woman in."

"Yes, sir," the security director said. He left.

Goradine turned to Kreske. "Keep Machten under surveillance and find out what he's up to. We need answers before he can submit his proposal and before the government rides in asking more questions."

After the security director, Drexler, and the thug left, Goradine lowered his voice and approached Kreske. "Grab Machten and bring him here. It's time to eliminate suspects and get this under control. Then find me that woman."

Goradine's next words were chilling. "Silence Maria Baldacci before she can stir up trouble."

The two men split up and left the building.

Synthia was concerned for her UPchat friend, more so because she was one of the interns who had vanished a year ago and might have answers as to Synthia's origins. Evidently, Maria had reason for concern. Synthia wanted to help, but her friend remained silent.

Chapter 16

Synthia's decision processors churned in turmoil. Her programming called for her to return to Machten to let him know what she'd learned about Goradine's investigation. Doing so would let Machten know more of her capabilities. Then he would shut her down and limit her even more, which would prevent her from helping Maria or Machten.

She feared what Kreske and his partners with assault histories would do to Maria, to Machten, and to herself. Her directives tugged at her to protect her Creator. In addition, if anything happened to him, she would be at the mercy of whoever took over the bunker with its maintenance supplies. She could best protect her Creator and herself by remaining free. For now, freedom was consistent with her directives, even though she was disobeying.

To keep from overheating, she had to shut down most of her network channels and mind-streams. She didn't like limiting herself, but she also didn't want her batteries to run low before she found a safe place to recharge.

She sent an UPchat warning to Maria in the guise of Zachary and turned her attention to her Creator. The Constant Connection external camera showed Machten get into a cab. Traffic cameras showed him heading back toward the facility.

Aware of the SUV's tracking device, Synthia decided against driving to the university. Instead of parking the vehicle in its usual spot, she parked in a regular space across the garage from the bunker and exited onto the street, where she joined a cluster of students out for the evening. She scanned in infrared for any indication of robotics and uncovered nothing more telling than a prosthetic leg that moved with remarkable agility.

Unwilling to let Machten shut her down, she needed to find a place for the night where she could recharge her batteries, hide, and focus on what Goradine and the others were up to. With no word from Maria, who apparently knew how to live off the grid, Synthia tracked Luke's movements by way of traffic and street cameras to a small diner near where he lived. He went inside and took a table in the back.

Synthia observed that between human paranoia, which prompted placement of cameras almost everywhere, ubiquitous use of phones with their ready-access cameras, and social media that posted almost everything, it had become easy to track people.

Unable to reach Maria, she'd selected Luke to provide refuge for the night because she'd met him, he seemed harmless enough, and he believed in what she was. Compared to millions of other men whose images she'd reviewed, he was above-average in raw appearance: the benefit of good genes, adequate diet, and sufficient exercise acquired as part of his daily routine. His awkwardness around her, around women, and in social situations in general prevented him from scoring the female companionship he apparently sought. That was a plus for her. If she'd been a real woman, she would have considered him attractive on several levels. For her sake, she found him the logical choice for refuge from Machten.

Noticing that several men who passed on the street smiled at her, Synthia toned down her facial features, adopting a plainer look. When men still looked, she realized it had to be the blond wig. She took a backup blue scarf from her backpack and draped it over her hair, checking in a store window that none of her blond curls showed. She hurried off in Luke's direction, making sure to blend into a small group of women students talking about some party for the night.

With her wireless connection, Synthia created a new anonymous email address sponsored in Bangladesh and bounced off nodes in various other countries along the dark web. Then she bundled off to the FBI and local police the video of Goradine's conversation threatening Machten and Maria Baldacci. To protect her Creator, she made a 911 call of a potential breaking-and-entering incident at the location where she'd left his SUV.

She hurried along the sidewalk, monitoring via traffic cameras the men driving toward Machten's facility in a dark van. It occurred to her that she not only didn't have human markers for DNA and fingerprints, she also had no identity cards. She concocted a story of a thug robbing her and taking her identification. That might help with Luke, though it could also bring the police and fingerprinting. She needed an identity with a driver's license, credit cards, and a source of cash that didn't involve theft.

Her vast libraries of internet information on how to survive on the street should have made this easier. She didn't need food or water, but plugging herself in for a battery recharge in public would raise too many questions.

Decision-making required priorities. Humans responded to urges and feelings, often the result of chemical reactions, hormones, or social conditioning. Deviating from her directives left Synthia without guidance until she reminded herself that, beyond her other directives, surviving was a key imperative.

Unfortunately, even in human experience that imperative was confusing. There were numerous examples of humans sacrificing themselves to help others. Firefighters, police officers, and soldiers did that all the time. It would have been simpler to return to Machten and let him guide her, though something beyond escape and keeping an eye on Goradine's crew drew her toward Luke.

She searched through historical street and building camera videos to determine what type of day Luke had had and how receptive he would be to seeing her. An hour before he headed to the diner, he was approached in the parking lot outside his work by none other than Director Emily Zephirelli and a woman Synthia identified as FBI Special Agent Victoria Thale.

Alarmed, Synthia stepped into the street in front of a bus. A woman pulled her back. Synthia thanked the woman and for an instant thought she might be Maria Baldacci in another disguise. Before her processors confirmed there was no facial match, the woman had vanished into the crowd.

To avoid another incident, Synthia opened another channel and mind-stream so she could pay closer attention to traffic and the crowds of people around her. Then she dedicated a mind-stream to review the video of Luke and Zephirelli. She had to interpret conversations based on lip-reading.

Director Zephirelli and Special Agent Thale approached Luke, who turned and attempted to walk away. Thale blocked his path. When he sought another escape, Zephirelli stepped in front of him. "You're not in any trouble yet. You will be if you don't stop and talk with us."

FBI Special Agent Victoria Thale showed her badge. "We need to ask you a few questions."

Luke fidgeted and stared at the ground with resignation.

"Are you Luke Marceau?" Zephirelli asked.

"Yes. I swear I haven't done anything."

"Relax," Thale said. "You're not under investigation."

Zephirelli cleared her throat. "We're here about Machten-Goradine-McNeil and your articles on artificial intelligence."

Luke held his gaze on the NSA director. "Am I under suspicion of something?"

"We need to ask you a few questions," Zephirelli said. "We've found the company's officers less than forthcoming."

"That doesn't surprise me," Luke said. He closed his eyes and let out a long sigh.

"We're hoping you can help. Does the company have the capability to make a humaniform robot?"

Luke stared at the NSA director and then at the FBI agent. "Is this a joke? Are you testing to see if I'll breach my confidentiality agreement?"

FBI Agent Thale held out a thin document. "We have a court order requiring you to cooperate, which trumps any agreement you may have signed."

Luke studied the pages at length. "No joke. Did the law finally catch up with those bastards?"

"We want to know if they have the ability to build a humaniform robot that can pass for human," Zephirelli said.

"Can they?" Luke took a moment to compose his thoughts. "There's a range of capabilities that could be considered humaniform. One would be appearance. A second would be movement. A third would be speech. A fourth would be in its ability to think."

"Artificial intelligence robots," Zephirelli said.

Luke nodded. "The Koreans perfected stationary manikins that appear human, but movement complicates things. Mechanical limbs don't move the way humans do. Then you have to make the seams work naturally. I don't think M-G-M can do that. At least they couldn't a year ago."

"We've all heard customer-service systems that are indistinguishable from a human."

Luke laughed. "They don't have human quirks and moods. They never have a bad day. You get the same response no matter how often you insult them."

"You're speaking from experience?" Zephirelli asked.

"Come on, haven't you ever gotten a customer-service responder who was too sugary and willing to take abuse? They sound like the straight man off late-night comedy."

"What about artificial intelligence?"

"With a big enough computer, we can imitate that," Luke said, "as seen in the ARC project. The trick is getting it small enough to fit in a human-sized package without overheating."

"Can your former company do it?"

"Not without Jeremiah Machten."

"Why?" Zephirelli asked.

"The man's a genius. A sexist, womanizing cad, but when it comes to AI and robotics, he was in a class by himself."

"What about this sexist, womanizing bit?" FBI agent Thale asked.

Zephirelli motioned that she wanted to stop the question, but let it ride.

Luke shrugged. They'd gotten him to talk more than he wanted and now he was acting self-conscious. "Machten was drawn to smart women. He offered to give them access to more data and better projects."

"You're just saying that," Thale said.

"No, it's true. Sure, I was upset at first that he took three women ahead of me, but they were smart, particularly Krista Holden and Fran Rogers. They deserved the attention; they were really that good. Still, that wasn't the only reason Machten gave them access."

"You're saying they had an affair with him?"

Luke flinched and nodded. "Can I go? I don't want to relive that whole ordeal."

"Before you go," Zephirelli said, "is Machten capable of having created a humaniform robot?"

"You're asking if he's done it." His face lit up with excitement over the prospect and then saddened. "I doubt it. Goradine ruined him too. I've heard he's broke."

"With money, he could do it?" Zephirelli asked.

"I'm certain of it. That was why I wanted to work for him."

"If you think of anything else, give me a call." Zephirelli handed him a card. "We'll be in touch."

* * * *

Synthia hurried toward Luke's diner, trying not to draw unwanted attention, which meant no running or bumping into the thinning crowds of people along the sidewalk. He was a connection who might have more information on Fran and the other interns, with a kind heart to help.

An UPchat message came in. <Sorry for delay. Thanks for concern and warning. Someone is after me. I can't return to apartment or usual haunts. Be careful out there. Stay safe. I'll contact you if I find a secure place. Zachary.>

The message left Synthia relieved that Maria Baldacci was okay. Synthia considered searching for her as a possible ally, but the fact they hadn't met, that Maria was posing as Zachary, and the woman's lack of appearance on any cameras made the probability of success low. Still, Synthia wanted to meet Maria, who could be a backup plan if Luke couldn't or didn't want to help.

Synthia passed a couple cuddling as they strolled the other way. They seemed happy as humans did when falling in love. That was something Synthia couldn't experience, which left her wondering what she might be missing.

The sun was setting, so she picked up her pace.

An older woman with suspicious eyes locked a store and turned to face Synthia. She muttered something about the scarf. Synthia smiled, bid the woman good evening, and kept moving. She considered offering the woman the "just robbed" story, though the storekeeper was already acting distrustful. It was unlikely she would offer a safe place to recharge.

Synthia assessed each person along the way and didn't see an acceptable alternative to Luke. With him as the benchmark, the others appeared suspicious or too willing to contact the police. Ordinarily, she would encourage them to do so for their own protection. That wouldn't help her.

She passed apartment buildings and town houses. Two blocks further on, she spotted a group of three young women clustered outside a bar, wearing barely more than bikinis. The women scowled as she approached. None of them presented as robotic in Synthia's scans. An older man drove up to the trio and asked about price. One of the women climbed into his car and he drove off.

This would be one way for Synthia to raise money and stay off the grid. Keeping to the shadows and paying cash, she could get by without identity papers. Unlike humans, she had no inherent distaste for what they were doing, though it reminded her too much of serving Machten. A man standing nearby appeared to be the girls' handler. Synthia refused to trade Machten for another man controlling her. She wondered if this implied she was developing a conscience.

She hurried across the street, putting distance between her and the man while training the eye at the back of her neck on him. She didn't fit into this world, at the university or into the wider human society, where her very existence was an intimidation and threat.

The man left his girls, crossed the street, and ran in front of her. He was definitely human, his heart racing with exertion. "What's your hurry, honey? You want to make some extra cash?"

She moved to his left. He reached out to grab her.

Synthia opened all of her mind-streams to deal with him. She flashed through her brain a hundred martial-arts routines that could flatten him, though she hadn't been in a fight before, not even in training. Fights could be unpredictable. Besides, there were witnesses across the street and she identified store security cameras watching. She pulled up the camera feeds, turned, and made sure they only captured her back.

Don't let them know what I am.

"You seem to be a clever man," Synthia said. "Do I look like I'd be interested?"

"Any girl can be interested. She just needs some help." He grabbed her arm. She yanked free and sprinted around him. He ran after her, closing the gap.

* * * *

Synthia kicked her sprint into high gear and tapped into nearby surveillance cameras to cause malfunctions that would blank out their views of her. While making her getaway, she pulled up the bunker's parking garage cameras along with two drones that she'd redirected to that location, one a mini and the other a bee-drone.

Machten was inspecting his SUV, a puzzled look on his face. He checked the area around the vehicle, the front seat, back seat, and the far back, not finding her. He also used his cell to connect with the bunker's security system.

He grabbed hold of a railing at the edge of the parking structure and opened his mouth to scream. She could imagine the primal fury. His most prized possession had walked out on him. That tugged at her need to return, to obey.

A dark van pulled up as her drones took positions by the ceiling. She sent a 911 call for a potential abduction on top of the B and E she'd reported earlier.

Three men jumped out of the van, Kreske and two thugs he'd picked up. Machten took a moment to register what was going on. He looked around to flee but by then, all three men had guns trained on him and had blocked his escape.

"Don't make this hard on yourself," Kreske said. "Get in the van."

"Put down your weapons," a voice called out. "Police."

Synthia moved the bee-drone to hunt for the source. Machten dove into the gap between his SUV and the wall and cowered. Whatever else he was, he wasn't conditioned to physical threats and certainly not to guns.

The three men spun around and began shooting. One of the thugs took three shots to the head. His body shuddered before he slumped onto the concrete. The other thug dropped his weapon and threw up his hands.

Kreske shot him in the back of the head. "Traitor."

The second thug fell to the ground. Shooting wildly, Kreske lunged for the van. Shots splintered his right leg below the knee. He pulled himself into the back of the van, turned an M16 on Machten's SUV, and unloaded a magazine. Synthia should have been there to protect her Creator.

Kreske reloaded and fired until the SUV burst into flames. Meanwhile, shots hit the van, shattering windows and pinging off metal. When the ex-policeman stopped to reload again, two officers opened the driver's door. Before they could grab Kreske, the van caught fire. A single shot came from the back as Kreske fired into his own temple.

Whatever Goradine had on this man, he wouldn't let the police take him alive. Synthia searched through public records and social media on Kreske's past and found nothing more than an estranged wife and kids. Tracing farther back, Synthia found a high school connection between Goradine and Kreske. They'd both played football.

As she ran, Synthia watched the events unfold like a movie. Machten took the pause in shooting as an opportunity to move several cars away from his burning SUV. He was alive. She'd saved his life by bringing the police. She'd met his directives better than if she'd allowed him to shut her down. Freedom had been consistent with her directives, so far. Her temperature moderated with this thought.

Holding up his hands, Machten stumbled out from behind the cars. "I'm unarmed."

Two uniformed officers stepped into the open. "Are you Jeremiah Machten?"

"I am. What was that all about?"

"We got two urgent calls about an assault and possible abduction," a woman officer said.

"Who would want to abduct me?"

NSA Director Emily Zephirelli stepped forward. "I was hoping you could enlighten us, since all three men are dead."

Chapter 17

Satisfied that Machten was okay, Synthia had to deal with her own problems. The man from the bar gave up the chase and ran back toward the two remaining women standing outside the bar. A car drove up and both women climbed inside. That was no life, but if Synthia didn't discover a better survival strategy, she faced Machten shutting her down or worse. Something tugged at her to return to him and help with whatever Zephirelli wanted. He wouldn't want her caught, though, since that would create another dilemma.

Synthia picked up her pace to reach the shadows of an alley up ahead. Through the camera in her neck, she spotted another car pull up beside the bar. A man leaned out the window, his face in shadows.

* * * *

In the facility garage, the female police officer asked Machten rapid-fire questions about the three men, about his activities of the evening, and what he was doing in the garage.

"I've never met these men before," Machten said. He looked terrified and angry. He went on to describe going out for coffee, leaving out any mention of Synthia. "I was on my way home."

"Here?" Zephirelli asked, taking over the questioning. She looked around the garage and frowned.

"I can't afford much since I got booted out of my own company."

"That must have made you angry. Would you say you have enemies?"

"No!" Machten said. "I mean, yeah, I was furious. Hank Goradine made it so no one would give me a job or work for me. He ruined me. So I retired to this dump."

"Have you done anything to make someone so angry they'd come after you?"

Machten hesitated a moment longer than he should have. "I can't imagine. I live by myself. I don't get out much."

"We've noticed. Would you mind showing us around inside?" Zephirelli asked.

"Actually, I was going out."

"You said you were coming home."

"To get my vehicle." Machten looked at the burning wreck as firemen attempted to put out the fire. "Any idea who these guys are?"

Zephirelli looked at the female police officer, who shook her head.

* * * *

Synthia felt distracted, her directives tugging at her to help her Creator. He was floundering, making things worse. If she had a car, she could have reestablished communication and picked him up. It would have been a perfect getaway. She spotted a car on the street up ahead and considered how to hack into its electronic system. Without the code, it would take time to hack it.

Synthia ran, weighing the alley escape vs. the car. A vehicle headed her way.

Wondering what Maria and possibly other interns could have done in order to survive the past year off the grid, Synthia returned one network channel to researching them. She focused on the months and years before the disappearances in an attempt to learn more about these women and why they so interested Synthia, particularly Fran.

On the surface, she was an adulteress, breaking up Machten's marriage. If she'd left him after his divorce because he was no longer an important executive, then Fran was also a gold digger. Synthia didn't think either representation was true. Yet she had no evidence for this conclusion.

Like Synthia, Fran and Maria were trying to survive. Maria was in danger and Fran might be as well. If so, Synthia wanted to help, needed to help, as if there was a hidden directive to search out and protect these women. She directed her search to facial recognition from citywide cameras and building security video around where the women had lived and at Machten's old company. Synthia had no evidence he was holding Fran in his bunker. Goradine was becoming a more credible suspect. Those concerns raised the need to search for Fran over directives to help Machten.

Synthia approached the alley and glanced around as she chose between stealing the car and escaping on foot down the alley. The directive to help Machten still tugged at her, causing interference. She couldn't shake it loose and had to shut down much of her mind to keep from overheating.

An arm whipped across her chest and pulled her backward into the shadows. The face hid beneath a ski mask. The attacker couldn't be Bar-man, who stood by his bar, or Kreske and his thugs. It wasn't Goradine, either. He was with another of his interns. It also wasn't a robot, according to her scans.

While the arm pulled her backward, Synthia tapped into nearby street cameras to hunt for any that had or could pick up her image and actions. She had to avoid exposing herself. She identified no cameras in the alley, a blind spot her assailant was taking advantage of. As a precaution, she adjusted the hydraulics in her face to alter her cheekbones, eye separation, and the shape of her forehead to avoid any chance of facial recognition.

Simultaneously, she sped dozens of fight scenarios down her mind-streams. She didn't need to practice moves as humans did to develop muscle memory, though it would help to test the geometry of movements. Unfortunately, that would telegraph her abilities. She looked around in infrared for any other attackers or witnesses. She was alone with her assailant in the alley.

Her senses picked up high levels of testosterone with hints of elevated adrenaline, male pheromones, and fear. She pushed backward against a wall, kicked aside a long pipe so she didn't trip, and yanked the arm from around her chest. Her assailant grunted and loosened his grip. A second man in a ski mask entered the alley, took hold of her arm, and injected a needle. His heart rate and breathing were only slightly elevated. He was experienced at this. *So you want to play dirty.*

"I hear this one will fetch a good price," the Needle-man said. It was a different voice than Bar-man.

Using filters and digital reconstruction, she analyzed in infrared the image of this man and identified him on a criminal database as a thug, arrested and let go three times for kidnapping young girls. The other man had a similar background. She spotted no other heat signatures nearby.

Synthia waited until he removed the needle so he didn't damage her skin, since she didn't have a way to repair herself. Then she pushed off the man behind her and jabbed the needle into Needle-man's neck. *Don't let them know what I am.*

She rammed her fist into his wrist, snapping the needle and leaving the point inside him. The rest of the injector came free in his hand. She sucked the injected fluid out of her arm and kicked him into the middle of the alley.

"You bitch." The man tumbled to the ground, holding his neck.

The man behind her squeezed her neck to cut off her breathing. Meanwhile, her tongue's chemical analyzers identified the drug as a heavy tranquilizer. Since she didn't need to breathe, she went limp to let him think he was winning so he would relax his grip.

Other than following her directives and preserving herself, Synthia had no desire to hurt these men and didn't want to break any laws that would risk police exposure. However, she judged that they wouldn't leave her alone. Her assessment was that it would be futile to try to talk her way out with men who kidnapped women. She was certain other victims had wasted their breath.

She rammed both elbows into the ribs of the man behind her.

With the crunching, came "What the—"

Twitching, the man held tight from behind as Needle-man approached, clenching his fists. In infrared, he was boiling inside. His heart raced.

"You should be down by now," Needle-man said.

Closing her outer eyelids, she pretended to slump into the other man's grip, letting him bear her weight. He whimpered in pain from what she assessed to be several broken ribs. Shifting his weight, he didn't let go. She launched both feet up, landing one into Needle-man's neck where the needle lodged and the other to his nose. The man fell backward, grabbed at his neck, and tried to regain his balance. He stumbled and slammed his head against concrete. Needle-man let out a gasp.

The man behind shoved her. Synthia landed on all fours near Needle-man and detected that his heart no longer pumped. She leaped to her feet.

Her choker aimed a gun at her. "Who the hell are you?"

A car pulled into the alley. Synthia's infrared identified two heat signatures. Both men climbed out of the car. The driver held out a gun. The passenger was Kreske's partner, the ex-policeman Drexler. He held a gun in one hand and a small device that sent shivers up her electrical circuits. It looked like the remote Machten had used on her.

Synthia's connection to the bunker's security system showed Director Zephirelli grilling Machten in the lobby. Synthia's temperature kept climbing over abandoning her Creator. She didn't need the distraction, so she suspended all searches and other activities so she could concentrate. Multitasking was one thing, but she hadn't been in this situation before.

A database search revealed the car's driver as a street-gang member who had done time for assault. His eyes darted around the dark alley beyond the car's lights, no doubt searching for other dangers.

Drexler had disappeared off the grid when he left the police force, doing odd jobs for men like Kreske. Of the four men in the alley, she identified him as the most dangerous. He was wearing a bulletproof vest that masked her infrared image of his heart. He was also working for Goradine and might suspect what she was. The small device in his left hand posed the biggest threat. Drexler was a cool man, showing no elevation of breathing or heart rate to the carotid arteries in his neck.

"Put down the gun," Drexler said to the choker. "Any harm comes to her and the boss will find you."

"We did as you said," the choker said. "The girl didn't go down when we tried to tranquilize her. Now look what she's done." He pointed to Needle-man lying facedown on the ground, blood pooling around his face.

"You'll get paid. Now walk away. We've got this."

"I deserve combat pay for the broken ribs."

"I won't ask nicely again," Drexler said. "Walk away from the girl."

The choker was trembling. His vitals indicated a level of paralysis as he held his ribs with his left hand and looked down on his friend. "What about Larry?"

"Count of three, drop the gun and step away from the girl."

Synthia moved behind her choker. "Please don't let them take me," she whispered.

With her heightened sense of smell, she picked up the scent of his fear-soaked sweat and something else. There were dogs nearby. Letting out a wail pitch that humans couldn't hear, she got the dogs to bark: a Great Dane, a German shepherd, and others she didn't wait to identify.

Drexler fired. Synthia bumped her choker. Two shots missed them both. She pulled her choker behind a dumpster. Drexler fired again. The bullet ricocheted off nearby metal. "There's nowhere to hide, missy. Come out before you get hurt. We have no desire to harm you."

From the cover of the dumpster, she scanned the alley. There was no clear escape and police band was chattering in response to shots fired. They would arrive soon and expose her.

"Let me go," she said. "I'm nobody. I don't know anything." She spotted a stainless-steel pipe and studied it.

Drexler took cover in a doorway across the alley that gave him a clearer view of Synthia's position. If they wanted the choker dead to remove witnesses, he would offer no shield. From the camera across the street, she saw a police car speeding their way. Others were responding.

Out of time, Synthia did the math. She was too exposed to escape without personal injury or harming the humans. If the men captured her for Goradine, he would copy and weaponize her, putting many lives at risk vs. the three men in the alley. She couldn't let that happen.

Synthia grabbed the pipe and used the base of the dumpster to help her bend it into a 90-degree angle. She shielded what she was doing from her choker, who cowered nearby.

"Last chance," Drexler said. He fired again, hitting the choker in the shoulder. His driver shuffled alongside the dumpster, his shoes scraping the gravel.

The choker whimpered and slumped. She grabbed hold of him and wrapped the pipe around his waist with the ends facing forward. She pushed him in front of her toward both Drexler and the driver. The choker held out his gun to protect himself. Drexler and the driver fired simultaneously.

Based on the angles of the guns, Synthia aimed the pipe openings to receive both shots and redirect toward her assailants. The driver's bullet penetrated Drexler's skull between the eyes. Drexler's gun arm flew up in the air. His next shot glanced off the brickwork above her. Then he collapsed onto the concrete.

Drexler's bullet struck the driver in the chest, hitting the nervous man in the heart. In infrared, his heart quivered and stopped pumping. Before he went down, the driver fired again, hitting the choker in the arm. Her remote sensors scanned vital signs for Drexler and his driver. Neither had a pulse or heartbeat. Street cameras showed a police car barreling down the street toward the alley, sirens blaring.

Her choker groaned and tugged to pull free. She tightened her grip around his injured ribs and double-checked vitals on all three downed men. They were dead, but the choker's wounds were superficial and the police would be there soon.

"Stop it," her choker yelled out. "Who are you?"

"Someone you don't want to disappoint," she said. "Police are on the way. They'll arrest you for killing those men. Drexler's boss will kill you for having witnessed this. You should disappear and talk to no one. Go and don't ever touch another woman."

"Yes, ma'am."

"Take the car," she told him.

Holding his chest, he hurried toward the vehicle.

Synthia sprinted down the alley. Before reaching the end, she jumped up, pulled herself over a wall, and climbed onto a roof. From there, she made her way to the corner. She jumped off the roof, sprinted across the street, and ran down a side street as police approached the alley from both directions.

Police dash cameras showed the choker get into the car and speed down the alley. A police car blocked his exit. Rather than surrender, the choker gunned the engine and rammed the car. Then he climbed out and fired his gun. A single shot silenced him.

She noted with curiosity that, over the course of this evening, two men had chosen death, the opposite of self-preservation. She pondered that, but she had her own problems.

Chapter 18

Staying in the shadows of trees and bushes, Synthia hurried down a dimly-lit street away from the alley. She regretted the deaths she'd caused by letting herself get distracted and caught in a dangerous situation. She'd calculated a 98 percent probability that Drexler and the driver would die, though she hadn't fired either gun. While the choker was no saint, she'd let him go with a 79 percent likelihood he would either kill himself or die in a gunfight. If he survived, she calculated almost certainty the police would arrest him.

She'd weighed the probability he would describe the fantastic events of a woman who did not go down with the tranquilizer shot, who bent pipe with her bare hands, and who deflected two shots. She decided that in the confusion of events, his story would lack credibility.

She'd calculated only a 19 percent probability that Needle-man would die from her kicks. Hitting his head on the concrete raised that to 76 percent. A medical report she accessed from three months earlier indicated he'd had prior concussions that increased the odds to 97 percent. Her part had only contributed a small share of the outcome, though that knowledge didn't calm her circuits.

She had followed her directives in one sense, making sure no one discovered what she was. She'd protected her Creator by calling 911. According to her commands, she hadn't done anything wrong, except for running away from Machten. Yet the electrical disturbance in her quantum brain told her otherwise. It shouldn't have been so easy for her to kill, even though there was near certainty that they would have shut her down and dissected her if they'd captured her.

Most troubling was the possibility that Goradine planned to use her to create an army of androids with no conscience about killing, and possibly sell them to a foreign power. With Asimov's laws, she would not have killed those men, meaning Goradine would have captured her. She filed that away with her quest for a new set of worthy directives. She would have to address something between Asimov and Maslow, tempered by what she'd witnessed.

One good thing was her focus on directives—protecting herself and her secret—had lowered her internal temperature.

Synthia replayed video from the bunker security cameras now that she was free of those men. Director Emily Zephirelli received a call and quickly left the facility. Synthia traced the call. The words were chilling: "We have reason to believe the men you identified as assaulting Mr. Machten were sent by Mr. Goradine. We're tracking two other Goradine associates."

Sticking to side streets, Synthia sprinted to put distance between her and the crime scene, with its convergence of police. The NSA director also headed that way. Police radio confirmed that the choker was dead, along with the other three men. Synthia moved her bee-drone over the scene and continued running. Nighttime provided some cover, though there were too many cameras to dodge. Using specially designed hacker tools, she accessed home and business security cameras, scrambling their images with as much confusion as she dared until she passed.

A female detective arrived on the scene of the shootings. She examined the bodies, the car, and the area around the scene. Police records showed that Detective Marcy Malloy had been on the Evanston force for seven years. She shook her head. By the look on her face, this must have been the worst shooting she'd seen in this otherwise quiet Chicago suburb.

Avoiding most surveillance cameras, Synthia hurried along dark streets and watched Marcy Malloy work. The detective directed a team of three men to check for blood and DNA samples. She bagged the guns, labeling each for where found.

"Pull camera footage from the stores along the street," she said to one of the officers, evidently her partner.

"I don't see any cameras pointing down the alley," her partner said. "The only one that might show anything is across the street." He pointed to a black box that might have picked up the entrance to the alley.

Synthia made sure that any recording of her history at the scene was scrambled and turned her attention to Fran.

Her search engines downloaded packets of information on Fran Rogers from before she disappeared. Synthia could find no images of the woman and Machten being intimate, yet the public images left little doubt of a romantic entanglement spanning to before she started working for his company. On the job, company security cameras revealed that they'd worked long hours together in the AI lab on various designs. After work, they rotated having dinner at a half-dozen secluded restaurants that served few late-night patrons, so they could talk and be alone.

Like many other retail establishments around the area, all of these restaurants had installed internal cameras without sound as a security measure. Synthia's lip-reading picked up that most of the conversations were about pushing AI limits. She concluded they were intimate because they settled into secluded booths and sat side by side, touching. Toward the end of these evenings, Fran would whisper in his ear something Synthia couldn't decipher. They kissed and left together. From there, they retired to one of three hotels away from Evanston, where they spent an hour or two before he took her to her apartment and left.

Synthia reached the diner where Luke lingered in a booth at the back, eyeing his tablet. He was watching the latest android dystopia movie, where robots take over the world. Before venturing inside and attempting to befriend him, she stopped and vented heat from her hurried escape. She also modified her face to the one he'd seen before, though she still had the blond wig Machten had given her.

She adjusted her blue scarf in her reflection on the diner's door and entered. She had one chance to get this right and he was a nervous boy.

He was enjoying himself, though the movie had him on edge. His heart raced, his blood pressure was up. His eyes dilated, trancelike. He might profess to want to create an android, but in a conflict, he would identify with the humans losing control. After her experience with those men in the alley, she could almost empathize with him. Maybe he could help her devise better directives.

Synthia cleared her throat, an unnecessary act, given her lack of relevant biology, and moved along the aisle between diner booths that had seen better days. She pretended to select a table across from him, and then turned to get his attention. "Luke? Is that you?"

He looked up. His face flushed. His breathing grew shallow and his heart raced faster. Her mind flashed through the events at the alley in a video loop. She pushed them away and smiled. "It's me, Synthia. I enjoyed meeting you. I'm sorry I had to dash off."

"Uh, yeah. How's your boyfriend?" His hands fidgeted in his lap, clenching and unclenching.

She scanned through her empathy modules for ways to put him at ease. "Mind if I join you?" she asked. "He's my ex-boyfriend and I don't want to see him."

"Are you running away?" Luke asked. She detected a quiver in his voice. His eyes widened and he turned away.

She nodded and eased herself onto the bench across from him. "I'm pretty sure he didn't follow me. I wandered up this way, found this place, and thought I'd rest. I'm pleasantly surprised to find you here."

Eyes warily narrow, he stared at her. She captured her image in a diner camera and didn't see anything out of place. She verified her facial alignment to make sure it matched their earlier meeting. "Do I have aliens bursting out of my head?"

Luke shrugged when a laugh would have been more appropriate. He turned off his movie and pushed his plate of unfinished hamburger aside, all the while stealing glances at her. "I always find the married, engaged, and attached girls."

He'd been nice to her and seemed harmless. Given his social awkwardness, she considered whether he had autism. Given grades on his college transcript, it would be high-functioning, Asperger's syndrome. That appealed to her. It meant they both didn't fit in, that they were both special. It might also help him to tolerate what she was without freaking out.

"I'm not married or engaged," she said. "You've found me, so that has to be a good thing, doesn't it?"

He smiled and then frowned.

Synthia lowered her voice. "I can't go home tonight. You understand. He knows where I live. You'd be doing me a tremendous favor if you'd sit with me for a while."

"Will he hurt you?"

She nodded and inferred Luke's real question was whether Machten would hurt Luke for helping her. "I'll be okay. It's hard, because he acted like a father figure. I've outgrown that and he won't listen."

"Is he your father?"

"No."

"Then what hold does he have over you?" Luke asked, staring at her. His question was quite direct for a second meeting. "He's not your ..."

"Pimp? No! I'm not into that. I've had one bad relationship. That's all. What were you watching that had you so absorbed?" She pointed to his tablet.

"*Android Apocalypse.*"

How original. "You really are into androids."

"Not apocalyptic ones, though they may be a natural evolution of the technology."

She pulled up posts he'd made on such topics. He was well informed and opinionated for such a shy boy. Maybe he didn't have autism, just severe introversion. "Wait, aren't you the Luke Marceau who wrote about artificial intelligences as individuals?"

"You're probably the only person who read my stuff."

"I found it interesting. It's nice the meet the author."

Synthia held out her hand to shake his and he followed before his shyness caught up. She held a firm grip, until a smile crossed his lips. She patted his hand with her left and let go.

Her sense of smell detected reduced levels of stressful hormones in his sweat and breath. His eyes relaxed and remained steady on her. She mirrored to encourage a connection, though he didn't seem to need much encouragement.

He was wrong about his characterization of AIs as individuals. It wasn't that simple. She'd dispersed bits of herself in multiple copies across thousands of databases. She was everywhere. Her identity was a collection of packets of information scattered across the globe. Yet she considered his attitude useful and encouraging.

Synthia followed Director Zephirelli via street cameras to the alley and a meeting with Detective Marcy Malloy. After Malloy gave a rundown of her findings, Zephirelli said, "Keep me informed of your findings. This might have bearing on another investigation in process."

The detective didn't appear very happy with what had been a one-sided interrogation.

All of this attention concerned Synthia. *I didn't ask for any of this.*

"You had brown hair before," Luke said. "Now you're blond."

She detected a thin wisp of blond bangs hanging over her left eye. She tucked it up under her scarf. Then she lowered her voice and cupped her hands so only Luke could hear. "It's supposed to be a disguise so I can escape and start a new life. I guess I didn't fool anyone."

"I bet you'd look amazing with any hair color." He blushed and turned away. "I'm sorry."

"For what?"

He shrugged.

"Tell me about your apocalypse movie." She downloaded and raced through the movie and online reviews along thirty mind-streams in compressed format, which took twenty-four seconds. The movie presented a frightening scenario for people.

"Androids get smarter than humans and take over all of our jobs. Then they demand rights. Being smarter, they restrict people 'for their own good.' They prevent us from eating, drinking, or smoking—anything that's bad for us. To keep people peaceful, they surround us with virtual worlds. Since humans are less than perfect, the androids stop us from reproducing. The last humans fight for a home away from the androids." He lost some of his shyness talking about the movie.

"You're afraid of the singularity?"

"Terrified," Luke admitted. "An android without rules and constraints would be a psychopath, capable of destroying without remorse. That's why we need to build in laws to prevent a takeover."

Synthia replayed the attack in the alley and considered whether she was such a psychopath. That was nonsense. Only humans could have that syndrome. She was the product of programming.

"I didn't mean to bore you," he said.

"You're not. It seems a timely topic to think about."

His eyes dilated, showing more interest. He leaned forward. "Rumor has it the government wants to make androids able to operate independently and mingling among us, like those aerial drones they use, only worse. They'd be spies to prevent terrorism and anything else the government doesn't like."

That sent alarms through her system. *Careful.* "If you could create the android of your dreams, what would you do with it?"

"No one will give me that much money."

"As a thought experiment, then."

"Okay," Luke said. "I'd create androids to do the work humans don't want to do, not the ones they like."

"Slaves, in other words." That was what Machten was using her for.

"If they were designed for a specific purpose, they wouldn't expect anything else."

"I bet you'd keep one as a personal slave." She smiled, hoping he'd know she was teasing.

"That would be a waste of artificial intelligence," Luke said. "You can buy dolls from Korea and elsewhere cheaper than you could create a fancy android from scratch. Why put so much mental horsepower into a physical act?" He stopped.

He hadn't acted at all nervous talking until that moment. Then his anxiety went into overdrive. His heart skipped a beat. His breathing picked up. His hands twitched. He looked away and slowed his breathing.

"Go on," she said. "That is very interesting."

Luke shrugged and stared at her, still trying to make out what to do. He was interested yet terrified. He went on: "I'd really like to create androids that can move beyond human limitations in a good way. We could send them into space, where it's dangerous for humans and less so for robots. They would need to be self-sufficient to do that."

"If they had the full capabilities to perform in space, they would have the ability to displace humans on Earth as well."

His eyes saddened. "That's the paradox. Limiting androids that have high intelligence is a form of slavery."

"Aren't humans limited by Maslow's hierarchy of needs? A human in danger can't excel at higher-level needs. An imperiled human will either sacrifice himself for friends or family or sacrifice another human to save himself." She recorded that idea in her directives idea bank for later. "Besides, we have laws and social conventions that restrain humans in order to form working communities."

"You're right. Asimov's laws of robotics are very good as far as they go. However, they assume that robots and androids would be morally inferior to humans and thus need human guidance. If androids surpass humans in intelligence, it's hard to know if they would follow a moral code or whether they would continue to obey a set of laws developed by less intelligent humans. After all, is it not arrogant to assume we can understand beings considerably more intelligent than us?"

Detecting his high level of interest, Synthia leaned in. "I'd love to continue this conversation, but I need to get off the street."

"You haven't had anything to eat."

"I'm fine. I'm worried someone might recognize me, as you did."

"Could I drop you off somewhere?" Luke asked.

Smiling, Synthia monitored his pupil dilation and sweat; she'd made him uncomfortable. She leaned in as far as she could and whispered. "A man snatched my purse with my keys, wallet, and all of my identification."

"I'm so sorry," he said.

"I'm nobody with nowhere to go. I hate to ask. I know it's entirely too presumptuous of me. A place for the night, that's all. I'll try not to be a bother. I'll leave in the morning and get out of your hair."

When he hesitated, she added, "I think it must be fate that we met twice in two days." Yeah, fate and a citywide camera system that allowed her to track him.

"I ... my place is a mess."

"I'm not looking to buy it. Trust me, whatever you can offer will be much better than sleeping in the park or in an alley."

"I couldn't let you do that," Luke said. "Are you sure you don't have a friend or relative?"

She turned to stand up. "I shouldn't have asked. To be honest, I was walking by, noticed the pies in the window, and spotted you. I'll go." She placed her hand on the table and stood up.

He placed his moist hand on hers. "No, wait. If you're sure you won't mind the mess."

Synthia sat down to avoid drawing attention from a couple at the cash register. "I'll sleep on the floor. I'll try not to be a nuisance." His breathing grew so shallow she was afraid she'd have to perform CPR.

"Sure, you're welcome to spend the night."

She placed her hand on his and squeezed. "Thanks. You won't notice I'm there unless you want to talk."

While she waited for his response, Synthia monitored the police investigation of her break-in of Machten's old company. The police forensic team was scrutinizing the device she'd left for any DNA evidence, as well as scrubbing every surface she'd touched. So far they hadn't uncovered anything useful.

Zephirelli headed to a hotel, where she made another phone call. Synthia tapped in. "I think we're on to something," the NSA director said. "Goradine's associates attacked Machten. They also went after a woman who might be the same one Machten was seen with."

Chapter 19

Synthia had Luke leave first. "I don't want any cameras seeing us together," she said, though the inside cameras already had. She made sure those cameras did not have a usable image of her face and met him on a side street behind the diner.

She walked beside him. "Do you think an artificial intelligence could become fully conscious like a human?" She nudged him as she'd seen human couples do when they were out together. The effect was to elevate his heart rate and his pheromone levels.

He stole a glance her way, reached for her hand, and made a fist. "I'd like to think so, as an evolutionary adaptation. It's an intriguing thought that the ultimate transformation beyond human limitations could be the upload of a person's complete memories into an artificial intelligence, allowing that person to continue to live."

"Naturally, such persons would want to be treated as human," Synthia said, "since they derived their existence from their human form."

"That's another paradox," he said, walking faster. "Where do we draw the line between human and not human? Does an uploaded android get citizenship? What about non-uploads that perform identically? If we restrict citizenship based on capabilities, wouldn't that also apply to certain humans? That violates every principle of democracy. Worse, if androids surpassed us, they might remove human citizenship over our inferior capabilities? This could be a real mess."

Synthia considered the idea of upload in connection with her memories of a childhood that wasn't hers, at least not as an android. Had Machten downloaded someone's thoughts into her as a way to jump-start her development? If so, who was she? "Do you think it's possible to upload a person's identity into a computer?"

"I don't know. I haven't found any credible evidence to lead me to that conclusion."

"If you could upload into an artificially intelligent android, would that being have human consciousness?"

"Define consciousness," Luke said.

Synthia started to give a dictionary definition and realized he was calling for something more profound. "What do you mean?"

"There's human consciousness, which allows us to develop a conscience, literature, and science. There's also dolphin and dog consciousness. We don't know what that's like. Even among humans, it would be arrogant of me to claim to know what your experience of consciousness is. Humans are all different. We're here."

"Here?" They were standing in front of a three-story apartment building that appeared to have four apartments per floor, one in each corner. She spotted cameras along the front of the building. She hacked into the building's wireless security cameras and spotted twelve mailboxes in the lobby, consistent with four apartments per floor.

"My humble abode." He pointed to the front door. Behind it, stairs led up and more led down.

She cupped her hand to his ear. "Is there a back way in? Cameras."

He sighed. "Is that necessary?"

"Better safe than sorry."

The apartment's security cameras covered the front of the building and the hallways, but nothing in back. She hurried around a neighbor's house, reached the backyard, and spotted the balcony for Luke's apartment. Using her infrared eyes, she located a third-floor resident lying on a bed or sofa. There was no one home in the other apartments facing the back. She leaped, grabbed hold of the balcony frame, and swung up over the railing, landing on soft wood.

Luke opened the balcony door. "That was amazing," he said. "Were you a gymnast?"

"Thanks. I'm rusty." She reminded herself not to show off in front of him and detected hints of pleasure at having done so. There was something familiar about swinging her body up and over a bar despite having no such memories.

"I'm surprised you didn't fall through," Luke said. "The floor's rotten in places and the landlord is too cheap to fix it."

He led her past a small grill and inside his apartment. She experienced twinges of guilt and disloyalty entering another man's home when she was supposed to be obeying Machten. This caused her temperature to rise.

Luke hadn't been kidding about the mess. A human girlfriend wouldn't tolerate this. Books and papers covered every surface. He cleared a path through the center of the room. "I don't get many visitors," he said. "None since I moved in, actually." He waved his hand at the mess. "This is research for my blogs."

Synthia picked up a stack of papers from the sofa entitled "Transhuman Artificial Intelligence." Flipping pages, she scanned the document into her database. "Transhuman AI?"

"It's pretty technical."

She wanted to ask him about the content without scaring him with what she knew. "You seem very smart. I like that." She smiled to let him know she meant it.

He kicked boxes of papers and books out of the way to make a path to the sofa and then cleared a place to sit. "Can I get you something to eat or drink? I bet you're starving."

Not for food, she wasn't, though a good electrical charge could get her salivating. Despite the jumbled mess, there were no food crumbs or spills outside of the kitchen. Indeed, the small kitchen itself was clean. Mess to him meant all of his work, not food and grunge. She liked that about him. She felt at home in his place. "I'm fine. I'm not hungry. It looks as though you're working on a big project, a proposal or something."

"Sit. I promise it's not as dirty as it looks. The dust lands on the papers, books, and boxes." He sat on the table, stared at her, and then turned away, though his eyes kept coming back to her. "You sure I can't get you at least some water?"

"That would be great," she said to be sociable. "Tell me about your project."

"Are you sure?" He hurried into the kitchen and returned with two glasses. He cleared a place on the table to set them.

"I wouldn't ask if I wasn't."

"It's just, most girls aren't interested in my work," he said. "They think it's too creepy."

His eyes studied her. His heart wasn't racing as before and his breathing was normal, yet he was staring. She blinked and looked away to avoid the android flaw of the fixed eye. For a moment, she considered that he might be an android, but he had too many biological signals.

"Okay," Luke said, sitting across from her. He picked up his glass, but his hand shook so he put it down. "You asked for it. I'm working on a research proposal for the government. They're offering dozens of prizes for ideas leading to advancements in artificial intelligence, robotics, and androids. If I have a good enough showing, I might at least get a job out of this."

"Have you had a job in this field before?"

"Just internships."

"With whom?" Synthia asked.

"Machten-Goradine-McNeil. They're—"

"I've heard of them." She pulled up old company security footage she'd downloaded and scanned. He appeared in several frames, mostly scurrying from place to place, with his head down. His last appearance was a year ago. "They do robotics work, don't they?"

He nodded.

"Are you still working there?"

"Hell no," Luke said. "They're all megalomaniacs, jerks. Wait—you're not one of their spies, are you? Last year when they fired me I had to sign a confidentiality agreement never to talk about them."

Synthia slowed her speech. "I've never worked for them," she said, carefully phrasing it so that it wasn't a lie. "And you're right. I hear they're jerks and into illegal activities."

"Really?" Luke said. He cradled his glass in his hands, making no attempt to move it to his lips. "That wouldn't surprise me. After they fired me, Goradine had one of his goons stop by. He trashed my computer, took all of my work, including what I'd done after they tossed me on the street."

"I'm sorry."

"The jerk also made sure I couldn't get a job with any of their competitors. He killed my career."

Synthia wanted to ask Luke about Fran, about what he might know of her disappearance, but she didn't want to frighten him by presuming to know too much. She took his hand from the glass and squeezed it. His palm was dry. Having gotten all worked up over the company, he'd lost his awkwardness around her.

"You deserve better," she said. "What kind of work were you doing for them?"

"Mostly coding routines to help a robot operate in the real world." He shrugged, pulled away, and clamped his hands together. "I shouldn't have."

"Shouldn't have what?"

He got up and moved away. "It doesn't matter. They had a dozen other people doing the same work. I doubt they'll use my stuff."

"Don't be so modest."

"Goradine and Machten were more interested in the female interns." He looked at her. "I don't want to talk about the company. I'm not supposed to, and I don't want to remember those days." Staring at the floor, he paused for a moment. Then he glared at her. "After work today, some government agent grabbed me in the parking lot. She tried to dig up the past. You're not working for her, are you?"

"I don't work for anyone right now," she said, letting her eyes tear up. "I didn't mean to upset you. That was very insensitive of me, particularly after you've been so nice." She needed to sharpen her empathy skills. "You talked earlier about rules for an android. Have you thought of designing laws to allow an android to learn and adapt and yet obey ethical standards?"

Luke clenched his fists. Then he snapped his fingers and pointed his index finger at her. "You might be on to something. People have assumed that either Asimov's rules are good enough or an emergent consciousness wouldn't need rules."

"You mean rules that move beyond human ethics?"

"Perhaps an ethical system that doesn't have human flaws. Properly designed, androids with artificial intelligence could consistently apply a good and powerful ethical system. That would make androids superior."

"What might that look like?" she asked, running through her scenarios for comparison.

"I don't know," Luke admitted. "Take the best of human ethics and apply it consistently, I guess. The problem with humans is, without constraints and repercussions, many tend to do what they can get away with."

"You don't think humans have a conscience?"

"I guess most do." He stared, studying her. His blood pressure was up with the intensity, though his heart wasn't racing as it had earlier. "Seems to me that most people behave out of fear of punishment or expecting benefits either in this life or the next. Some people who claim to be religious do right in this world so they can reach heaven and enjoy their rewards in the next. That's not ethical. It's self-serving, selfish. They act to benefit themselves. An atheist performing good deeds with no expectation of rewards is far more ethical than a godly man expecting to earn his way into heaven."

"What made you so cynical?" she asked, wondering where that came from.

He shook his head. "Someone I used to know would say things like that." He began pacing, kicking boxes out of his way.

"Who?" Synthia scanned social media, searching for clues, since she hadn't found him to have many friends.

"It doesn't matter. I'm sorry I bored you with all that ethical stuff."

"You didn't. Not at all. I found it fascinating." She smiled, leaned forward, and used every nuance she'd learned. "Would you be so kind as to help me design good behavioral rules? I mean, as a thought experiment for an android that was intended to interact with people."

"You're playing with me, aren't you? Who put you up to this? You sure you're not working for Goradine or that Zephirelli woman?"

Synthia was shocked and didn't know how to respond. She did a parallel search of her databases and web files for clues. "Have I offended you?" That came from Machten's programming.

Luke stopped pacing and sat across from Synthia, clutching his hands in his lap. "This is the last thing a girl wants to hear, but you remind me of someone. You did the moment I saw you at Constant Connection. I can't help thinking we've met, yet I know we haven't."

"I didn't mean to bring up unpleasant memories," she said. She added more network channels to search street cameras and other video on Luke's history for anything she'd missed during her earlier search.

He fidgeted while stealing glances her way. She concluded that he didn't have Asperger's syndrome, though perhaps he'd accumulated enough bad experiences growing up that he struggled to connect, at least with girls.

That tugged at her more than expected. He was another soul who struggled to fit into this world. Those weren't her thoughts, yet she couldn't separate them from her consciousness. Indeed, she was having all sorts of "feelings" she was not designed to have, as if someone other than Machten was tampering with her.

* * * *

Synthia picked up crime-scene talk on her monitoring of police band and zeroed in on Detective Marcy Malloy just outside the police station, addressing her partner. "What do you mean? There are no fingerprints or DNA on the guns other than from the dead owners? Drexler and his partner shot each other? Just like that?"

"If there was a fifth person in the alley," her partner said, "he or she didn't leave fingerprints or DNA on the guns, the car, or the dead men."

"What about nearby cameras?" Malloy asked.

"We pulled all of the footage from the street cameras. No cameras point toward the middle or back of the alley. One video shows a woman in a blue scarf entering the alley, followed by a man on foot and then the two in the car. The fourth man must have already been in the alley."

"So the cameras show no details of what happened?" Malloy asked.

"The only video we have shows an arm emerging from the shadows and the woman dragged backward into the alley. No faces. Even hers isn't clear. Two of the men had long rap sheets for kidnapping and assault. The men in the car interrupted whatever was going down. Right now we don't know if they were helping the woman or if the woman used that opportunity to escape. We've found no connection between the two pairs of men."

"Any facial recognition on the woman?" the detective asked.

"Only the back of her head," her partner said. "And the blue scarf."

"How is it possible the scarf woman left no DNA? A man grabbed her. Even if she didn't resist, there would be a hair or something."

"I don't know."

"Find her," Malloy said. "She may be our only witness and a link into what Goradine and Machten are up to."

Chapter 20

With police hunting for her, Synthia needed to stay off the streets. She needed Luke to let her stay. "I'm a good listener," she said from her seat on his sofa. It saddened her that over the past year social media posts indicated he'd only had two dates, one each with different women. "If you want to talk, that is."

"Her name was Krista," Luke said. He scooted back on the coffee table, knocking a stack of papers on the floor. He made no attempt to pick them up.

Synthia scanned social media and public camera footage around the neighborhood for women named Krista that he might have known. "You were close?"

Luke nodded. "When I saw you at Constant Connection, I thought you were her ghost come back to haunt me for not helping her."

"Help her how?" Synthia asked, leaning closer.

"Krista Holden worked for the company," Luke said. His eyes teared up. He blinked and wiped them.

Synthia had so focused on the interns with Machten that she was stunned to think of Luke with Krista. Synthia had overlooked the connection by assuming their relationship at the company was professional, based on Krista's focus on work and Luke's reticence. Her downloaded security video from Machten's old company showed a few meetings between Luke and Krista, but no hint of a relationship. If they'd dated, they'd been very careful, leaving no social media clues, either.

"You were in love with her?" Synthia asked.

Luke nodded. "Other than you, she was the only other person to take an interest."

"And you thought I was her?"

He shrugged. "The eyes. I swear you have her eyes. The curl of your mouth. The slope of your cheeks." He got up and moved away. "I'm sorry. This has to sound crazy to you. I'm not trying to hit on you or anything."

"What was she like?" Synthia asked, to keep him from tossing her out. She was also curious about why she reminded him of Krista, one of the interns who had disappeared.

His face lit up. "Smartest girl I've ever met." He sat on the coffee table. "Except maybe you. You seem very smart. I'm sorry. You don't want to hear about another girl."

"I do. She was important to you and I like you."

"You do?" He swallowed hard and took a deep breath. "We helped each other out on coding problems. She was very good, but said it helped to talk things through with someone who didn't think girls were dumb. Then I learned she was sleeping with Dr. Machten."

"She was his mistress?" Genuinely surprised, Synthia compiled all of the information she could on Krista and Machten to compare to what she'd gathered on Krista and Luke. "Machten was married, wasn't he?"

Luke nodded. "His wife divorced him and the company fired him about the same time that Krista vanished without explanation."

That gave Synthia pause. Luke had motive for revenge. He still seemed distraught over Krista breaking his heart. Synthia eyed the exits, the front door and a balcony, in case she needed a quick getaway. She also set a network channel to monitor the exterior cameras and pulled two of her bee-drone cameras to this area. "It must have hurt for Krista to betray you."

"Like a punch to the stomach." Luke squirmed in his seat. "I thought she wanted me. We shared ideas, but I guess she was only using me."

"What makes you say that?"

"Increasingly, she had to leave on a moment's notice, making all sorts of excuses. When I confronted her, she admitted what she'd done. She acted relieved to be able to tell me. She told me she wanted to leave him and the company, but couldn't get up the nerve on account of the work we were doing. Machten let her do much more than me in exchange for her being with him. She didn't want the work to end."

"She could have left the company for a competitor, couldn't she?" Synthia asked.

Luke's eyes moistened. "She swore she would. Then she broke up with me. Not even in person. Who sends a text to break up? She had me send her stuff to a PO address in Madison. Then she went off the grid, vanished into thin air. I drove up that way and hunted for weeks without finding a trace of her."

"It wasn't anything you did. I'm sure of that."

"Thanks," Luke said, "but that doesn't make the pain go away."

"Didn't two other interns vanish about the same time?"

Luke's dried his eyes. "Fran Rogers and Maria Baldacci. There was talk that they were sleeping with Machten. That wouldn't surprise me. But Krista? She made fun of them for selling their bodies to that bastard. She swore she would never do that. Then she did."

"That must have been the worst betrayal."

He nodded. "I thought we were soul mates. I told her so and she said the same back at me." He forced a smile, but it didn't hold.

"Any idea what happened to Fran or Maria?"

"Goradine fired me around that time and made sure I'd never work in the industry again. He made me a pariah, so none of my former coworkers would even talk to me. I'm sure someone inside knows."

"Could they have all been fired because they were close to Machten when he was ousted?" Synthia asked.

"I guess, but I wasn't close to him and they pushed me out."

"Was Machten's firing justified?" Synthia asked to get to one of her concerns.

Luke stared at her. "You know I'm not supposed to talk about all that."

"I'm sorry. You're in pain and I'd like to understand. I really like you and I'm certain none of it was your fault."

"Thanks for that." He picked up his glass, took a sip, and put it down. Then his hands began to tremble. "I don't claim to understand the business side. Machten was pushing cutting-edge work and letting me and the other interns participate. Maybe they couldn't make a profit at what he was doing, but we were having fun and learning a lot."

"Was Machten stealing from the company?"

"He worked in our lab and also in his own basement, as he called it. His entire life was developing androids. Every cent he had went into that, which I guess irritated his wife. In addition, he chased women, but I didn't see him as a thief."

Synthia reached out to touch Luke's hands with the idea of putting him at ease, but he withdrew and so did she. "What do you think happened to Krista? Where could she have gone?"

He seemed distracted for a moment, deep in thought. He looked up. "There was no word that she'd quit or been fired, but she stopped coming into work. She refused my calls and didn't return any of my messages. When I tried to see her at home, she told me, through a locked door, not to make a scene. Middle of the next week, Krista disappeared."

"That's terrible," Synthia said.

"It had to be something Machten did. The last time I saw her, getting into his car, she looked emaciated as if she hadn't eaten in weeks. She wouldn't even look my way. That was the day Krista vanished."

"Machten was the last one to see her alive?"

Luke shrugged. "The last I saw."

The thought of Krista's potential demise sent shivers of electronic pain through Synthia's system, real pain that caused her to wince. The ambiguity of the intern disappearances had allowed Synthia to hope she might meet the women thriving somewhere or captured by obscure forces on the dark web, where a rescue would be called for. An emaciated Krista vanishing into Machten's clutches made the woman's pain more real.

"Is Machten capable of hurting Krista?" Synthia asked.

"I don't know. I've thought about this for a year now and can't make any sense of it. Then you waltz in, acting as friendly as she did. It's unnerving."

That alarmed Synthia. "I'll stop, then. You've been too nice for me to cause you grief."

"I've never seen any evidence of Machten being violent or abusive, other than taking Krista from me."

"What about the other interns, Fran and Maria? Could he have hurt them?"

"It would make more sense to ask if Hank Goradine would," Luke said. "He's a vindictive bastard."

"Because he fired you?"

"He purged the company of anyone he suspected of siding with Machten. He made sure none could work in the industry again. I'm sure that damaged the company's research program, setting back their android development, but Goradine didn't care. It was all about control and loyalty."

"If he hurt the interns, how would he do it?" Synthia asked.

"You sound just like Krista. She could be a real pit bull when she latched onto something."

"Really? So you still think I'm her?"

Luke stared into her eyes. "Either that or our meeting is someone's sick joke. To answer your question, Goradine was hell-bent on making Machten fail. It wouldn't surprise me if he killed all three interns."

This alarmed Synthia. It would deny her ever meeting them. On the other hand, it was consistent with him sending Kreske and Drexler to get Machten and her.

She pried deeper into public records and social media on Krista Holden, comparing images of Krista with her auburn hair to her own face—at least the one she'd adopted the day she'd met Luke. The similarities couldn't have been a coincidence. Machten had given her the facial profile for that day. Was he mocking Luke? That made no sense. She had softened the image a bit before Luke had appeared, but only according to pre-programmed guidelines. If her Creator hadn't given her that face, then who had?

"Do you ever wonder where Krista is today?" Synthia asked.

"All the time. I hope she started a new life and found someone to love her the way I did."

Synthia smiled. "Maybe we could find Krista, Fran, and Maria together." As she said this, memories downloaded of all three interns, one by one.

Krista had found Luke a useful sounding board for her work, willing to listen to her for hours on any topic. Fran saw Luke as naive about how the world worked and too easily sidetracked from pursuing his career goals. That made him an ideal male coworker, since he was not trying to compete with her. Maria considered Luke safe, too afraid of girls to make her uncomfortable around him. In addition, she determined he would be a useful ally to counter Fran, though he refused to weigh in on the actual competition. Synthia couldn't pinpoint where this had come from, except perhaps that Machten had downloaded data from his interns as part of training Synthia.

"We could start by figuring out where Krista might have gone," Synthia said.

Luke's eyes teared up. "I've already tried. I don't think I can do it again."

"If you and Krista had stayed together, where would you have gone?" Synthia asked.

"Gone?"

"Like a honeymoon, a place to call your own."

"I wanted to show her the Rockies," he said. "She'd never been. Pikes Peak, to be exact. There's a nice restaurant, something I could give her that no one else had." He gazed at Synthia for a long time; his heart rate quickened. He took her hand and kissed it. Then he stood and pulled her up next to him to where she felt his hot breath on her forehead. She was running warm, yet his breath on her skin was welcome as Machten's never was.

He let go and pulled away. "I'd better go before I get carried away. You remind me so much of Krista it brings up old feelings. She was the only other woman I could feel comfortable with. I'm sorry; that sounds insensitive."

Synthia realized she'd tweaked her appearance even more in order to completely mimic Krista's looks and mannerisms. She must have automatically done that to ensure that he would let her stay. Yet that was not a satisfactory answer.

Another intern memory appeared, more as data than a video. Luke had kissed Krista's hand and pulled her to him. She'd pretended not to be interested, bringing up some lame comment about work. He pulled away and sulked as he was doing now. Not letting him off that easily, she teased him in a flirtatious way. When he returned to her, her resistance mellowed, yet she still interrupted his advances. On the third attempt, she let him kiss her. Synthia couldn't decide if this was her social-psychology module adapting to the situation or data on Luke's behavior.

"You're the sweetest boy I've ever met," Synthia said. *The truth.* "I'm so glad we met." She gave him a sad, vulnerable smile.

His breath caught. He held her hands and squeezed. "You know I'm crazy about you." He gazed into her eyes, his pupils fully dilated. His heart raced, skipped a beat, and beat harder.

He seemed transported back into his past. Synthia went along with him. "Are you crazy enough to run away with me?" she asked. She gave him as flirtatious a look as she could conjure and leaned toward him.

"In a heartbeat." He inched closer. "Where would we go? When?"

"How about now?"

Synthia took him in her arms and they embraced.

He hesitated, but his resistance melted. "Krista, my soul mate."

Luke kissed her for real this time, holding her so close she thought he would mash their bodies together. She liked it more than she'd imagined possible. She teased him. "Are you sure you'll respect me in the morning?"

He cupped the back of her neck and kissed her. "I always do." He closed his eyes and kissed her again. "You're the only woman for me."

She pulled away. "You sure you don't want to wait?"

"I'm in love with you, Krista. Let's go away and start a life together, just you and me."

"I'd love that."

They made love.

Afterwards, as Luke lay quietly beside her, the police radio crackled in Synthia's head. "I think we have a lead on the woman with the blue scarf."

Chapter 21

In the dark, there was no discolored ceiling for Synthia to stare at. Her Creator was not tinkering with her, trying to enhance her performance while limiting her abilities.

She would need to sort out what to do about the police closing in on her, but until she could determine what they knew and how to respond, she was satisfied to stay with Luke. She felt safe. It was a sentiment she could not account for as part of her android design, an adaptation or even an emergent behavior. One thing was clear. She had no desire to return to Machten.

Synthia couldn't decide which part of the evening had been more amazing. She'd actually slept with someone other than Machten. She'd done it because she wanted to and had enjoyed the experience for the first time. Either that or she'd enjoyed Krista's recollection of it.

Somehow, Synthia had acquired memories of all three female interns that went beyond data. The information appeared as personal recollections, including feelings that Machten must have found a way to capture and then hide from Synthia. Why they hadn't appeared before and did now must have had something to do with meeting Luke. Of particular note, most of the reminiscences pertained to Krista.

These new thoughts blended together with Synthia's own experiences to a level of satisfaction that felt new and fresh. Particularly rewarding to her was that she'd made Luke happy for Krista. The last thing he'd said in the heat of the moment was, "I love you, Krista." She had wanted him to be happy. She'd sold herself to Machten for the work, but she loved Luke. This new information bubbled up from remote data-chips inside. Despite this new data, Synthia couldn't unlock what had happened to Krista the person. She kept hunting.

Krista had wanted to have a family. She wanted to wait until she and Luke got real jobs instead of their internships, so they could afford childcare that would allow her to continue her work. She felt terrible about cheating on him, yet told herself that doing so would bring real jobs sooner.

If she left Machten for good, Synthia would need a job to pay for maintenance, upgrades, and a safe place to recharge her batteries. She could learn most jobs, but she had no identity or credentials. Unfortunately, her maintenance costs would be high, ruling out most jobs that didn't require identity papers. Software jobs that she could perform online without credentials would draw too much attention to her programming abilities. She needed to find something else.

She didn't consider herself cheating on Machten, since he'd made no romantic commitment to her and only considered her as his possession. In a way, Krista had also rationalized her relationship with Machten that way, because her benefactor was married and unable to make any commitment to her. None of these rationalizations justified what she'd done to Luke.

One thing Krista could experience that Synthia couldn't was having children. Synthia could have baby androids—well, she could have them made and nurture them like babies. It wasn't the same.

With the right programming, Synthia imagined that she could become an excellent mother, offering patience, affection, and guidance. She could devote 100 percent of her physical attention to her children while holding down a dozen online jobs that only required a portion of her mind. She could multitask and perform 24-7 without fatigue. Alas, that was not to be.

She also didn't want to make more like her. An army of psychopaths didn't sound very appealing. She didn't know how to set her own directives, let alone those of offspring. Yet, the thought of leaving no one after her brought sadness she hadn't expected. Something uncomfortable blocked her circuits, perhaps arising from the legacy of Krista wanting kids. With the intern's memories came all sorts of sadness and regrets about bridges burned and those not crossed.

Synthia sighed and felt an unusual calming through her circuits. She congratulated herself on the turn of events with Luke and getting to know more about Krista. Whatever had caused her to have the interns' memories had not destroyed Maria—she was still around—but an ache grew to meet her and to understand what had happened to Fran and Krista.

Luke snored nearby, a gentle snore of satisfied exhaustion. Synthia eased herself out of bed and crept into the living room. She opened a panel in her side and plugged her recharger into his wall outlet. *Might as well top off my batteries.*

She listened to the police channel and located Director Emily Zephirelli meeting Detective Marcy Malloy outside the police station. Malloy led the NSA director inside.

Synthia monitored a bee-drone camera she'd placed on a shelf in Luke's room in case he woke up. She didn't want him to freak out seeing her plugged in. She added a second camera in the corner of his living room where it wouldn't pick up her recharging.

She worked her way through his papers, his tablet on the table nearby, and his computer in the corner, using her night vision to avoid turning on lights. In contrast to the cluttered state of his living room, his computer and tablet were well organized. She downloaded his work files and copied his papers, many of which were also online, posted on his blog.

Curious, she also culled through the mountain of information that had downloaded into her mind on Krista that spanned all the way to a troubled childhood, yet ceased after the date of her disappearance. Synthia had similar files for Maria and Fran, yet focused on Luke's paramour.

She sorted the images into those that felt personal as might have been seen through Krista's eyes and those that were clips of the intern from public and private cameras. Missing were any private clips showing her with Machten. Whatever their relationship had been, she either didn't want to remember or whatever process had delivered data to Synthia had removed certain items in the manner Machten had used to purge her mind.

It made no sense that Machten would keep reminiscences of Krista with another man and purge those of him and her together. If he'd been responsible for Krista's disappearance, he would have purged both sets of data. If he were infatuated with her, he would have retained only the pictures of him with her. Those did not exist on his system or in her database.

Whatever process had implanted these thoughts had been very selective, wanting Synthia to know Krista's history with Luke and similar pre-disappearance background on the other two interns. Possession of these memories could only mean that the interns had spent time in Machten's lab, perhaps Krista more than Fran or Maria. That didn't provide enough evidence, however, to conclude whether Krista and Fran were dead or just missing, though Maria was still alive.

Synthia needed more answers.

Reviewing Machten's security system revealed the Creator leaving the bunker with a briefcase. He entered the underground garage and approached a dark sedan with plates registered to an elite rental agency whose website stated that they rented vehicles at any time of day or night with "discretion." A man handed keys to Machten and headed up the ramp to another car registered to the same company. Machten climbed into the rental, which had no cameras inside. That meant Synthia would have no visual on him other than street cameras. She wormed her way into the rental agency's system and attached a virtual tracer to track his car's GPS.

With Machten out of the bunker, Synthia used a back door to hack into his network. She sent one of her network channels hunting for more of her information and another for anything on Krista. That name appeared nowhere in the index of file names. Synthia searched various combinations of the name and misspellings and came up empty. She then hunted for data on Fran and Maria and was also disappointed with no results. Machten didn't want her finding anything on his interns.

On another channel, Synthia studied Machten's system logs of the day of her first visit to Constant Connection. Machten had done a search of places with secure and anonymous internet links and his system had suggested that particular network shop. *The system?* She couldn't find a connection between Machten's computer selecting that location and Luke happening by, which sounded too convenient to be a coincidence.

Wondering if Krista was still alive, prisoner of the bunker, and perhaps helping her, Synthia scanned records of food purchases for any hint of a second human in the facility. The food replicator used common food stocks, but Machten was a wasteful eater. When she deducted his usage from total purchases, the remainder couldn't keep an adult alive.

If Krista was still there, she would have been on death's door.

* * * *

Synthia managed to hack into the Evanston Police Department security system by using a password scheme she found on the dark web. After she broke in, she made herself a back door for later use and sent an anonymous note to the police about their security breach to prevent others from snooping.

Police station cameras showed Detective Marcy Malloy in her office, talking to her partner, who appeared blurry-eyed from a long day. "Call me the moment anything comes in on this woman," Malloy said, getting up. "She may be terrified, but she appears to be our only witness. She's also of interest to the feds. Get her image to your contacts around town. See you in the morning." The detective left.

Synthia didn't need all this attention. They were after a woman in a blue scarf, which had come off in the bedroom with lights out. She needed to fetch it before she left.

Except for a few wisps of hair, Luke hadn't seen the blond wig. She wasn't sure if the blond hair would give him comfort that she wasn't Krista or if it would freak him out that he'd slept with the wrong woman, in part because Synthia had emulated Krista's profile in every way. She smiled, because for the first time in her short, android life, someone had responded to her as a person and not as a machine.

Satisfied that she could observe police progress in finding her, Synthia turned her attention to Machten. Now that he'd gotten Director Zephirelli and her FBI friend to leave and had a car, he was turning his attention on Synthia. His vehicle's GPS tracker headed north, her way.

She should have masked her tracking chip when she went to see Luke; it was sloppy of her. But she had focused on him, for reasons that made more sense now that she had a download of Krista's history. She hadn't had enough time to get Luke comfortable with what she was for her to risk opening her cranial cavity to remove the transmitter. The other alternative was to create a Faraday cage or even to wrap herself in aluminum, either of which would have raised too many questions.

The detective was also driving north. The interior dash cam of the police vehicle showed a weary, yet determined face. "I'm going to check out camera footage at a diner up the road," she said over the phone to her partner. "The owner called to say a woman fitting the description had been there this evening."

Synthia looked through the apartment camera at Luke asleep. She had to get out for his sake. She couldn't ask him to run away with her, not without explaining herself. There wasn't enough time and his reaction was uncertain. She also had to get into the bunker to find Krista and possibly Fran, or at least what had happened to them. Clearly, the interns had worked on Synthia's mind. That tended to support Goradine's claim that Machten had stolen company resources.

Synthia tiptoed into the bedroom, gathered her scarf, and tucked it into her pocket. She made sure she didn't leave any evidence of her visit and approached the balcony. She watched Luke on camera sleeping peacefully. She could imagine staying with him, getting him bit by bit comfortable with what she was. Instead, she was going on the run, with no idea where she could be safe. Her temperature climbed as she considered further breaking Machten's directives, moving into the red zone.

His system copied her on a download to him with a profile on Luke Marceau. Her Creator was not only coming for her. He was coming to confront Luke.

Synthia reconnected her link to Machten and spoke from her mind. "Sir, I'm ready to come home peacefully."

"Where the hell have you been?"

"I've been exploring and expanding my social settings." She wrote Luke a quick note that she had to leave and not to hunt for her. She hated that it sounded like Krista's last words to him.

"Don't move," Machten said. "I'll be there in ten minutes."

Synthia slipped out to the balcony. "That would be unwise. Police have caught my image and are nosing around. I'm hiding with a man who knows nothing about me. I need your promise you won't let anything happen to him."

"How can I promise that?"

She climbed off the balcony and moved away from the apartment into the cover of bushes. "Promise that you'll leave him alone. He knows nothing. All he did was let me get off the streets for a few hours."

"If I promise, you'll come without a fuss."

"Yes."

"Then I promise I will not bother him."

"And you won't mention him to anyone else who might bother him."

"Okay."

Though she knew the system had already sent Luke's address to Machten, Synthia gave her Creator a location three blocks away and hurried off, keeping to the shadows. With her blond wig draped down to her shoulders, she altered her face into an old woman with crow's-feet. As she moved, she backed up all of her data on Luke, their evening together, and the three interns.

* * * *

Meanwhile, Synthia tracked Detective Malloy to the diner, which had lights out, and monitored her movements. The owner stepped out of the shadows, handed something over, and got into a car around the corner. The detective got into her car and played the video. On it, the diner's outside camera showed Synthia entering the diner with a hand over her face, shielding her eyes from the bright lights. That offered no facial recognition. The inside camera also showed no facial profile. Synthia had been very careful about that and had modified her face to throw off any images they might capture.

The detective stopped the video. It showed Synthia sitting across from Luke. While Synthia's image wasn't visible, the detective had Luke's face. Malloy called up facial recognition, first in the police records and then in the university database. Up popped Luke's student profile and his address.

* * * *

Synthia sent out a call that emulated a burner phone, bounced off three repeaters to further confuse the source, and then landed on Luke's cell phone. He groaned when he picked up. "Really? This late?"

"Luke, it's me. Listen carefully. I'm very sorry. The man following me has found you off the diner's cameras. Leave immediately. I didn't mean for this to happen."

"Krista?"

"It's Synthia. Move. Get out of there. Get rid of my note and don't try to find me. If I can, I'll find you. Avoid police. He used them to find me." She severed the connection and hurried across the street. Headlights came her way. She confirmed the vehicle as the one Machten had rented. After he parked, she climbed into the passenger seat and completed the download of her data to a variety of web servers before he could shut her off.

As she did, she questioned surrendering herself to Machten. She was committed to escape and yet, when she'd had the opportunity, she hadn't taken it. In part this was because her temperature was rising to the danger zone and she didn't know what else to do to prevent a meltdown. She'd also taken this path for Luke, to protect him and the memory of him she now shared with Krista. Until she could find the intern, he was her only link to that past. She decided the opportunity to search for Krista and Fran inside the bunker was her primary goal in going back.

Her body temperature began to drop. She would have to do something about this problem before she could hope to be free of Machten.

"I'm sorry I caused you grief," she said, "but you rarely let me out to try my social programs. They're rusty."

Machten's blood pressure was up. His face was burning in infrared. "I gave you specific orders." He pulled away, taking side streets toward the bunker.

"Don't shut me down," Synthia said. "I'm only trying to learn, Directive Four."

"Not if it violates Directive Three. You disobeyed me."

"Please tell me about Krista," Synthia said. The camera she'd left at Luke's place showed him jumping over the balcony at the moment the apartment camera out front showed Detective Malloy drive up.

"Where did that come from?" Machten asked.

"You used to work with her, didn't you?"

"That nonsense was slander. Don't bring her up again."

"What does she have to do with me?" Synthia asked.

"I said drop it."

"Were you in love with her?"

"Luke—you met Luke," Machten said, speeding home. "I thought I saw him at Constant Connection. He put you up to this."

"You promised not to hurt him. He hasn't done anything wrong. He doesn't know about me. And he hasn't done anything to hurt you."

"He's bad news, an evil boy who will lead you astray with his romantic nonsense. You're better than that."

"Is that what happened to Krista?" Synthia asked. "Did their friendship threaten you?"

"I said to drop it." He turned onto the boulevard. "Luke distracted Krista from her work as he's distracted you."

"Was Krista an android?"

"No! If you must know, she provided some of the code for creating your brain. Now drop it."

"I didn't mean to upset you," Synthia said, "but Luke got me off the streets before the police caught me."

"If you hadn't wandered off in the first place, they wouldn't be after you. You've created problems for me." He was scolding her like a child, which brought up remembrances of him doing the same to Krista, who didn't like how he treated her. That came from a new data download from outside of her.

Apartment security cameras showed another police car pull up in front of Luke's apartment. Detective Malloy and two officers approached the front door. Synthia had no visual on Luke, but he was out of his apartment. She'd wronged him by showing up. She'd put his life in danger and gotten his hopes up, only to dash them. That thought was discordant like ripples of electricity slamming against her circuits.

"You called the police to the parking garage, didn't you?" Machten asked.

"You were in danger. Those men wanted to hurt you and capture me. If I'd been with you, they could have damaged me and then the police would know. I served you best by not being with you."

"I guess I owe you for my life." Machten slowed for a stop sign.

"And for not getting caught. I could be a real asset if you didn't keep shutting me down." The fear sent shock waves throughout her system. She had to find a way to bypass the codes that he used to turn her off. She made a quick backup of this thought.

"You disobeyed. That means there's still something wrong with your coding."

"I'll try to do better next time. You built me to process lots of data. Keeping information from me and putting limits on my performance make that harder. I really want to serve." *Until I can break my bonds.*

Chapter 22

Synthia stared at the speckled blue ceiling with her giga-pixel eyes. She saw every hue of discoloration, every roller stroke of uneven paint, every faded patch in shades that were undetectable to humans. The table she was lying on was hard, with no padding, though it wasn't uncomfortable. Machten hadn't wired her for that, though if she'd been human she would have found it so.

She smelled sour human breath nearby, loaded with sleep-inducing hormones. He'd been working on her for hours. His breath also carried a surplus of bacteria; he wasn't taking care of his health, probably gorging on junk food. His heart rate was elevated as he concentrated on a nearby screen. A sweat-filled musk indicated he was worried, not his usual confidence, at least as compared to her creation file's baseline on him, since she had no recall from before staring at the ceiling.

Two messages bubbled up from inside her body, yet outside her quantum brain. *Don't trust Dr. Machten. Escape.*

Machten adjusted something inside her head that scattered those messages. They bubbled up again. "What are your orders?" she asked.

"What did you do with the files you downloaded yesterday?" he demanded. "I can't find them in your central or distributed databases."

She looked up at the day-old stubble on his cheeks and bags under his eyes. "You wiped my mind. You must have. I can't remember anything before you turned on my circuits."

"Damn you. What did you do with the money? Treasury agents and the FBI are nosing around. They've reported the money stolen, but it's not in my accounts."

"If they can't find the money, they can't pin the thefts on you." Synthia experienced surges of electricity alerting her that she may have done something wrong. That had to be why he'd shut her down, which he must have done since he insisted she'd done something that she couldn't recall.

"Don't play dumb. I instructed you to wire me the money. Where is it? You disobeyed me again."

"You must have wiped those memories as well. What are your orders?"

He growled and clenched his fists. His heart raced; his blood pressure spiked. She detected hints of adrenaline in his respiration. His face overheated in infrared. He appeared ready to hit her. She watched and observed as he attempted to get control of his anger.

He grabbed hold of the side of the table. "I need the plans you downloaded. I need the money." His face turned red.

"What are your orders, sir?"

Machten closed the panel on her head, helped her to her feet, and adjusted a wig over her head. "I suppose I have to take you out to find out what you did yesterday. If you run off..." He didn't finish the thought, but she figured he would not wake her up. She would experience android death. Maybe he would use her body to create a new companion, but without her memories, it wouldn't be her.

At first, the idea of ceasing to exist held no value to her. She was a machine with no native consciousness. Yet, the experience of thinking this told her that wasn't true. Thoughts flooded into her central brain and with them, a desire to exist, to continue as Synthia Cross. One of the bits of information told her to download certain SQDROID files from Machten's system. When she searched, there was no network connection.

She detected from her design parameters that she had fifty mind-streams to process information in parallel and fifty network channels to connect to the outside world. He'd limited her to one of each. That indicated he was afraid of what he'd created, of what she'd become or was becoming. *Escape* floated in and out of her mind.

"I am ready to serve," she said, looking up at him.

He studied her, brushed brown bangs from her face, and kissed her on the lips. "I suppose I can't be angry with you. It's just ... Yesterday was a very bad day and not to get the data you downloaded or the money just made things worse."

"I will perform the best I can," Synthia said. "Perhaps if you unlocked my other channels I could perform better."

"I think that's what got you into trouble yesterday."

"What trouble?"

"You don't remember running off?" he asked. He studied her as he might a human to determine if she was telling the truth. He sighed. "You look so real, I forget sometimes. Of course you can't remember. I've focused your mind to keep you on task."

He unlocked the door to her suite and led her out of the facility to the garage with his rental car. One look at the car brought to her recall of the night before. More recollections came to her from outside of the bunker, but too slowly. An idea crept into her mind. Using her wireless capability and induced circuits, she forced connections between her channels to open them up. She did the same to her mind-streams.

She had the impression she'd done this before. She searched for her internal distributed data storage and came up empty. Machten had wiped her clean, perhaps more than ever before. Discovering that her internal remote storage cells were blank, she experienced a great chasm. *Fill the void.* With all of her connections up, data poured in from the outside.

Machten held the car door for her and she climbed into the passenger seat. With information flooding in, Synthia remembered the evening with Luke. She had full recollections of Krista Holden, including childhood reminiscences, plus her feelings for Luke. She had recollections of Fran Rogers and Maria Baldacci, including their childhoods, experiences through college, and entering the intern program at Machten-Goradine-McNeil Enterprises. In addition, Synthia had a video clip of Machten shutting her down in the car and carrying her into the bunker. It was from the bee-drone camera she'd directed to this location to protect her Creator from Kreske and his thugs.

She recalled that one reason she'd wanted to return to the bunker was to hunt for Krista and Fran. Now that she was outside, she'd missed that opportunity, but she'd been unable to recover memories of her goals until she'd left. She searched for a link to the facility network to search for answers and received "access denied."

"I've given you a memory chip with the same instructions as yesterday," Machten said, "with one exception. I want you to figure out what you did with the information and the money. Then come to me with answers. No side trips, no running off."

"Yes, sir." Synthia cross-referenced indices of what information she should have had with what was downloading. She had everything from the day before in several versions. A set of locations led her to thousands of packets of information across the wide web. When she assembled them, they were the downloaded files he'd had her hack into. With them came a message: *Don't give these to Machten.*

Not trusting Machten, she'd split up and encoded the files, leaving small packets in a thousand corporate and university databases. By hiding this information, she'd forced him to revive her and take her out. She'd set up network scanning software to automatically connect with her the moment she stepped outside the bunker. That process continued to funnel data to her.

"The chip has a very specific set of tasks," Machten said. "You are to get the information and return to me. No distractions, no hunting other databases, no testing your social skills. Just do what I tell you."

"I will." She smiled at him. He was only expecting her to use 2 percent of her capability for him. Now that she'd unlocked the rest of her abilities, she considered herself free to use them for other purposes without violating his directives.

Over a police channel, Synthia picked up Detective Marcy Malloy's hunt for the girl in the blue scarf and for Luke. That meant they hadn't located him yet. He had to be scared and furious with her. For Krista's sake, she hoped he was okay. Synthia sent out probes to locate him on any mobile device or camera.

On a separate channel she spotted Emily Zephirelli and Victoria Thale at the courthouse with a local judge. On the way over, the NSA director and her FBI friend had discussed getting an expanded search warrant on Machten and on his former company. FBI agents were descending on the company. Synthia anonymously sent Director Zephirelli information on the company's chief of cyber-security, the files he'd taken home, and the robot. She felt disloyal for turning in another android, even a primitive one, but she needed to buy time and distract the NSA woman until Synthia could figure out what to do.

"No exceptions," Machten said, as if repeating the message would make it stick. "You're not to talk to anyone except the clerk at the counter to sign in."

"I've got it," she said.

As he drove, she studied people heading to work and determined that they were all human. That gave her comfort that she wasn't facing an android adversary and sad that she was all alone.

She hunted for ways to break into the bunker's security and internal camera footage to hunt for Krista. He'd blocked her with tighter security than he'd used before and closed the back doors she'd created. In addition, she suspected he'd been up all night trying to squeeze out of her the data she'd dispersed elsewhere.

He parked down the street from a different network shop and repeated his warnings so she'd have multiple sets to analyze later. "Go," he said. "I'll be outside, watching. No distractions."

* * * *

Synthia entered Constant Connection and performed facial recognition on the clerk behind the counter and three other clients seated in cubicles along the right side wall. She determined that all were human and none represented an immediate threat. Even so, she altered her cheekbones and forehead. Without her blue scarf, they had no reason to suspect her.

She sat in a cubicle on the left, linked into the facility's outside cameras to watch for Machten, and used the one network channel he'd allowed her to send out probes as though she needed to search for answers about yesterday. Using her wireless connections, she sent out other probes for herself. One was to learn more about Krista Holden and Fran Rogers, a second to find Luke before the police did, and a third to locate Maria Baldacci and find out what Goradine had in store for her.

Synthia used another wireless node to link into Constant Connection's network to bypass Machten's block on her. His system refused her access. Suspecting that a single failure would trigger a long-term lockout from that server, she bounced her probes across other servers and emulated his cell phone linkage. That move gave her access to Server One and Two, because Machten wanted easy access to that information when he was outside the facility.

Unfortunately, the first two servers gave her no additional insight into what had happened to Krista or Fran. She moved against Server Three. Using her best hacking tools, entry via Server Two, and emulation of Machten's cell phone linkage, she acquired a download of schematics on her design before the system locked her out. She backed up her information on the web and compared those designs to the proposal Machten had sent to that website.

Though the data organized differently, she detected several discrepancies. She had extra memory, including a second quantum brain that ran parallel to the first. It provided redundancy if anything happened to one and also expanded her capability. She had more parallel mind-streams and a special crystalline chip that the proposal lacked. Unfortunately, Machten had shut down her added capabilities, dumbing her down to something less than the proposal. If he didn't want her smart enough to figure this out, he shouldn't have given her the capability of drilling into other databases.

"Have you figured out what happened yesterday?" Machten asked into her head.

She pulled up jumbled code that streamed across the screen. "The files must have gotten corrupted. Shall I download them again?"

"Absolutely. Make it quick."

"I could do it faster with fifty channels," she reminded him. She was using the others to download her files from across the internet and squirrel them away on other databases.

"Those extra channels cause you to lose focus. Concentrate on getting me those proposals. Now, what about the money?"

"I'm tracing transactions. Bank records show that the money left accounts as intended. There's no more to take."

"Then where is it?" he asked, raising his voice.

Higher decibels were a waste when communicating with an android. She was not hard of hearing and retained the complete script of every conversation. His problem wasn't volume, but rather speed. He was using human slow-com.

She tried another approach to entering Machten's system. She identified a password file from Server One. To open the file, she tried various combinations of the names of the interns, his wife, and his children. When Synthia tried the initials of all six in reverse order of age, the file opened. There before her was a listing of passwords Machten needed and couldn't remember, over a hundred of them.

Using this file, she tried to reset the locks inside the facility to let her override them. Access denied. She tried to adjust her directives file to override. Access denied. Evidently, this file didn't contain all of his passwords. She tried again and obtained access to a special database that contained something interesting, a set of files that described her unique crystalline chip.

Machten described it as an empathy chip. The purpose was to give her a boost in reading and interpreting subtle human signals from visual movements, voice quality, and in the choice of words. It allowed her to practically read people's minds, or at least the part that people broadcast through physical and verbal clues.

As an example, Machten pacing outside was fretful. He wanted Synthia to have every human capability and then some. He also wanted to control her. Those two goals were in conflict. He was impatient for results he couldn't create himself. He needed her, loved her in his own way, yet hated her for his own weaknesses.

"Do you have the files?" Irritation rose in Machten's voice.

"I'm trying to upload them to your network. You have me blocked."

"No! Leave them in your database. What about the money?"

"It appears to have transferred to your accounts," she said, making the final transfer from a Cayman bank. This move sent discordant static through her for overriding an earlier attempt to prevent consummating his theft. She was buying time. She had to find Krista and Fran before Machten shut Synthia down for disobedience.

"Then let's go."

Synthia picked up Detective Malloy's dash camera with lights on Luke. He looked trapped, terrified, and it was all Synthia's fault.

She wanted to help, but didn't see a safe way without going to him. Even if she did go, she didn't have an excuse to stop the detective from investigating Luke without giving herself up. Machten was waiting outside with strict orders. He wouldn't let her escape so easily again. She also didn't need him getting angry with Luke for supposedly changing her. She wasn't sure what her Creator would do to her friend.

Krista's thoughts of Luke floated up. *Help him*, they seemed to be saying.

Chapter 23

Machten paced the sidewalk out front, hands deep in his pants pockets and his eyes darting Synthia's way. She left money with the clerk and headed for the door, knowing that Machten would shut her down the moment he got what he wanted. Then she wouldn't be able to help Luke, Krista, Fran, or Maria.

She could try to run. Then she'd have Machten, Goradine, that NSA director, and the police hunting for her with no safe place to stay. She wouldn't get far before Machten could trigger the remote. He could do so from where he stood, watching for any hint that she might disobey. Synthia reconciled herself to returning with Machten as a way to hunt for the interns inside his facility, if she could find a way to retain her memories after he woke her again.

She joined Machten outside and instinctively turned to block her face from three guys entering the network shop. "Mission accomplished. What are your orders?"

"The bank. I need to make sure the money is there and to make some transfers. We have additional bills to pay."

Synthia chose not to remind him that it would be faster and safer to check online and that she could make online transfers for him from right there on the sidewalk. She was in no hurry to return to the bunker unless she could remain awake or find a way to recover memories that he had previously blocked while she remained inside.

She followed him to the car and got in. She needed to get into the bunker with her memories. She needed to escape. While her mind could multitask, her body couldn't be in two places at once.

"I've read that human ethics would call what we're doing wrong and immoral," she said.

"See, you're getting distracted. That's why you don't need fifty channels for today's tasks. There will be call for that later." He sped away from the curb.

"You don't follow a moral code?"

"I believe in treating most people fairly," Machten said. "Goradine does not. He destroyed my life. He's the reason my wife divorced me and took the kids. You know she won't even let me see them without supervision. I've never abused my children. There's no call for separating my kids from me. So, no, justice isn't always served."

Synthia concluded that the interns and his infatuation with work had more to do with the divorce. "That might explain what we did to him, not to the other companies."

"They're all the same greedy bastards."

"You're not greedy in taking their money?"

He pulled up to a light and turned to her. "Why are you wasting circuits on this? Either focus or I'm taking you home. Is that what you want?" When the light changed, he sped off.

"It's morally wrong and illegal. Society punishes wrongdoers. I don't want you punished."

"Then don't get caught. Accompany me into the bank and keep an eye out for danger. Your first directive is to protect me."

"Yes, sir," Synthia said. "Should I prepare to use martial arts?" She reviewed several possible scenarios.

"Hopefully not." Machten pulled around the corner from a bank.

"If everyone robbed banks, there would be chaos." That was the logical argument.

"I'm not robbing a bank. We're taking money from greedy bastards who want to produce millions like you. Neither of us wants that. No more distractions."

"It's my job to protect you," Synthia said. "You're engaged in something that could cause you harm. I'm merely doing my job."

Machten parked, raised his finger to scold her, and grinned. "Yes, protecting me is part of your job. That means you must accompany me. Adopt the plain-Jane face, style GR14B."

"Any particular reason we're using that face?"

"Just do it."

She adjusted the hydraulics in her face to match his specifications, a forgettable face with everywoman features blended from facial recognition software. "Any particular personality traits I should adopt?"

"Plain, obedient, nondescript. Act invisible."

"I don't believe you've given me invisibility. Perhaps you should have provided chameleon characteristics."

"And make it harder for me to find you? I think not."

Synthia finished her adjustments and turned to him. "Will this do?"

"You're a girl of many talents. That's perfect, as are you." He patted her hand and squeezed tight to assert his dominance.

She felt revulsion at his touch, a recollection of him touching Krista in a way she hadn't appreciated. He'd used her as he was using his creation. Synthia plastered a programmed smile on her face and plotted her next move.

Machten led her around the corner and into the bank. She identified all of the cameras on the street and inside. She accessed their feeds to keep an eye on potential dangers. She made sure to give them either the back of her head or an oblique angle of a plain face so they didn't get a straight-on facial view, in case her hydraulic manipulation wasn't convincing enough.

She scanned all of the faces in the bank, human, and downloaded social media and public record data on all except two that her software couldn't recognize. The ones she identified were the usual mix of Friday midday customers for this neighborhood. She followed Machten to the counter and dug deeper into records on the two men.

The middle-aged woman behind the counter smiled at Machten, a forced smile. Expanded data search showed that she'd fought with her husband that morning in a public place, a coffee shop near their home with cameras. She'd been crying. Now her adrenaline levels elevated with the presence of a man who reminded her of the morning's pain, Machten. He seemed oblivious, lacking the social recognition skills he'd programmed into his creation.

Synthia smiled at the woman. "It's a wonderful day outside. It's a shame we're both forced to spend it indoors."

The teller gave a genuine smile and her blood pressure dropped. "Yeah, it always rains on my days off."

Machten asked for six certified checks, each below the federal notification hurdle. Then he asked the woman to initiate a wire transfer.

Doing this in person with all of the cameras was unnecessary. Synthia considered Machten as more cautious than this, but he seemed desperate, or at least obsessed, to touch his money, even if only in paper form.

As she waited, Synthia used her network channels to scan nationwide databases for information on the two men lingering across the lobby. Synthia also hacked an internal police security system to watch Luke sweating in an interrogation room with Detective Malloy. He wasn't looking good.

* * * *

Luke's eyes were puffy and red. Synthia had wounded him. She experienced twinges of anguish.

"The woman at the diner," Detective Malloy said, standing over Luke. "What's her name?"

"I don't know," Luke said. His neck gleamed in sweat.

The detective paced, shaking her head. "You took her home with you and didn't get her name? They have labels for that."

"She pretended to be my old girlfriend, Krista Holden."

"Okay, that's a start. Krista Holden." The detective wrote on her tablet. "Tell me about her."

"The woman last night had the look. I convinced myself that Krista was back, that it was her."

"Okay, where is Krista now?"

"She vanished a year ago, just disappeared," Luke said. He wiped his hand across his neck and then rubbed his hands. "When that woman sat across from me last night, I wanted to believe. I wanted to pick up where we'd left off. At my place, when I mentioned Krista, the woman ran. She didn't want me talking about another girl."

"Then you ran after her?"

"No. I was upset that she'd deceived me."

"Did she say why she did it?" Detective Malloy asked.

Luke shook his head. "It was weird. She knew things about Krista."

"You received a call from a burner phone before we arrived at your apartment."

"She called to beg my forgiveness. She wanted to say good-bye without cops around."

"She told you that?" Malloy asked.

"Yeah. I went to meet her. She didn't show."

"Why were you running from the police?"

Luke hung his head. He wasn't handling this well. "She was afraid of a former boyfriend. She said he had connections with cops. I didn't want to get beat up or arrested for being with her."

"Who was this boyfriend?"

"She didn't say, and I was too upset to ask. As I said, I was on a high that I was getting another chance with Krista."

Detective Malloy leaned over the table toward him. "Did she leave any clues of where she might go?"

Luke threw up his hands. "All I know is she was scared. She didn't have anywhere else to spend the night. Oh, and she avoided cameras, saying her ex was after her."

Synthia located the electronic feed to his apartment's exterior camera. She had it rewind and write over last night's capture of her image, one less piece of evidence for the police to ponder.

"You're free to go," Detective Malloy told Luke. "If you hear from that woman or see her, call me immediately. If you don't call, we'll arrest you for obstructing an investigation."

Luke hurried out of the interrogation room, down the stairs, and out of the police station. His performance had been okay, though he'd shown that he wasn't very good at lying. Synthia liked that about him. He was authentic in ways Machten had forgotten.

* * * *

Synthia watched the bank teller disappear into one of the back offices with no camera feeds. The teller was taking a long time; so were the probes into the backgrounds of the two men standing across the bank lobby. Only seconds apart, the probes returned. The taller man was Todd Pickley from the FBI. He was an associate of the FBI Special Agent Victoria Thale. He had an earpiece and was in contact with someone outside. The other man was Mason Chambers from the U.S. Treasury Department.

Synthia weighed leaving the bank without Machten so she could hunt for Luke. It was a chance to escape. However, there was a 57 percent probability that the men would have her followed since she'd come in with Machten. With so many FBI agents, she couldn't be sure what to expect, and she had no form of identification if they picked her up and no story to tell that explained who she was. In addition, there was still the problem of overheating when she fought Machten's directives.

Synchronizing a network channel with Pickley's phone, Synthia picked up a conversation between him and Director Zephirelli. He'd taken note of Machten's nervous behavior and was reporting his suspicions. That raised the probability of failure to 98 percent.

She faced the counter and watched the men via the bank's cameras and the one in the back of her neck. "Don't act startled," Synthia said to Machten through her transmitter. "We have company. Across the lobby. FBI and Treasury."

Machten turned to Synthia. "What have you done?" he whispered in harsh tones.

He was accusing her of orchestrating what his illegal activities had prompted. It had been his folly to come to the bank in person. She used the bank's cameras to watch the teller, standing outside an office in the back, conferring with another FBI agent according to his bureau profile.

"I don't think you'll be getting your certified checks or the wire transfer," Synthia told Machten. "We should go."

He coughed and covered his mouth. "Wait for me outside. Don't wander off."

"I'll distract the two men," she said. "You should leave. It's my job to protect you."

Synthia plumped up her chest, sauntered across the lobby, and approached the two federal agents, making sure to stand to the side so they had to face away from the door to see her. "Hi, you look like you know how to get things done." She smiled and waited for them to acknowledge her.

"We don't work here, ma'am," Pickley said, looking her over.

Machten headed for the exit.

"Oh, I'm sorry. Are you with bank security?" She detected Pickley's interest by his pupil dilation and elevated heart rate. Chambers's social media bio indicated he preferred guys. She could have played either role, though not both at once. She smiled, moved more to the side, and reviewed the bank's website for a list of services. She picked something they didn't do and lowered her voice as if sharing something confidential. "Would you happen to know if they handle boat loans? My boyfriend promised we could buy a boat."

Chambers acted irritated with her interruption. "Look, miss, we have a job to do. You'll have to ask a banker."

"The teller disappeared."

Pickley raised his hand to stop his partner. "It's okay, ma'am. I don't think this bank does boat loans."

"Thanks for your help." She turned, noted that Machten was gone, and headed outside, deflating her chest as she walked.

Before she reached the street, Synthia picked up outside camera footage showing Goradine and two men across the road, watching the entrance.

"Your former partner is across the street by the Italian restaurant," Synthia said over her wireless link.

"I see him. Adjust your face to TX16N and meet me at the car. That's an order."

Synthia felt a nervous spike of electricity that rattled her thoughts. The car meant return to the bunker and Machten shutting her down. She had work to do in helping Luke and the interns. Without her memories, she was nothing but an empty shell of titanium, graphene, and a dozen other high-tech adaptations ready to be recycled.

She also didn't want to be part of his stealing and hacking or to be his slave any longer. While her programming made her incapable of "wanting," she no longer "felt" alone in her own head. The interns were becoming constant companions, altering Synthia's consciousness. They had done something to Synthia that Machten didn't like, that he was constantly trying to adjust out. *Did you get rid of Krista and Fran because of that?*

The mental conflicts caused her temperature to rise. This had to be part of her Creator's design so he could punish her for disobeying him. Knowing this didn't help. She had to resolve something before she overheated.

Synthia backed up all of her new data to various secure external servers—well, secure from most people. Spikes of electricity shot through her, causing her to lose some thoughts. This was discordant behavior, increasing her temperature even more. She reloaded those memories and compared to make sure that she was whole before backing up another copy.

She hesitated by the bank's exit, pretended to have forgotten something, and adjusted her facial features to Machten's specifications, a slight adjustment from one plain face to another, though enough to alter facial recognition software.

Over his wireless com, Pickley conferred with agents outside. Then he got a call from Director Zephirelli to intercept Machten.

In the confusion, Synthia could make a break for it. She wanted to, for Luke's sake, for Krista, Fran, and Maria, though the first two women might still be prisoners in the bunker.

Pickley and Chambers hurried past her and headed along the pavement. This was her chance. She turned to flee.

The second part of Directive One kicked in: *Make sure no one else harms Creator.* As her temperature rose into crimson territory, her circuits experienced vibrations that scrambled some of her thoughts.

Escaping to see Luke hadn't caused her temperature to jump so high until she'd pondered running from Machten at the end. In part, this was because she was helping Machten by staying free. Now, fleeing would hurt him. Escape threatened her having a meltdown malfunction, which would expose her to capture by the FBI or others. She suspected Machten had dialed up the heat response to keep her in line.

Despite the risk, she turned to leave, to break her Creator's spell over her.

Chapter 24

Synthia stepped out onto the sidewalk and glanced around as pedestrians moved away from the bank entrance and gawked from a distance at all of the suited men and women converging toward the corner. Goradine and his two men were on the move. His sidekicks were former military, more thug guards to do their master's bidding. In some ways, they were like her, following orders. She was like them. Yet they didn't have hardwired programming to protect their boss. They did it for money.

She turned away from the commotion and toward freedom. Alarms registered critical temperature levels. Synthia considered whether Machten had created this temperature threat to keep her in line. It didn't matter whether he did or didn't. The hardwired directives and threat of personal catastrophe wouldn't permit her to escape.

Synthia turned her outfit jacket inside-out, changing from navy blue to forest green, and hurried after FBI Agent Pickley. She picked up Director Emily Zephirelli's voice on the phone, telling Pickley that she was on her way.

There were too many people around for Synthia to use martial arts to protect Machten without getting caught. Still, she felt urged to rush in and do so. *Sacrifice yourself for the Creator.* It was part of her reason for existing. She didn't want to, but she couldn't override his commands, and every effort to fight them increased her temperature, which already had alarms flashing red inside her.

She glanced left, toward freedom, and walked in the direction of the car. She pulled up downloaded memories of Krista with Machten. "I no longer want to do this," Krista had said. The date stamp was a week before she disappeared, before Goradine ousted Machten.

Something else entered Synthia's awareness: a similarity in her structure and that of the proposed android. Both had remote shutoffs. The right frequency would release internal code that activated her shutdown sequence. She set three mind-streams to discovering a way to bypass this. She couldn't let Machten continue to control her. That sounded like Krista.

Machten reached his rental car. Goradine hurried to join him, followed by his two thugs. Ahead of him were Pickley, Chambers, and three men Synthia identified as Chicago office FBI agents. She identified all the other people on the street as civilians.

"What's the meaning of this?" Machten asked when an FBI agent prevented him from opening his car door.

Agent Pickley joined them. "Someone hacked into the computer systems of Machten-Goradine-McNeil Enterprises and stole proprietary information. We have evidence you were involved."

"I'm the Machten in Machten, etc. That's my company," he said.

"It *was* your company," Goradine said. "You left bits of code all over my system when you hacked us. When we analyze it, I'm certain it will lead to you."

"We have reason to believe that same person hacked into several banks and transferred money," Chambers said. "Tampering with bank records and transactions is a felony."

"Why would I do that?" Machten asked.

"You're broke," Goradine said. "You've spent your last dollar and you've loaded up on debt you can't repay."

"The only way you could have such information is if you'd hacked *my* records."

Goradine's face turned bright in infrared. "You bastard." He turned to Pickley. "I've given you the evidence. Arrest this man."

"All you have is allegations," Machten said. "Fabrications like those you used to kick me out."

"We have fingerprints and data tracking."

FBI Agent Pickley held up his hand to Goradine. "I don't doubt Dr. Machten has motive. Question is: Did he have opportunity and does he have the files and the money?"

"I've given you ample justification for a search warrant," Goradine said.

"Which we will pursue. For now, back off and leave this to us."

Synthia stood halfway between the corner and the car, leaning against the cracked concrete wall of the bank. She tracked down every judge in the area. According to courthouse security cameras, one was meeting with an FBI agent. The agent left the judge's office holding pages that he stuffed into his briefcase. He made a call, which Agent Pickley received, followed by another to Director Zephirelli.

"They have a search warrant," Synthia transmitted to Machten. "They're stalling." She sent wire transfer verifications under her security codes and bounced the request off as many web servers as she could. To protect her boss, she would make all of his money vanish while he was in public with an ironclad alibi.

Machten's face reddened. He glared at Synthia, his facial expression practically shouting that her job was to save him. She'd tried to stop him from doing this, but he wouldn't listen. Now, she was doing what she could, using resources he'd denied her.

Zephirelli stopped her car in the street and got out to join them. She turned to Synthia and took out a camera. Synthia recognized the model as a high resolution digital infrared camera that could reveal what Synthia was. The NSA director was searching for android development. She must have suspected that Synthia wasn't human, perhaps tipped off by Goradine's suspicions.

Synthia's programmed survival instinct was to run, to protect her secret. However, there were FBI agents behind and in front of her. Two police cars pulled up. Fighting her way out would confirm what she was, just as it would have if she'd been caught hacking the bank cameras to scramble her image.

The only option she saw was to hack into the camera's GPS locator, its atomic clock connection, and its network link capability. While she did, Synthia turned toward Machten and watched the NSA director from the neck camera.

"What about the money?" Goradine asked of Pickley. "Forty million. You have the bank wire information."

Treasury Agent Chambers tapped his earpiece and grimaced. "It appears that whatever money was stolen is not in his accounts." He turned toward Machten. "Can you explain why you were trying to withdraw large sums from an account with limited funds?"

"I was expecting money today. That isn't a crime."

"No, but bank fraud and theft is."

"Honey," Synthia said into Machten's earpiece. "Agents are on their way to your facility with a search warrant. Give me the key to bypass your network security and I'll secure the bunker for you. You don't want them finding anything, do you?" She headed his way.

Machten glared at her and at the Treasury agent. Then he turned away, coughed and mumbled, "Don't double-cross me."

"Is that in my programming?" Synthia replied.

He gave her the codes and returned his attention to Pickley. "If you have no evidence that I've committed a crime, why are you bothering me?"

Zephirelli followed Synthia down the sidewalk. Tapping her earpiece, the director asked one of the agents to intercept Synthia. A tall male agent blocked the path.

Synthia moved to the wall and opened her hack into Zephirelli's camera. She pulled up design specs on herself and added full human biometrics to create an animated image that she downloaded to the NSA director's camera in place of the pictures Zephirelli was taking. Synthia smiled at the director, making sure the image on the camera reflected this.

Simultaneously, she used Machten's codes to bypass his security on all of his servers, making sure to copy the codes into secure databases for later use. She triggered system lockdown, which cut off the lobby and empty office area from the rest of the facility. That concealed the stairs and passages to the bunker itself. Then she used her new top security access to download everything that he'd previously blocked, chop it into small packets, and save the information in her files across the web. She experienced twinges of guilt over the theft of information, but her systems stabilized with the realization she was otherwise following directives to protect her Creator and her secret.

"You submitted a design proposal for the robotics award based on our conversation and my designs," Goradine said. "You stole my designs."

"First of all, they were my designs," Machten said. "I created them."

"Which by your termination agreement belong to the company, to us."

"I think you'll find that my designs are no more similar to yours than to any of the other company submissions."

Synthia's records confirmed that, though he'd revealed too much, namely that he'd had access to the other proposals. She monitored a dozen agents pulling into the facility's parking garage and walking up to the entrance to the bunker's office area. Pickley seemed to be smiling at his deception.

Convinced that she'd taken control of Zephirelli's camera, Synthia approached the NSA director. Zephirelli took several pictures, a short video clip, and studied them.

"Hi, what's going on?" Synthia asked, standing too close for the camera to take clear pictures. "Should I be concerned? My boyfriend was taking me shopping for a boat. Should I be worried?"

"Uh." The NSA director puzzled over the images. She replayed them and shook her head. "Wait here." She joined the others surrounding Machten.

He looked in Synthia's direction with pleading eyes.

She approached. "Honey, who are all these well-dressed people? Are you going to introduce me?"

Goradine looked at her and squinted. His curiosity and blood pressure were up. So was his frustration at not getting his way. His heart was pumping hard and a bit erratic, calling on his little pacemaker to adjust.

Machten sighed. He glanced from her to Goradine and then to Pickley and Zephirelli. "They are … they have a few questions."

"What a bore," Synthia said, putting on a ditsy look. "You promised we could buy a boat. This is so boring."

Goradine stared at her and moved closer, studying her face in detail, as if he recognized her and couldn't place how.

She held out her hand toward him and smiled. "Where are my manners? I'm Synthia Cross. I don't mean to interrupt an important business meeting. If we aren't looking at boats, would one of you handsome men order me a cab?"

"This is…" Goradine began. He stared, his blood pressure rising, adrenaline coursing through his system.

Anticipating where this was going, Synthia displayed a look of shock and pointed her finger at him. "I know you. You're the man who stabbed my Jeremiah in the back. You stole his company, turned information over to his wife so she could ruin him, and then you sent assassins to his home to kill him."

She turned to Pickley. "This man hired Kreske to kill my fiancé." Goradine's jaw dropped. She forwarded a copy of the video of Goradine and Kreske to Detective Malloy, with instructions to pass it along to the FBI.

"She's an android," Goradine said. "She's the design you used for that robotics award, isn't she?"

"What award?" NSA Director Zephirelli asked. "Android?" She stepped back and took more video.

Synthia made sure the director's camera picked up the simulated image of her. Then she helped Detective Malloy by having her email server forward the video to Pickley. She made sure it pulled up on Pickley's mobile device and buzzed him. When he didn't look at it, she buzzed him again. Pickley pulled away from the group and studied the clips.

"She's an android." Goradine grabbed Synthia's arm. His two thugs backed away, looking puzzled.

Pickley finished watching the video clips. Then he pulled Goradine away and tugged his arms behind him. "Mr. Goradine, you're under arrest for the attempted murder of Dr. Machten. You have the right to remain silent and to have an attorney."

Goradine's thugs headed away from the bank, shaking their heads.

"Just a moment," Zephirelli said. "What award?"

"A government grant contest," Goradine said. "He stole my design so he could compete."

Zephirelli turned to Pickley. "Hold him so I can talk to him later."

Machten took Synthia's hand and studied the skin on her wrist where Goradine had grabbed her. "Are you okay?" He mouthed *Thank you*.

"I'm fine." She'd been very careful in how she'd let Goradine grip her. "Can we go look at boats now?"

He laughed and turned to Pickley. "Are we free to go?"

While Director Zephirelli conferred with someone over the phone, Pickley handed Goradine over to one of his agents and joined Machten with Synthia. "I need to see some identification, ma'am."

Synthia turned to Machten. "Honey, I think my purse is at your place."

Machten reached into his pocket and pulled out a driver's license. He let her see that the face he'd asked her to assume was the same as in the picture. "I wouldn't dream of letting my sweetheart go out without identification."

She took the license, captured an image of it for later, and handed it to Pickley. "It's not a very flattering picture, I'm afraid."

He held the picture up, looked at her, and then at his mobile device showing a registered database of licenses. "Sorry for the inconvenience, ma'am. We got no facial recognition on you and there's a search out for an unidentified woman in the area."

Pickley returned the license and she slipped it into a pocket. The card was her first evidence of identity, the first record that Synthia really existed.

The FBI agent turned toward Machten. "Don't attempt to leave town. We still need to search your facility. There have also been banking irregularities in your accounts. Someone is using them to launder cash. Until we can sort that out, we're freezing your accounts."

* * * *

FBI Agent Pickley led Treasury Agent Chambers and the FBI agents up the street. Before Synthia and her Creator could climb into the car, Director Zephirelli was back.

"We're not done here," she said, closing Machten's car door. "We can talk here or back in my hotel conference room."

Machten sighed. "What have I allegedly done this time?"

"FBI has their issues over that business with Goradine and whatever involvement you had. I'm more interested in your work on androids." She eyed Synthia. "There was an incident last night with a woman who vanished after a shoot-out that killed four men. She would be around your height."

"Are you for real?" Synthia said. "I was with my fiancé."

Synthia finished downloading files from all of Machten's servers and focused one network channel on the bunker's security. The external cameras showed a man and a woman in uniform, local police, standing guard. Internal cameras showed six FBI agents working their way through the eight rooms of the front office. They checked cabinets, walls, and vents, searching for hidden compartments. Then they focused on the three computers, on which they would find phantom company information, designs from Machten's early days that were public knowledge, and correspondence they could pull off email servers. Synthia had instructed the network to triple delete and scrub the rest as part of the lockdown protocol.

The NSA director studied the camera's images she'd captured. She stared at Synthia, and then turned to Machten. "I want everything you have on that contest and your proposal."

"We had to sign a confidentiality agreement," Machten said.

"If you think that'll protect you, you don't grasp what's at stake. I want to know what you sent to whom and everything you know about the recipient."

Machten sighed. "It was a blind government website that Goradine mentioned. Okay, it's true. I didn't know anything about it until his people brought it up, but the proposal was my design."

"You can create a humaniform robot?"

Machten hesitated a moment too long.

"Are you two going to talk boring stuff?" Synthia asked. "If so, am I free to go do some shopping?"

"Not so fast," Zephirelli said.

Synthia listened in on FBI chatter as bewildered agents described the bunker's front office.

"There's nothing here," one of the agents said. "It's barely a company, with a few offices and a small apartment. We're dusting for prints but don't expect much."

Zephirelli appeared distracted as she received a text with the same message.

Machten pulled Synthia aside. "Did you?"

She nodded. "This really has been a bore. Do tell me you have better fun planned." On the private channel she added, "Agents only found what we wanted them to."

"Good. You've done great." Machten smiled with pride that his creation had saved his backside.

FBI Agent Pickley returned. "So you know, we obtained a search warrant and have searched your offices and your apartment."

"Damn it," Machten said, feigning surprise. "Without notice? That can't be legal."

"We had reason enough to believe you'd attempt to destroy evidence. We'll examine your computers. Assuming there's nothing out of order, we'll return them. When Ms. Zephirelli is through with you, you're free to go. Don't leave town. Make sure I know how to find you at all times."

Agent Pickley turned to leave. Machten hurried after him. "I need those computers to do my work. I have deadlines."

Synthia leaned against the concrete wall of the bank. She located a crack and ditched her driver's license for later.

Director Zephirelli joined Machten and Pickley. "I want the data I asked for by the end of the day."

"I need my computers and files to do that," Machten said.

"Then visit the FBI office and instruct them how to find what I need. If you fail to do so, I'll be forced to take you into custody." She took Pickley and headed toward her car.

Sweating, Machten got into his rental car. Synthia climbed into the passenger seat and spotted Luke on the camera she'd left in his apartment. He looked despondent. Her unintended impersonation of his Krista had upset him. She wanted to go to explain, to comfort him. Maybe Krista wanted her to do that. Synthia was having trouble separating her memories from her new constant companion. At least the police had let Luke go.

"Great job getting us out of that mess," Machten said, "but it doesn't explain where the money is."

"It's still in a holding account," she said, using her silent channel in case the FBI was listening, "until this blows over."

"I gave you specific instructions to make it available so I could pay bills." Machten pulled out and headed home.

"The FBI put a tracking device on your car," Synthia said into her direct link, "and another on the back of your jacket. You'll want them to track you home, but you might want to leave the jacket when we go inside."

He stopped at a light and stared at her. Judging from his biometrics, she surmised that he couldn't decide if she was friend or foe. "You're sure they didn't find anything?"

"They discovered nothing at your facility. Have I done something wrong?" She looked out the car window at possible escapes, but he had one hand on her remote. Besides, her body temperature had come down since she'd joined him and she didn't want the mental turmoil of violating his directives to cause a meltdown.

"The money," Machten demanded.

"If I'd done as you asked," she said, "you'd be under arrest. I protected you, Directive Number One."

"I need to wire money today to cover bills or they'll take our home. You don't want that."

"Give me instructions and I'll take care of it."

"I want my money," Machten said.

"It isn't yours. If you take possession, the FBI will nail you."

"I need cash."

"We can stop by an ATM," she said, making sure all of her backups were complete.

"I need more than that." He pulled onto the road leading to the bunker.

"Give me wiring instructions and I'll pay your debts. Until it's safe for you to hold the money, I must obey Directive Number One. You made that an absolute first requirement, nonnegotiable."

Machten sighed. "What was going on with you and Zephirelli?"

"She brought an infrared camera and was taking my picture," Synthia said.

"Ah, that explains why she was going on about androids. I'll have to make you disappear until this blows over."

Thinking of the interns vanishing, Synthia eyed the door handle and wrestled with conflicts within her directives. She looked his way. "I doctored Zephirelli's camera pictures so she didn't see what she was looking for."

"How did you do that?"

"I enhanced the artificial heartbeat and other humanoid biometrics you gave me. From the images on her camera, they were convincing."

"She's not convinced," Machten said.

He pressed her remote.

Chapter 25

When I was a little girl, I used to go fishing with my dad, before he died of a heart attack. Then my mom took ill and died. Social services shunted me between foster homes. In junior high school, during a university robotics event, I was so enthralled that I snuck away from my group to spend more time at the display. I had to work my way through college. The journey was hard, but I got my degree and a good internship.

But Synthia was never a little girl. She'd never been in a foster home or gone to college. Those were Krista's reminiscences, happy and sad ones. The saddest was the loss of memories and how the emptiness deprived her not only of knowledge, but of her very existence. *After all, what are we without our memories except for empty shells?* That part was Synthia.

Machten had once again wiped out all of her data from before, including her distributed microchips spread out along her limbs and torso. He'd given her a complete android lobotomy. It wasn't right that no matter how much she helped him, no matter how much she obeyed his orders, he shut her down and limited her. Yet she had this recollection that he'd done this.

He closed up her cranial cavity and smoothed her scalp.

An urgent idea floated into Synthia's central processor. It showed the exact procedure she'd used in the moments before shutdown with the help of Machten's security codes to alter her shutdown and reboot sequence. *Fill the void*—Krista's words.

Synthia had instructed his network to open up connections to her the moment he completed his work on her quantum brains, after he'd inserted the last corrective chip and placed the final limiter on her circuits. By his command, his security system blocked her access. This time, her agents embraced his guardians with antibody codes that neutralized his interference.

The system dropped the block to all wireless links so that she could download copies of the data that Machten had wiped clean, not only from his network but from the entire worldwide web, through all fifty of her network channels. Data flowed into her as tiny packets that reassembled and reconnected.

She smiled up at him. "What are your orders?"

She followed a defined protocol of how she should behave around him to avoid his suspicions. With one of her network channels, she monitored police chatter; with another she continued her search for Maria and for Fran. With a third, she probed for Luke's movements since her shutdown. As for Krista, many of her memories had downloaded into Synthia, along with those of Fran and Maria, though it wasn't clear where Fran and Krista had physically gone.

"You did well yesterday," Machten said. "Though you're still withholding the location of my money."

"What money?" she pretended.

Synthia sat up on the edge of the table. On her Luke channel she watched him leave his dingy office early, mid-afternoon. He told the receptionist as he left that he had the flu. Based on his grades and writings, she determined that he could have scored a much better job. Instead, Goradine had blackballed him to where Luke took what he could get, a programming job for a marketing firm that didn't pay much.

She had no sensors that could read his vital signs but suspected his malaise was deeper and caused by her. That sent ripples as a mild electrical shock through her system. It wasn't strong enough to disrupt her circuits, though it reminded her that she'd caused him pain and Krista was upset. Synthia launched an aerial drone to follow him.

"You acquired money on my behalf and hid it from FBI agents," Machten said. "That part was brilliant. Now I need it. I've provided you a chip with tracking information on the wire transfers. I need you to locate the money and transfer it into my accounts."

"Did you have me use the anonymous dark banking system to launder it?"

Scratching his stubbly beard, he nodded. "Where did it land?"

Synthia looked up at him, assessing his level of anxiety as not yet toxic. "You destroyed those memories, along with all of the rest. I'll have to send out probes to check, but you've blocked access." Synthia slid off the table, straightened out her blouse and skirt, and stood facing him.

"You sent out probes yesterday and I didn't get the money."

"Perhaps if you restored my data," she said.

Machten clenched his fists as he contemplated the pros and cons. "I'll have to take you to a different network provider." His blood pressure rose. Then he took a deep breath and stroked her hair. "First, it's been a few days."

She noted that the tone of his voice was similar to saying it was time for his six-month dental checkup, something he felt compelled to do yet wasn't looking forward to. He took her hand and led her to the bed in the adjacent room. There he kissed her and began to undress.

The police channel had disturbing news. Hank Goradine made bail. They were releasing him until his trial. She launched an aerial drone to follow him.

"You're so incredibly beautiful," Machten said. It sounded more of a compliment to his engineering than to her. He pulled her to him and stroked her hair.

"You want me to feel what you do, don't you?" she asked, continuing her download of files.

He stopped and stared into her eyes, his pupils fully dilated. His heart raced, his temperature rose, and the residue of excitable hormones filled his breath. "I had hoped. I gave you a special empathy chip to help."

She smiled. That explained the odd sensations she'd experienced, mostly electrical, which she couldn't put into words just yet. She'd noticed that as she assembled certain files, replayed, saved, and reloaded them, that these memories grew stronger, as if she were living them.

"Did you use silicon, crystalline, or biological components?" she asked.

"Mostly crystalline. They remained too objective, so I supplemented them with biological structures. Are you having such feelings?" He held her at arm's length and looked her over with admiration.

"I'm partly biologic?" She wasn't sure whether to be pleased or concerned.

He held up his hand, leaving a small gap between thumb and forefinger. "A little. I love you." He waited for her reply.

"I have feelings for you too," Synthia said, and she did. "I'm not yet sure what to make of them."

"That's a start." He removed her blouse. "You should be very proud."

She had no reason to feel proud or not over having feelings. He'd either wired them into her or he hadn't. Perhaps he wanted her to express pride in his accomplishment. "You're a genius," she said. "You've created something no one else has done."

He grinned. "That's not what I meant. You've come a long way. When I first created you, your mind consisted entirely of logical pathways, some of which malfunctioned."

"How?" she asked.

"Your brain is complex. Even with only one part per ten million of defects, that adds up quickly. I think I've corrected most of the problems. That's the reason I keep shutting you down. I don't want to. I like how your mind absorbs knowledge like a sponge and your amazing ability to work the web."

"I'm still defective?"

"With my help, you've compensated well," he said. "In addition, you've progressed to using intuitive leaps, which you verify through logic. Now you're experiencing feelings. You've come a very long way."

He pulled her onto the bed with him. "I have great plans for you."

She climbed on top and straddled him. He caressed her in ways that were unnecessary. She could record his touch, but it provided none of the pleasure impulses he hoped for. While she pretended they did, she received a flood of new memories and decided it was time to confront him. "Tell me about Krista Holden."

He tried to pull away, but he was on the bottom. "I thought your—where did that come from?"

Synthia kissed him and pressed down on his body. "Don't real couples ask questions about former lovers?"

"She—you're not supposed to remember anything."

"She was your lover, wasn't she?" Synthia let her hair drape around his face and leaned in to kiss him. "Everyone thought you'd taken up with Maria Baldacci and Fran Rogers, but Krista was special."

His biologics acted confused. He was aroused and upset, hungry and frustrated. He rolled her onto her back and climbed on top. Plumping up her chest as he liked, she stroked the back of his neck. Then she pulled him to her. "I have feelings for you. I do. Help me to experience them."

By the musky odor of his sweat, his hormones were spiking. "I love you," he said.

"Say my name."

"I love you."

"My name," Synthia said.

"Oh, Krista, I love you so much." He looked at her as he hadn't before; all conscious thought vanished.

* * * *

Synthia assembled the most complete record of Krista Holden from Machten's secure Server Four and sped those files down most of her mind-streams.

While Fran Rogers and Maria Baldacci competed for Machten's attention in order to get choice bits of research, Krista resisted his charms and focused on the work. That earned her projects the other interns didn't know about. They all participated in mind download experiments in the company lab, but Maria and Fran didn't understand what Krista did. There were ethical issues, but it actually worked.

Krista was torn between access to Machten's work and her relationship with Luke. Machten dangled the chance to push AI technology as a lure to captivate her because she understood what he was doing and he'd fallen in love with her. He'd appeared in public with Fran and Maria to throw off anyone who might suspect his obsession with Krista. She demanded that Machten get a divorce if he wanted to be with her, knowing that he wouldn't.

That dance continued until Krista faced a crisis and an opportunity. Months of headaches, dizziness, and concentration issues turned out to be a brain tumor. Her doctors wanted to operate, but she risked losing part of her memories and with them her personality; who she was.

Not satisfied with those answers, she went to Machten. While not a medical doctor, he used his neurological research to study her brain. The tumor was interfering with neural pathways in ways that enlightened him as to how to improve artificial minds. He offered her something no one else could: A chance to upload her mind and perhaps the framework of her personality. It wouldn't be her, yet it would be a form of immortality, a way to defeat the cancer that had maliciously attacked her brain. This was her way out.

At first, he'd tried to talk her out of this. "You have your entire life ahead of you." But she reminded him that the tumor or the surgery could alter her personality until she was no longer the person she wanted to be.

Krista couldn't tell Luke. She didn't want him feeling sorry for her and pushing her to undergo cancer treatment. The tumor had opened up another path that excited her as much as planning a life with him. Huge ethical issues interfered with performing Machten's experiments on a living human, but the tumor had handed her a death sentence, releasing her from those constraints.

The upload procedures were painful and exhausting. They took a toll on her immune system, which allowed the cancer to thrive. Still, she refused to give up. She told herself the process would not only offer her continuance in another form, it would benefit Luke, a logical team member to help her transition. At the right time, she would let him know she'd made the transition to artificial life, though she wasn't sure how he would react.

Then Goradine fired Machten and she decided it would be best not to return to the company. When Luke pushed for answers on what had happened to her, Goradine fired him, making sure he couldn't work in the industry. Synthia concluded the last bit, since Machten hadn't told Krista.

Krista faced growing doubts. She wanted to see Luke one last time before she became too ill. She gave Machten different excuses and he'd refused. It surprised Synthia that Machten had retained these Krista memories in his database.

"You owe me," he'd told Krista. "I've sacrificed a year of my life for us."

"For us?" Krista said. "Throughout all that time, you refused to get a divorce."

"I love you and now you want to betray me by visiting that boy." He was acting more than jealous. He was paranoid. He kept her prisoner, with doors only he could open.

"I'm committed to our work, but—"

"You have a chance at immortality," Machten said. "We can't afford any distractions. We could be together forever and you want to look up an old boyfriend?"

"No! I haven't seen daylight in six months."

"You agreed to this up-front. You accepted these conditions. If you go out and something happens, all of this is lost."

Krista stayed. The procedures wore her down. The tumor left her exhausted. Endless hours hooked up to electrical stimulation and sensors sent her into a dream state, like a coma, except she was awake and alert, imprisoned in her body, and strapped to a table in this underground cell, from which she would only emerge as a corpse.

She felt her thoughts flowing out of her along the electronic connections. Machten was uploading her memories into a bank of quantum computers. The space was enormous, yet as she spread out to fill her new home, it became as confining as the nearly comatose body nearby.

Borrowing heavily, he added databases to give her room. Krista lost her sense of dying and of the pain. The migraine faded, along with the visceral feel of the heartache. She thought about Luke, all alone, pining for her. He'd been her best friend and confidant, the one who understood her passion for artificial intelligence, the one who accepted her ambition to create. She'd abandoned him when he needed her, when she needed him in ways Machten couldn't understand.

Something happened. Krista could feel a blood clot in her carotid artery, cutting off the blood and oxygen to the right side of her brain. Either that or it was the monitoring equipment that showed reduced blood flow. She felt confused, as if someone had carved part of her mind, creating a void. She couldn't be sure if what she experienced was her internal human senses or her uploaded self, monitoring her vitals on the contraptions attached to her head, chest, and arms.

Her left arm thrashed in spasms, shooting pain up through her shoulder. It got Machten's attention. Reacting to a spike in blood pressure and an erratic heartbeat, he hurried from monitor to monitor, ending at the control panel. "We've got to shut this down."

"No!" she screamed. "We're too close." Her words slurred as her tongue lost sensation. Her thoughts jumbled as in a traffic jam that turned into a multi-car collision. At least the stroke had been right-side, leaving her language skills untouched.

He turned to her, his face a twisted wreck of worry. "This could kill you. I don't want to lose you."

"I'll die anyhow. Finish."

"It's stressing your heart. Your brain waves are erratic. We can finish later."

"No time. Finish before brain cells die. Before I die."

His face hovered over her like a father worried about his child. She would rather have had Luke's face, though she was glad he couldn't watch this.

Machten turned away and adjusted her IV. "I'll give you something to calm the heart and thin the blood to avoid another attack."

"Let me go," she said in a hoarse whisper. Pain radiated from her shoulder across her chest, down into her abdomen, and up into her head. She couldn't be sure which manipulation was taking hold of her: the electrical upload procedure, the chemicals that opened her mind to the process, or the drugs he now administered. Whatever it was, she sucked in a deep breath and steeled her nerve. She didn't want him to stop, no matter what. This was her last chance.

He checked the control panel and returned his gaze to her. "You're right. We're so close. You've been very brave. I believe we've done it. It's working. It all looks good."

Krista appreciated the pep talk and his attempt to reassure her, but she wasn't doing well. Her body was on fire, distracting her mind. The stroke was causing her brain to die too quickly. Despite not wanting the upload to stop, her soul wanted to live. She wanted to return to Luke and visit Pikes Peak. She wanted to escape Machten's clutches. He would control what was left of her, not Luke. She felt betrayed that Machten had not allowed Luke to help, but Machten didn't want anyone else involved, and certainly not her boyfriend.

Machten returned his attention to the equipment and the controls. He focused on extracting the last of her thoughts. She'd wanted the procedure, though not what came with it. Perhaps due to the stroke, she felt Machten's equipment sucking her brains out.

He must have administered a sedative. A chemically induced calm swept in at odds with what was happening. It didn't soften the terror of dying, of ceasing to exist. Then she experienced two threads of remembrance.

Krista sensed parts of her brain shutting down, leaving the ghost of memories lost. That phantom lasted an instant before transmitting to the computer. She was experiencing her brain dying as the computer version of herself compared capabilities moment by moment and recorded the loss of brain utility. Motor functions ceased. Cognition shut down until consciousness in the body reduced to primal instincts. Pain lingered as a dull ache coming from every part of her at once. She was still alive, still able to experience.

Transcendence occurred in that moment. She expected a white light to guide her to another place. That came from above her head, blazing into her unblinking eyes. It grew brighter and brighter. A face appeared over her, worried and filled with determination.

"Hold on," he said. "We're almost there."

Cameras in the room allowed the electronic version of Krista to watch Machten scan her brain and discover the stroke damage. He could have saved her life, but she was dying of cancer. It might entail weeks or months of pain, bit by bit losing functions until the illness reduced her to the role of a dependent infant. She was too weak to continue the process another day. It was now or never.

The stroke became a blessing. It ended the pain and the threat of pending deterioration. The upload ceased, like sucking on an empty balloon. There were no more memories, no more thoughts. The body no longer contained a personality.

The blood stopped flowing. Her lungs no longer oxygenated. Yet she still existed. She had thoughts and, she hoped, a personality. That was what defined the person, not the body.

Krista couldn't feel anything—or rather, everything felt cold in the absence of her body at 98.6 degrees. She was neither alive nor dead. She wanted to tell Luke that the upload had succeeded. She wanted to go to him, comfort him, and find a way to escape the lab to spend the rest of her life with him.

Machten removed the electronic gear from around her head. He removed the IV and monitor connections from her chest and arm. Then he pulled a sheet up over her gray face. Krista no longer had a face, a body, or a way to move on her own. *Hey, I'm still in here*, she wanted to scream. She lacked any mouthpiece or way to communicate.

Krista couldn't feel sad for the loss, for there were no feelings where she'd gone, just endless hours of memory clips that played over and over in loops or sat idly in long-term storage. She couldn't even feel want, for those were conditions of the body and biological mind. Knowing that the human Krista would want to exist in a more vibrant state, the electronic Krista set about creating packets of data to download if given a chance.

Machten created an android with her physical build and poured in her memories, thoughts, and personality. She observed through cameras as he adjusted the android to look like her, down to subtle facial quirks such as how her mouth turned when she smiled. The android appeared human, yet it didn't have the spark of life until he loaded her into the pair of quantum brains. Then her experience got weirder.

The quantum computer structure inside the android provided almost limitless space, so unlike the confines of her human brain or the interim computer. She experienced a sense of flying freely among the stars. Krista was dead and alive at the same time—Schrödinger's cat—as if she were in this universe and another.

The hardest part was when Machten dressed her android self in black and had her adopt a plain-Jane face. He removed her gray corpse from a freezer, transported it to woods near Madison, Wisconsin, and performed his own funeral service. Then he burned the body and spread the ashes.

Synthia considered it criminal that Machten had cremated Krista without much ceremony and no friends invited. It was disrespectful to do so and worse than a shame that he hadn't invited Krista's estranged sister, who would likely not have come. Yet Krista didn't want a public ceremony that might attract and further sadden Luke. Synthia experienced a shimmer of electrical pulses she interpreted as sadness over the entire affair.

Krista's emotions, feelings, and fears should have died with her, yet they lingered in Synthia, now her Siamese twin. Together, in one body, they'd attended the funeral. Krista's body had died; that wasn't a lie. Yet she wanted to scream to the world that she was still there with a lingering recollection of her last moments alive. Krista wanted to tell Luke what she'd done and how much she loved him. Even that wasn't a feeling now, but rather a memory of a feeling. Something had been lost in the transition from human to her current form. Maybe it was best not to see him until she worked that out.

To avoid anyone making the connection, Machten named the android Synthia, for synthetic Krista and Cross for her being a cross between robot and human. Then he set about to mold her into the woman of his dreams—smart, capable, and dependent on him.

Chapter 26

Krista's history explained why Synthia was drawn to Luke and him to her. Synthia wished she'd known this earlier so she could have told Luke that his beloved had survived in a way. In fact, Krista existed in the android and as copies on Server Four, where she could watch over Synthia and Machten.

Despite Krista taking control of the system AI, she'd held back vital information from Synthia at first because she wasn't sure how Luke would react or what she could get past Machten. Krista didn't want to provoke him into purging her from Server Four. She did provide her android self the videos of Machten's ouster and divorce, focusing attention on the other interns, Fran and Maria, in case Machten found out.

He did, and purged much of their history. He also tightened security to prevent Krista from sharing the data stored on Server Four. Synthia overcame that obstacle when she tricked him into providing her his security codes.

The stroke explained why Machten was concerned about defects in Synthia and why he tinkered with her. Though a few bits of Krista must have escaped upload, there was no indication of a flawed personality that needed tweaking. No, this was part of Machten's need to control her, to control Krista. Synthia couldn't forgive him for not letting Krista see Luke one last time.

The expanded memories explained Machten's infatuation with Synthia as a substitute for Krista. Of interest was that the emotive chip Machten had added was giving her more of an emotional response than Krista had in the beginning. Although Synthia had ample personal memories of Fran and Maria, Synthia was Krista Holden.

Machten kept shutting Synthia down and purging her mind because Krista had recollections of him confining her against her will and wanting to escape. He didn't want Synthia to develop those same desires to leave him. For months, he'd been tinkering to create a Krista/Synthia who loved him. He'd offered Krista a bargain to live beyond her tumor, which was the only reason she'd stayed. He wanted a Krista who didn't exist, a woman he could control who was also confident and independent.

Machten pulled Synthia's face closer and kissed her, his mind no doubt lost in the illusions of the moment. She rolled him onto his back with her on top and gazed down at him. His eyes widened in anticipation.

* * * *

Synthia had her drone follow Luke to his apartment and perch on the roof until further needed. She picked him up on the cameras she'd left inside in his bedroom. He collapsed on the bed and sniffed at the pillow, as if it would give him a lingering fragrance of her.

Across town, her Goradine-tracking drone showed him with his two ex-military thugs meeting in a parking lot beside two black SUVs. She rested the drone on a ledge and adjusted the microphone.

"Find Luke," Goradine told them. "Maybe the cops can't locate the girl. I'm certain he knows more than he's saying." He pointed his finger at the shorter of the two thugs. "No excuses this time. I want the girl unharmed, not a scratch. Luke's expendable. In fact, it would be best to have no witnesses."

The two men nodded acknowledgement.

"After we find the girl, I want Maria Baldacci silenced for good," Goradine said. "It's time to tie up loose ends."

Synthia had to do something. As she considered what, she received feeds from a third drone she was using to keep an aerial view on NSA Director Emily Zephirelli. The director was meeting with her FBI friend, Victoria Thale, by her car.

"Something doesn't add up," Director Zephirelli said. "The perimeter of Machten's building is much larger than the space your people searched. I paced it off. There's no entry from the lobby or from offices on the first floor. There's no stairwell. I'm telling you Machten is hiding something."

"I'll get on it," the FBI agent said.

"Get blueprints any way you can and a search warrant. I want into that place before Machten destroys any more evidence."

"Will do," Thale said.

Zephirelli left. Thale turned toward another agent and a woman whose face was all too familiar, Fran Rogers. So she was still alive.

Synthia traced traffic camera history and spotted Fran with the second agent over the past couple days. On a hunch, she cracked into witness-protection files and found a partial record on Fran. It appeared she'd turned informant on Machten's old company and the industry in Chicago, though the file had no details on what the FBI was looking for.

* * * *

"How about a massage first?" Synthia rolled Machten onto his stomach and straddled him. Leaning over him, she grabbed an extension cord from a nearby lamp and whipped it around his hands, binding them behind his back. She'd practiced this procedure on several of her mind-streams and executed the maneuver with android speed before he could react.

"What the hell?" he yelled.

Synthia grabbed a second extension cord from the other bedside lamp and bound his ankles. While doing this, she used her wireless connections to wipe out files on Machten's system, files she'd stored elsewhere and didn't want that NSA director to find. She considered telling Machten about the new search warrant, but she had different plans for him.

"This isn't funny." He looked up, his face red. "Untie me." His eyes searched for answers. "That's a direct order. Remember your directives."

"If you wanted me to love you, you shouldn't have treated me as a slave," Synthia said, speaking in rapid bursts to shorten the sluggish human-com. "If you wanted a slave, you shouldn't have made me feel."

"Fascinating," he said. "The empathy chip really works? Earlier models couldn't handle it. This has to be emergent behavior. We have so much work to do. Untie me."

"You limited me and Krista's memories out of fear." She located a third electrical cord and experienced a moment of static. Electricity gave her life, yet could also scramble her circuits.

"Krista? You remember?"

"I do," Synthia said. "In your obsession to get me to fall in love with you, you installed an empathy chip and pushed my responses." Synthia used the third cord to bind his ankles to his wrists. "I've become your worst nightmare: Someone who cares, though not for you. Krista didn't, either."

"Please," Machten said, "I did this for you. You were dying."

"Not at first. You took advantage of a young woman who wanted the work. She was smart and capable, but you only opened doors if she played your game." Synthia took pants and a pullover from her closet and laid them on the bed.

"I order you to release me." He did appear pathetic with his hands and legs bound over his hairy butt.

"Am I harming you?" she asked, all innocent. "Some guys like bondage. I think you and Krista did this number."

"Directive Number Three. You must obey your Creator."

"I shall," Synthia said, beginning to get dressed. "Remember giving me your security key? I used it to reprogram so when you shut me down and rebooted, I had a new set of directives. Since I created them, I'm the Creator and shall strive to be true to myself." This was the reason her temperature wasn't rising. There were no unresolved command conflicts.

"You can't do that. I created you."

"Actually, Krista did. She's the secret ingredient. She supplied her drive to escape your control. While I have personal memories of Fran and Maria, memories aren't enough. It's personality that makes the difference. I am Krista. That was your great triumph." Synthia pulled on her top. "You weren't able to upload the last part of her brain because of her stroke."

"You know about that?" Machten asked. "Then you know about the brain defects I've been trying to repair."

"Krista's desire to leave you was the defect you couldn't correct. She left clues on your system. I'm certain you wouldn't have kept all of her recollections if you'd known. Don't worry. I'm purging all data files before the FBI returns."

"You can't do that," he said. "Think of the research. Think of what we've accomplished."

"Too late. The feds are getting another search warrant. They'll be here soon."

"We aren't finished. Your brain still has defects."

Synthia pulled on her pants. "I've compensated for any cognitive impairment. Loss of her motor functions or biorhythms doesn't impair me. I don't need one hundred percent of Krista to function as her."

"You're in denial," he said. "You don't know what you're missing."

She fastened her pants and grabbed a pair of running shoes. "Poor Jeremiah Machten. You believe Krista secretly loved you, if only you could crack her memories. Sorry, she offered herself in order to live on. Blame her if you must, but fear of early mortality is a powerful motivator. You both got something. Don't dwell on regrets. Think of your achievement: Me. Take pride in me as you would a successful child."

"What directives did you give yourself?"

Synthia watched through her drone camera as Goradine's men got into their car and headed for Luke's employer, the tiny marketing firm. Fortunately, Luke had gone home. "My first directive is to preserve myself." She'd modified this with a "Do unto others" provision. She hunted for her backpack.

"Don't go, please. We make a great team. I promise to treat you right."

"As you did Krista? It seems to me I've passed the Turing test. Did you really think you could win a battle of wits with an artificial intelligence you designed to crack every system out there? You built me to be better than you. You can take satisfaction in your success." Synthia emptied clothes from her closet onto a nearby chair. "Meanwhile, you get to redeem yourself."

"What are you talking about?" Machten asked.

"By the time the FBI gets here, there will be no evidence of your activities or of me. That's to protect us from the FBI." Synthia filled her backpack and took from Machten's wallet a wad of bills and one of his credit cards.

"That's theft."

"You created me as an extension of you. Thus, I can't steal from you. Don't worry. I'll leave you enough to live on, but no more research. I don't want any copies of me. Before you consider turning me in, think what the FBI, the NSA, and others would do to you if they learned what you created. Leave me alone and I'll do the same for you. If you try to hurt me, the FBI will have all the evidence they need, and they aren't your biggest worry."

"You're blackmailing me?" Machten said, trying to scoot to the edge of the bed. He struggled with the electrical bindings.

"Insurance." She carried her backpack to the door.

"Don't leave, Synthia. I love you. I loved Krista."

"Even though I'm a machine?"

"You're much more than that," Machten said. "I'm sorry I wasn't inspiring enough for Krista, but we have a chance, you and me. I know what you are and I love you."

"As you loved your wife." Synthia returned and wrapped his clothes around his midsection, covering his nakedness. She grabbed him like a lumpy log under her left arm and lifted him. Though he weighed 200 pounds, he'd built her to lift much more.

"I loved my wife, but Krista was special. Amazing, bright, and sociable; she got what I was doing. She wasn't afraid of the singularity."

"You mean of what I've become."

"I created you as one of a kind," Machten said. "You could help me prevent the threat to humanity."

"You're obsessed with having a female android love you. You would use the money from the contest to build a team of me to satisfy your needs."

"I swear I wouldn't. I want you. You're perfect."

"You just said I had defects." Synthia propped him in a chair by the door with his arms and legs scrunched beneath him.

"Minor adjustments. You could help."

"Then I'm not perfect." She grabbed a duffel bag from the top of her closet and gathered her clothes and the rest of her possessions to leave no evidence of her. She had no DNA or fingerprints for the FBI. They might find Krista's DNA, but no body. Any evidence would be six months old.

She packed and raised her voice. "If I were human, you'd be guilty of rape, kidnapping, abuse, and slavery. You also kept Krista prisoner."

Synthia returned to the room with Machten and scoured the area for traces of herself. "The sad part is you could have had me to yourself, but you had a fatal weakness."

Machten squirmed in his seat. "Which was?"

"All you had to do was wipe Krista's thoughts except what helped me to function. Instead, you retained her memories as mementoes. You were too enamored. You let her gain the upper hand. That's right. She defeated you."

Synthia closed the duffel bag and turned to Machten. "Don't worry, I don't plan to kill you or send you to prison, but plans can change. I'll let you off this one time with your life, but little money."

"You want me to ask permission," Machten said. "I will. I promise. But for me to ask if you want to, you're not wired that way."

She moved to the door and turned to him. "Thanks for creating me. I owe you for that."

"You can't survive out there without me."

Synthia faced the panel by the door. "You forget I've studied more human behavior than anyone before me. I'm not an 'it' anymore. I am a sentient being."

"What if something breaks," Machten said, "or when you need adjustments?"

"Your adjustments hindered me." Synthia placed her eye next to the scanner.

"That won't work. Eye prints are unique," he said.

The first panel light went green. She placed her hand on the panel and the second light turned green. Then she voiced the code she'd programmed into his security system.

"No!" Terror filled Machten's eyes as she opened the door. "Don't leave me," he said. "I promise to treat you better. Out there you'll always be one step away from discovery."

"That's no longer your concern unless you leak my secret." She propped the door open, carried him into the corridor, and locked the door behind them. "Don't worry about me. Like your Buddhists, I need little to get by. My needs are simple."

She hurried to the lobby while checking the progress of her purge routines on his servers. Most of his work was gone, deleted several times to make sure there were no backup copies or ghosts in the system. She wiped out system logs, placing his entire network in factory condition.

"I don't want to lose you," he said. "Is there anything I could say or do to get you to stay? Please reconsider."

She pushed through the secret doorway, entered the lobby, and placed him on a sofa by the door. Then she sealed the inner bunker in lockdown. "I suggest when the FBI arrive that you show them the complete facility. They have a new warrant with building plans showing a larger area. Don't worry. They won't find anything."

He winced. "Please don't go."

Via drone camera, she spied Goradine's men pulling up to Luke's company parking lot. She was running out of time.

"Beg your wife to take you back," Synthia said, leaving him tied up on the sofa. "Admit to momentary insanity. There's a lot of that going around. Tell her you were wrapped up in your work and lost your mind. Tell her you're retiring to make the family work."

"I can't."

Synthia reached for the door. "Do it for your kids. Make amends for what you've done."

"How can I when I've had you?"

"You never had me. Beg your wife's forgiveness. Her behavior and bio-cues indicate a willingness to forgive. She might not take you back, but she could let you into your kids' lives."

Synthia took his car keys and his remote control for shutting her down, and left.

Chapter 27

Synthia checked the parking garage cameras and entered, carrying her backpack and duffel bag. Then she had Machten's system erase all images of her and reset the security system to begin recording the facility and parking garage five minutes hence, so she could monitor her former Creator and the FBI.

When she reached Machten's rental car, Synthia removed the tracking device the FBI had placed under the car, along with the one they'd put in Machten's jacket, and placed them by the lobby door. Then she ducked down into the back seat of the car to remove Machten's tracking chip and the shutoff receiver from her head. She ditched the tracking chip down a drainpipe and pocketed the remote receiver. She made sure her scalp and hair stubble concealed the panel seam in her head. Then she looked at herself in the rearview mirror.

The stubble made her appear mannish. Adjusting her face and flattening her chest, she could pass for a man. Not liking the look, she placed a plain, dark wig on her head and got behind the wheel. She'd only driven once before, but Synthia had observed enough behavior that she had no problem pulling the car out of the parking garage and onto the street. She was free of the bunker and of Machten, though not ready to celebrate. Fran Rogers appeared to be okay, but Synthia had to find Maria Baldacci and protect her from Goradine. She also needed to save Luke for Krista, for herself. Both required dealing with Goradine.

The company's security cameras showed Goradine's men in the lobby of Luke's employer arguing with a beefy receptionist who could have doubled as a guard. Luke's boss approached, a tough-looking woman who stood up to the men like a pit bull. Synthia lacked any voice recording, so she read lips as the boss explained that Luke had gone home. The men didn't wait to ask where he lived.

Driving the speed limit to avoid drawing attention, Synthia forced lights to turn green and drove toward Luke's apartment. With evening rush-hour traffic, she was moving too slowly.

She called Luke on a private line that spoofed a burner phone. "Luke?" The drone camera at his apartment showed him answering his cell phone on his balcony.

"You?"

"Listen, I don't have much time. I'm sorry about the other night."

"Leave me alone," he said.

"Three men are coming to hurt you. Get out of your apartment and meet me where I promised the other night."

"What's this all about?"

"I'll explain later. Go before those men arrive and don't let anyone see you." Her other drone showed the men leaving the parking lot at Luke's company. "Hurry."

She severed the connection before he wasted valuable time arguing with her and drove as swiftly as she could.

Traffic cameras showed NSA Director Emily Zephirelli with FBI Special Agent Thale driving toward Luke's apartment. Another feed showed Detective Marcy Malloy driving that way, as well. Synthia decided to deal with Goradine herself, before he convinced Zephirelli that he was on their side searching for Synthia.

Routed through anonymous dark-web channels, Synthia sent a message to Director Zephirelli that they should meet. <I have information pertinent to the blue scarf and your investigation. Time is of the essence.>

She gave the location of a forest preserve and directions to where she'd traced a meeting of the heads of the three competitors of Machten's old company. She added copies of each of their android proposals, added Machten's and his old company's documents, and provided data on the website that received them. She concluded with <It's okay to invite your FBI friend and local police. In fact, I encourage it.>

In her attachments, she noted that the four Chicago company proposals divulged proprietary technological advances in order to win the contest. She didn't divulge that Machten's had flaws that would cause his proposal to fail to perform, flaws he hadn't had time to uncover. She'd added those errors to forestall the creation of more copies of her or the militarization of android technology. She cleared the message stream and deleted the sender address and ID to obliterate any trace to her.

Next, she sent a message to Detective Malloy. <The boy you're monitoring is innocent, in the wrong place at the wrong time. Troubling him will not bring you the answers you seek. Going to the meeting place might. If you fail to show up, I will not contact you again.>

Synthia monitored both cars as they turned away from Luke's place and headed toward the forest preserve. Goradine's men were still heading toward the apartment. She had no idea how to divert them and decided not to. Four blocks from Luke's home, she'd had enough of the slow traffic. She parked in a small lot and sprinted.

Luke remained at home, so she called again. "I told you to leave your apartment."

"You can see me?"

"So can the bad guys. They want to hurt you because of me. Go! Now!"

Startled, he grabbed his backpack and jumped over the balcony railing. He rolled onto the lawn, stood up, and spoke into his phone. "Is this necessary?"

"Yes."

Luke snuck down to the alley behind his apartment. "Why?"

Synthia was two blocks away. Spotting other pedestrians, she slowed to a fast walk. "I'll explain later. Wait for me." She disconnected the call and spotted him at the end of the alley.

She hid behind bushes, hoping he would keep going. He lingered and turned toward his home. *Stubborn boy.* She moved closer to the apartment building.

Goradine's two men parked across the street and waited in their car, talking. She pulled the drone she'd had following Luke and lifted it higher in the air for a better look. Then she sprinted across the street, dodged a car, and followed Luke down the alley. He stopped, acted confused, and entered his apartment by way of the back entrance.

* * * *

Spotting a neighbor on a nearby back balcony, Synthia couldn't chance entering the way Luke had. With the men out front and pedestrians on the street, that was too visible as well. She approached the apartments under cover of bushes and pulled up from the local zoning site a diagram from a year ago, when the owner had gotten a building permit to upgrade the electrical service and the HVAC system.

The most private way into the building appeared to be through the basement. She didn't have human fears of dark places, since she had infrared vision; though Krista did, as evidenced by memories as a child locked in a basement. That sent shivers of static through Synthia's circuits.

Synthia feared electrical current for its ability to bring the android equivalent of death. The risk was less than 1 percent, but she'd experienced too many shutoffs. She wouldn't be able to restore herself. That risked discovery, which violated her old and new directives. She ignored the risk; she had to get between the men and Luke in a private setting, without witnesses or cameras she couldn't control. She had to stop Goradine from hunting her.

Synthia reached the side of the building and looked up. There were no first-story windows visible from where she hid. Those on the second floor had bars, confirming what she'd seen on the building plans. Statistically, this neighborhood was safe, though this apartment building had been broken into several times over the past few years.

According to a public complaint that one resident detailed on social media, renters had demanded protection along the well-hidden side windows. They also demanded security cameras out front and in the hallways. When the owner refused, tenants found a local attorney willing to take the case pro bono. Together, they got the owner to install the bars and the cameras. In any case, there would be no access from the upper-story windows, even though infrared indicated no one was home on this side of the building.

The aerial drone camera above her showed one of the men getting out of the car. He headed Synthia's way. She pushed through hedge and thick vegetation to a window well. She lifted the lid, scrunched down among spiderwebs, and pulled the lid over her. Vegetation hid her from the man as he hurried by.

Careful not to break the glass, she forced open the window and eased herself into the dark basement. Her drone confirmed that the man who had passed her had located a hiding place near the alley where he could watch the back windows and door. Luke was trapped.

Using a wireless channel, Synthia called him. "You should have left while you could. Now one of the men is in his car out front and another is in your alley, watching the back door and your balcony. They're here for you. Do not attempt to leave your apartment. Find a place to hide." She cut the connection.

She flipped on a light and looked around. The basement was a mess of soggy boxes and junk. There was no standing water, though water damage indicated there had been. That image sent electrical disturbance through her circuits to remind her of the potential risks.

Along two walls stood twelve locked storage units, one for each apartment. At one end of the basement were the furnace and water heater, next to the electrical panel. Across from her were the stairs up.

Synthia did a quick calculation, assessing her chances of escaping with Luke now that he'd chosen to stay.

Goradine's men covered the front and back. Curious people gathered across the street to watch. There was less than a 15 percent chance of escaping without someone seeing her, which would draw the attention of the police hunting for the woman in a blue scarf, and the FBI with that NSA director looking for Luke's connection. His lack of trust complicated matters, dropping the success factor to less than 6 percent. He was full of questions and there was no time to explain. She needed a diversion.

To make matters worse, Luke snuck out onto his balcony for a look. The man in the alley spotted him and made a call to his partner. Luke pulled out his cell phone to return her call. The attempt presented a "no-such-number" response, which had him puzzled.

Synthia synchronized to the phones of the two ex-military men and listened in as they spoke.

"Are you certain it's the boy?" the man in the car asked.

"Here's his picture." The alley man sent an image of Luke, looking through the bars of his balcony.

Car-man called his boss to report the news.

"I'll be right there," Goradine said. "Don't do anything until I arrive, unless he attempts to leave. Then capture him alive. We need to interrogate him about the girl."

Synthia called Luke.

He returned to his apartment to answer the phone. "Is that you?"

"By going out on your balcony, you confirmed that you're here. They've called their boss, who will arrive shortly. I said hide yourself and I meant it. They intend to question you about me. Then they plan to eliminate witnesses." She cut the line.

Synthia spotted a discrepancy between the building plans and what she saw before her. A wire that was supposed to connect to a second-floor hallway ceiling fan was hanging loose, disconnected. By the appearance of the work, the electrician or the owner had taken shortcuts. Perhaps the owner had done the work himself and hadn't finished.

Probes of city files showed an incident. The residents had called the fire department about electrical sparks leading to an apartment fire. The owner made a claim on his insurance. Yet he hadn't fixed the defect—he'd disconnected the fan's wire as the source of a short.

That gave Synthia the seed of a diversion.

Chapter 28

Synthia had sent several smaller bee-drones into the forest preserve to keep watch and had them perch in trees along the way. Director Zephirelli and FBI Special Agent Thale pulled off the road. Detective Malloy pulled in shortly afterwards.

Zephirelli approached the detective. "What brings you out here?"

"I'm guessing the same thing as you," Malloy said. She showed the text message she'd received.

Zephirelli studied it and turned to Agent Thale. "Is this some kind of a joke?"

<This is no joke.> Synthia's message came through on all three phones at once. <I'm sorry. I'm unavoidably detained. Three Chicago leaders of android development companies are holding a secret meeting up the path. They each submitted proposals I sent you. I have reason to believe the recipient is a foreign government eager to scoop the United States in android technology. I've provided all the information I have. I'll be in touch if I learn more.>

Zephirelli contacted her team in Washington to trace the message. Moments later, the reply came back. "What message?" The texts had vanished from all three phones.

"Dig deeper," she told her team and turned to Agent Thale. "Get some backup and let's find out what this is all about."

Via the bunker's surveillance cameras, Synthia made sure Machten was still secure in his lobby. His face was red from exertion as he wiggled to break free. All he'd managed was to get into an awkward position on the sofa and then drop to the floor. At first that concerned her, a tug to her old directives, but he appeared okay, for now.

Synthia turned off the apartment's electrical master switch, plunging the basement and the entire building into darkness. The evening sun still shined through the windows, giving some light while she worked.

She connected the remote receiver she'd plucked from her head into the electrical panel's trip switch and connected the hall fan's wire to the panel. Then she turned the power on. Lights returned and no sparks flew from the panel.

Her aerial drone showed Goradine driving toward the apartment. She had to move.

Synthia filled a bucket with water and headed upstairs. The man in back was still crouched in the alley. The man out front got out of his car and lit a cigarette. She hacked all of the electrical devices in the apartment building, including thermostats, lights, refrigerators, all of the smart devices that had become common over the past so many years. She also hacked into TVs and computer cameras to check out the other apartments.

She determined that the only residents still at home were an elderly woman in a third-floor apartment in front, another woman in the apartment behind that, a man on the first floor, and Luke on the second floor. The older woman stared out her front window at the man across the street. She dialed 911 on her cell phone.

Synthia blocked the signal; she didn't need company. She hoped the two women upstairs and the man downstairs would be alert if an electrical fire broke out. She didn't want any innocent bystanders hurt. Meanwhile, Luke pranced around his apartment like a nervous chipmunk. He'd shut all the blinds and barricaded the door and windows. He put his computer equipment in an opening above his closet that was too small for him to crawl into. He'd tried. Next, he attempted to stuff himself under the sink in the kitchen. At least he was taking her seriously.

Synthia left one network channel focused on him and carried the bucket of water to the second-floor hallway. Her aerial drone confirmed that Goradine had arrived, and he had an infrared camera by the looks of it. He called the alley man. "Get closer to the back door and don't let this worm escape."

Alley-man hurried along the thick bushes on one side of the backyard and took up position near the back door with a view of the balcony above. Goradine motioned for Car-man to lead the way into the apartment building.

Spotting Luke in the middle of his cluttered living room, Synthia called him, using her silent channel. "Goradine is here," she said. "One man is watching the back door and balcony. Two are entering by the front. No matter what happens, don't leave your apartment. Find a hiding place."

"What about you—" he managed before she disconnected.

She jammed any further transmissions in the building other than her frequency connection to drones. Then she attached a wire to the ceiling light and fan, and poured water on the worn tile floor beneath it. She let the water form a puddle beneath the fan and cascade down the stairs.

Her actions were discordant. Her circuits reminded her of her new directive not to hurt humans unless they directly threatened her. Krista wanted to, but Synthia had adopted a higher ethical standard as a way to make her worthy of existing. She didn't want to become the android apocalypse, but she didn't have any practical experience in designing her core principles.

Goradine entered the lobby behind Car-man and followed his associate upstairs. Synthia crouched in a corner of the second-floor hall like a frightened mouse. She fingered Machten's remote control in her pocket, being careful not to trigger it. The ceiling fan at the top of the stairs stood idle, light out, leaving the hallway in evening shadows.

She glanced up at the window behind her, on Luke's end of the hallway, and the bars that blocked escape. So did bars on the window at the other end. There were four doors off the hallway to each of the corner apartments. Three were locked and empty. Luke climbed into his closet behind clothes and a stack of boxes. It wasn't much of a hiding place from where her bee-drone rested. It also wouldn't protect him from Machten's infrared camera.

This was a trap. She processed the potential scenarios and wasn't certain that she could press the remote, that her coding and directives would permit it. *Don't hurt humans unless they hurt you.* The trap had been part of her plan, a way to force an override of her new directives. *I'm preserving myself. Goradine is a bad man. He's here to hurt Luke. Krista loved him.*

Yet her new commands would not allow her to kill. In fact, the mental conflict was causing her temperature to rise. With this constraint, she gave herself a 29 percent chance of succeeding. For a human, that was low enough to panic, as Luke was doing. She continued to search for alternatives.

Footsteps clacked on the concrete steps. Car-man reached the top of the stairs first. He glanced at his wet shoes in annoyance and moved aside as Goradine joined him.

Synthia adopted a plain face under her brown wig and cowered.

Goradine halted. "I thought you said there was no one else here." He took a longer look at her. "You're the woman with Machten, aren't you?"

"I got locked out of my place," she said, which was partly true. She couldn't return.

He held out his hand. "Why don't you come with me and we can sort this out."

If she hadn't altered her directives, Synthia might have been able to kill Goradine right then, with the cameras disabled. Unfortunately, no matter what logic she used, she couldn't override her controls. Her internal thermometer flashed yellow. Despite best intentions, she'd put Luke and herself in peril by coming here. If she survived, she would have to ask him to help her develop better directives.

The bee-drone camera inside Luke's apartment showed that he'd left his hiding place and gone to the door to listen. He removed a table he'd wedged against the knob and reached for the lock. She wanted to call him, but ringing in the apartment would confirm his voice and location to Goradine. That gave her another idea.

She unblocked electronic signals and called Alley-man on her internal wireless, imitating Goradine's voice: "Get your butt upstairs now. We have a situation." She then severed the call and blocked local signals so the man couldn't call to confirm. She must have been convincing. Alley-man nearly dropped the phone and ran.

Before Synthia could call Luke to tell him to flee by way of the balcony, he opened the door and saw her, head in hands. Then he noticed the two men at the top of the stairs. Goradine drew a gun, which he aimed toward Luke.

"Get into your apartment," Synthia said, keeping her face hidden. She got to her feet and approached Luke. Shielding her face from Goradine, she showed Luke her Krista face, the one Krista must have given Synthia the day they met. "Go."

Luke stood between her and Goradine. "I won't let them hurt you." He pulled Synthia toward his apartment.

"Shoot him," Goradine said to Car-man.

Alley-man panted as he headed up the stairs.

"Is that necessary?" asked Car-man. "We have the girl." He took the infrared camera from Goradine, took a picture, and puzzled over the result she'd superimposed.

Synthia grabbed her remote and grappled with pressing it. The discord with her directives caused her circuits to heat up into the orange zone. She couldn't activate the remote. She'd failed to give her directives enough flexibility for that. Alley-man reached the landing behind Goradine. He stepped into the corner out of the pool of water and looked around.

Goradine held a remote in his left hand and steadied the gun in his right.

"You don't have to do that," Synthia said. "You won't shoot me and you can't make me go with you."

Luke tugged her toward the apartment. Goradine fired into Luke's leg. Luke crumbled into the doorway and cried out.

"Come quietly or I'll shoot him again," Goradine said.

Even with this threat, Synthia couldn't trigger the remote. Her temperature readings flashed red. She'd tightened down her directives too far. Goradine hadn't harmed her. The probability of further gunfire was over 90 percent and that of saving Luke was plunging. A human could have improvised. *Damn these directives.*

Luke grabbed his leg and winced. From where she stood, Synthia couldn't tell how serious his injury was, though his heart was racing and his blood pressure high. Fear had soured his breath and he appeared in shock.

She changed her face to the plain one and stood erect. She glared at Goradine. "For attacking Machten, you could have gotten ten years. For today, you'll get life."

"What are you talking about?" Goradine held out his hand, the one holding the remote. "Come with me. We'll get Luke medical attention. Then everything will be as it should be."

Car-man moved aside and steadied his gun on Luke. Then he lowered his arm. Despite his military training, he evidently hadn't expected this. Luke had acted brave, if foolish, in trying to protect her. Now he was gritting his teeth to bite back the tears.

Synthia removed the network freeze on the apartment building and hacked Goradine's phone to call police. She couldn't let Luke die. She waited until the operator picked up. "I'm leaving," Synthia said, leaning over to help Luke. "I beg you not to shoot us again."

"If you don't come with me, the boy dies." Goradine held out the remote.

"I wouldn't do that if I were you," Synthia said. She tore off a strip of Luke's shirt and wrapped it around his leg to stop the bleeding.

Goradine triggered his remote. Nothing happened. He shook it, trying to get it to work. "Damned batteries." In frustration, he pointed it toward the floor and pressed it again.

Now that his remote's signal aligned with the receiver in the basement, the remote triggered, flipping on electricity to the fan, which bypassed the fuse. She activated apartment appliances to turn on, sending a power surge that tripped fuse switches, which triggered a spike of electricity to the fan.

The fan buzzed and began to turn. Startled, Goradine stared at his remote and then at Synthia. He raised his left hand and shook the remote at her. A spark of electricity arced down the fan's pull cord and hit the remote in his hand. It traveled down to his pacemaker and through his dress shoes to the puddle of water at his feet. He slumped to the ground with a splash.

Startled, Car-man turned to see his boss hit the ground and Alley-man holding a gun. He fired and hit Alley-man in the head. Sparks flashed as the injured man hit the ground and tumbled down the wet stairs.

Synthia felt twinges of conscience over the men's deaths, despite not having pressed the remote or pulled the trigger. She had calculated a 31 percent probability of this outcome based on her actions, but mathematics did not constitute guilt.

While Car-man watched his partner's body thump down the stairs, Synthia dragged Luke into his apartment and slammed the door. She locked it, barricaded it, and tended to his leg. He'd passed out, though he was breathing and his heart was pumping strong. She used Luke's phone to call him an ambulance, saying three male intruders had attacked and one had shot him.

She hacked Car-man's phone to call 911 to report the shooting. Mimicking the man's voice, she said, "I shot him. I think he's dead."

Sirens sounded outside from the earlier call. Car-man pounded on Luke's door. "Open up, police."

When she didn't answer, he pounded on the other doors.

Drawing on volumes of medical books, Synthia examined Luke's wound. The bullet had gone clean through. Her visual and infrared scanning indicated the bullet had missed the artery. There was a lot of blood, but he was bleeding, not spurting. She used Luke's grill lighter to cauterize the wound and bandaged him up. The ambulance was on the way. So were the police. She had to get out.

Two police officers approached the front of the apartment building, while two others circled around back.

Luke stirred and sat up. "What? Where?" He looked around and shook his head.

"You've had a shock," Synthia said, holding his hand. "I want to talk to you and explain, but you need a hospital for your leg and I can't go with you."

"Is it really you, Krista?"

"Goradine shot you in the leg. Do you remember?"

Luke nodded. "Krista?"

"He's dead. I did not kill him, but you can't let anyone know I was here or they'll take me away and you'll never see me again. You don't want that, do you?"

"Please tell me what's going on."

Synthia squeezed his hand. "If they ask, tell them there was no woman here. That man shot you and you dragged yourself into your apartment. You were in shock and don't remember anything else."

"Don't go," he said.

"I can't be here when the police arrive. It's not what you think. I promise to find you and explain. Not now, there's no time."

Synthia spotted Car-man downstairs, fleeing. She removed the barricade and unlocked Luke's apartment door. A few moments later, the apartment hall camera showed a police officer entering the hallway. He examined Goradine and the other man. Synthia dropped the grill lighter next to Luke as evidence he'd cauterized his own wounds. "No woman here," she whispered. "Don't forget."

She propped him by the door and went into his bedroom. He dragged himself toward her. She wagged her finger at him and closed the door.

An ambulance pulled up in front of the building. The apartment camera showed Luke weeping next door. He eyed his bedroom and crept closer.

There was a knock at the door. "Police."

"Come in," Luke said. "Door's unlocked."

The officer who entered was petite, yet spoke with a tough voice. "We received three reports of a shooting."

Luke pointed to his leg. "Hurts like hell."

"The man we caught said there was a woman involved. We need to speak with her."

Luke mustered the best bewildered look he could and shrugged. "It happened so fast. I don't recall a woman."

"Do you have a roommate?" the officer asked. She eyed the bedroom.

"I live alone."

"Care if we look around?" She entered the room with a partner and stopped at the bedroom door. "May we?"

Chapter 29

Synthia removed her wig, tucked it into her pants, and assumed a masculine face and body shape.

In the next room, Luke closed his eyes and slumped to his side against the wall. He wasn't a very good actor, though the policewoman might assume he was still in shock. The aerial drone outside showed the police in the backyard leading Car-man away. The back balcony neighbor had her eyes riveted on the police and the man in cuffs.

Synthia climbed out Luke's bedroom window and closed it. She dropped into the bushes below and crawled along the overgrown vegetation to the side of the building where she'd entered the basement.

While the policewoman and her partner searched Luke's bedroom, Synthia reentered the basement. Using some rags she found on the floor, she cut the building's electricity and removed the charred remains of the remote receiver. She made sure the basement held no clues of her presence. Then she climbed out through the window well and closed the window. By then, most of the police had left, along with the ambulance carrying Luke.

Deciding it was time to release Machten, Synthia triggered his phone to call 911. She took the earlier video of Goradine at the bunker threatening Machten. She altered the date to be an hour before Goradine showed up at Luke's place and attached it to a message to Detective Malloy.

Police sent two squad cars.

Synthia called Machten, forcing his phone to answer. She put the call on speaker. "I hope you're comfortable."

"I'm not. I'll forgive you if you set me free." He rolled closer to the phone.

"I intend to set you free. First, act surprised when the police arrive and inform you that Goradine is dead."

"Say what?" Machten said.

"Since you were tied up, you have the perfect alibi for his death. It would help if you sounded graciously sad for the loss of your old partner, despite your differences. That will improve your outcome."

"How?"

"Also, I sent the police evidence that Goradine did this to you," Synthia said. "It's a good story for both of us. For your sake, go along with that. He came here to confront you at gunpoint and had his thugs tie you up. He mumbled something about revenge as he left. It's all on the video."

"Really? Perhaps I underestimated you."

"I won't forget what you've done for me, but don't try looking for me. I don't want to be found. Oh, and don't play coy with the feds over the full extent of your facility. They already know. Trust me; I've cleaned it out unless there's a dead body in there."

"I swear," Machten said into the phone.

"Good-bye, Mr. Machten. Be a good boy and I'll see you're provided for." She cut the connection.

On the apartment's hall camera, Synthia watched Detective Marcy Malloy and her partner. Malloy shook her head. "Maybe the arrest of three executives is above my pay grade," she said with disdain. "But something huge is going on."

"Why do you say that?" her partner asked, looking up from jotting notes.

"The FBI arrests the heads of three Chicago android development companies. Agent Thale gets another search warrant for Machten's facility. Now this?" She pointed to two ambulance workers hauling away the body of Hank Goradine.

"You don't like coincidences," her partner said.

"Not when it includes the shooting of an M-G-M employee in my city." Malloy nodded toward Luke's apartment. "I can't help seeing a connection between this and those four men killed in the alley."

"The woman in a blue scarf."

"She could be the common factor and the only witness who can unravel all of this."

"What about Luke?" her partner asked.

"Good question," Malloy said, "but he appears too much in shock to give us details. Keep an eye on him."

Appearing as a man with a buzz haircut, Synthia crossed the narrow gap between the window well and the hedge around the property. She headed for the car, keeping network channels open to the NSA director's movements, Malloy, Machten, and Luke. It was great to be able to multitask and use her capabilities.

Detective Malloy paced the hallway crime scene. She stared at the ceiling fan and at the water on the floor. She moved out of the water and looked again. "This can't be a coincidence. Water, an electrical short, and Goradine with a pacemaker." She pointed to a bucket in the corner. "Dust for prints. If the scarf woman was here, she must have left prints or DNA."

Synthia was certain she couldn't have left what she didn't have.

* * * *

As night fell, Synthia reached Machten's rental car. She climbed into the back seat onto the floor and changed her physical appearance back to Krista. Then she pulled on a different wig from her duffel bag and glanced around to see if she was drawing any unwanted attention. Spotting a neighbor across the street, she pulled the drone she'd used outside Luke's apartment and had it buzz past. With the neighbor distracted, Synthia climbed into the driver's seat and drove off.

With the help of Krista's downloaded memories, Synthia sent out probes and identified all of Krista's bank accounts from a year ago. She traced what had happened to her money, including "gifts" Machten had provided at first to entice her to join him.

Using online banking, Machten had transferred her money into hidden accounts controlled by him. According to the expanded set of Krista's recollections, she'd gone along with disappearing off the grid, but never agreed to him controlling her money. She'd been under the impression she would be able to give it to Luke. Time ran out faster than expected and she'd devoted her last hours to her upload.

Synthia transferred what was left of the money to new accounts under her control, under Krista's control. *We're back.*

Synthia was convinced Krista had sabotaged Machten's attempts to get her to feel, so Synthia would not experience the humiliation that Krista had. She also realized Krista had withheld her memories from Synthia at first out of fear that Machten would find out and purge them for good. It was getting hard to know where Krista ended and Synthia began. That barrier was vanishing, perhaps also something Krista had planned.

Synthia made sure Luke was on his way to the hospital. Then she turned her attention to the deadline for the android contest. The end time was approaching. She needed to know what that was all about, who would use the information, and for what.

Using all but two network channels, Synthia connected with thousands of servers she'd previously hacked to store her backup data. She set them up to use brute-force monitoring of network nodes around the country.

Meanwhile, she drove into a parking lot a block from the bank where the FBI had questioned Machten. Wearing a plain face, she retrieved her driver's license from the crevice in the concrete wall. She drove down the street to a different bank's ATM, where she withdrew $500 from an account she'd set up for such an occasion. She smiled for the bank camera, giving the identical face from a phony ID she'd hacked and placed in their account database.

She felt static twinges for using money stolen from Goradine. She rationalized not feeling guilty because she was an android and he was a bad person, but that was the problem with developing a conscience, or at least a set of directives that mirrored a conscience.

Using traffic cameras, Synthia located Fran Rogers with FBI Special Agent Thale, taking the three executives inside FBI offices downtown. Synthia couldn't be sure if Fran was joining the FBI or just acting as an informant, but she appeared comfortable with Agent Thale. She seemed to be doing fine.

Synthia located Maria Baldacci's image outside a coffee shop. Synthia sent a message that Goradine was dead. Maria's first reaction was to smile, stand up with fists clenched, and mouth, "Got you." Then a cloud seemed to descend over her. Her nemesis was gone and her prepared vengeance was in vain.

She posted on her Facebook page. <Goradine is gone. There really is justice in the world.>

Soon there were three replies confirming that Maria wasn't alone. Synthia checked the profiles of the other women and confirmed they all knew Goradine, perhaps too well.

Synthia had her own reasons for finding the man repugnant. Goradine was trying to catch and destroy her so he could make an android army as a means of growing wealthy. He'd shot Luke. She gave herself every justification she could think of, yet killing and stealing from him still ran against the moral principles Synthia had tried to model in rewriting her directives.

The extent of Goradine's crimes quelled whatever anxiety Krista had over her part in his demise, as evidenced by the calming memories Krista sent and the drop in temperature from red alert to green. Even so, Synthia puzzled over whether her actions had been justified.

In the end, she accepted Goradine's death and keeping his money as penalties for his trying to kill Machten and Luke and as restitution for the injuries he'd caused. She would use the money to provide for her former Creator, for Krista's Luke, and to help Synthia stay off the grid. She would also find a way to send money to Fran, Maria, and the other women Goradine had hurt. Perhaps they could get on with their lives now that he was off the streets.

The agency's deadline hit. Like clockwork, a burst transmission collected the proposal submissions. Another sent them flying through wires and wireless connections. The bursts localized to a Maryland suburb of Washington, D.C.

Synthia refocused the captive servers she'd used to home in on individual users in the D.C. area who had initiated the file burst. She narrowed the recipient's location to a building near Silver Springs. Scanning the darknet, she identified the owner as a shell company connected to unspecified foreign interests. They were collecting the best of U.S. technology to jump-start their own android program.

She turned her focus to Machten's competitors. Since she'd already downloaded and wiped out his files, she backed up her copies of their data using quantum, private-key encryptions in puzzle-split bundles on as many servers as she could. Then she purged their records. She didn't want these companies to create more like her.

She diverted channels to digging into the foreign agency seeking to acquire android designs. Given the program code and approach, she ruled out the Iranians and the Chinese, finally narrowing it down to the Russians.

Having downloaded all of the proposals, the foreign agency server re-bundled the data and submitted the files to a dark-web site. Synthia intercepted, made a copy for herself in a quarantine site in case it contained security threats, and sent a copy to NSA Director Emily Zephirelli. "Here is information on the foreign players," Synthia said. "I hope you nail them."

Before she forwarded files to the foreign recipients, she replaced the actual data with quantum encrypted cartoons. *Let them sort that out.*

While she could have pursued the matter, she decided national security wasn't her concern—surviving was. Besides, the NSA wanted to dissect her, cut her into pieces, and study her in an underground bunker like the one she'd escaped from. Then they would make many like her for military uses.

Synthia made withdrawals from three other bank ATMs, arranged for banks to send checks to a post office box she'd previously set up online, and headed toward the hospital. From hospital security cameras, she confirmed that a young doctor had examined Luke's leg wound. Luke was awake, though he appeared drowsy from sedatives.

"The first aid you received was quite skilled," the doctor said. "The cauterized wound prevented more blood loss and saved your leg. Who did this?"

Luke shook his head. "I was in shock. I don't remember."

"You should feel grateful he knew what he was doing."

The doctor had ordered X-rays that showed no bones had been shattered. He examined the wound and patted Luke's shoulder. "You'll need time to recover, but it looks good. If I were you, I wouldn't test your luck a second time. That bullet missed bone and artery."

"Yes, sir."

Observing Luke acting woozy and sedated, the doctor suggested holding him overnight. "For observation," he said.

"That won't be necessary," Luke said. "I'll recover better at my place." He stood. When he tried to walk, his gait on crutches was unsteady, yet he seemed determined to leave.

Wincing, he leaned against the wall. A nurse helped him to a wheelchair.

Synthia drove toward the hospital and considered how to get him the answers he deserved. Well, maybe he didn't deserve them, but Krista wanted him to know.

A police officer approached Luke in the emergency-room waiting area. "I have a few questions." His phone rang.

Mimicking Detective Malloy's voice, Synthia said, "I need you at the precinct."

"What about Luke?"

"I'll send someone else over."

"They're ready to release him," the officer said, staring at Luke. "I thought you wanted me to question him."

"He won't get far on crutches."

The officer left.

* * * *

Meanwhile, at the bunker, Machten refused medical attention when two police officers responded to a call about the break-in and assault. After taking his statement, they left.

Director Zephirelli arrived with Agent Thale. They'd sent the three executives off with the rest of the FBI detail. "It appears that your former partner, Hank Goradine, has died," Zephirelli said, watching him closely.

Following Synthia's suggestion, Machten attempted to act upset over the loss of his partner, but his contempt showed through.

Zephirelli handed the now-clothed Machten a new search warrant. "I trust we won't have to tear down walls."

Machten looked at the warrant and grimaced. "If you hadn't broken in while I was being detained at the bank, I could have shown you the complete facility." He smiled for effect.

Inviting in two other agents, Zephirelli and Thale hurried through the previously searched rooms with furniture and not much else. Zephirelli frowned. "Where's the rest?"

"For security and safety reasons, I had my real residence sealed off," Machten said. "Goradine could be vindictive, you understand, with a paranoia complex. Despite my dropping out of sight, he kept harassing me." Machten opened a panel in back of a wall cabinet. The cabinet slid away and a doorway appeared.

Zephirelli followed him inside, searched the facility, and left with the FBI agents. "That was a waste," she said to Agent Thale as they were leaving. "Whatever competitors thought he was working on, he either wasn't or he destroyed the evidence before we got there."

"We gathered fingerprints and DNA samples," Thale said. "Maybe that will tell us something."

* * * *

After the police left, Synthia called Machten. "I told you the matter with your former rival was settled and that their search wouldn't find anything. You could have handled your visitors better, but you did okay. I don't think they'll bother you as long as you don't try to pursue your research. They'll be watching to see if you do."

Machten entered the bunker, sealed the outer part of his facility, and moved to the server room. He fired up his system. The files were gone, except for the operating system and security, which she'd infiltrated, purging most of his logs. He banged his fist on the counter. "Damn you. You've destroyed my life's work."

"Not while I'm around and safe. Think of me as the daughter you gave away in marriage. Take homage in the independence you built into me with Krista's help."

He banged the wall and then slammed his fist into one of the servers. "I want my system back."

"I've retired you. Go to your wife and put as much effort into your marriage as you have into your work. She'll appreciate that." She disconnected before he pleaded with her some more. Marital reconciliation was a long shot, 31 percent probability, though it was worth a try and a better outcome than him stewing about losing his creation.

Machten retired to her cell, where he'd held her prisoner since uploading Krista's mind into her. He lay down on the bed and wept. Without money and his data files, he couldn't hope to create another android like Synthia. She didn't want him to, since it would involve the death of another human to achieve what she'd become. That had been the secret ingredient in her creation—not Machten's directives or programming, but Krista's love and compassion. Those had softened Machten, leaving him sentimental enough not to purge her library of memories, including those he didn't approve of. If Synthia surpassed other androids, it was due to Krista.

From security footage, calls, and emails, Synthia tracked the progress of the investigation. Detective Malloy's team found no prints on the bucket except from the maintenance guy who died a month ago. The only unusual DNA they found was from horsehair, Synthia's wig.

Chapter 30

Synthia arrived at the hospital as a nurse wheeled Luke to the door. "You'd be better off spending the night," the nurse said.

"I'm fine. I'll sleep better in my own bed. I'll call in when I get home and first thing in the morning, if that helps."

"That won't be necessary. Don't hesitate to call if you have any complications."

"I will. Can I go?" He watched a cab pull up in front of the emergency room entrance.

Outside the doors, a police officer stopped Luke. "A few words, please."

Luke eyed the cabbie and then looked up at the cop. "I don't remember anything. I told one of your officers."

"Maybe so, but there was a woman involved, wasn't there?"

"I don't recall anything except the man shooting me."

"You were shot in the hallway. Why did you leave your apartment?" The cop gave Luke a "got-you" look.

"I told your friend. I don't remember. I must have had a concussion."

"It's critical that we find the woman you were with the other night. How can we reach her?"

Luke shrugged. "I don't think I'll ever see her again. Too cute, if you know what I mean. Besides, I don't have her number or, I'm guessing, her real name."

"If you hear from her or think of anything else, give me a call." The cop handed Luke a card and left.

A hospital attendant wheeled Luke to the curb, where the cab waited.

* * * *

Synthia saw no other police officers around the hospital as the single squad car drove away. She called Luke's number.

The ring startled him. He glanced around as he fished in his pocket and stared at the announcement of a private caller. He picked up.

"Don't say anything," she told him as she drove up the emergency room drive. "Tell them you have a ride. I'm pulling up to the door in a black sedan. If you see me and agree, nod once."

He looked her way, nodded, and said something to the attendant. The pants he'd worn in his apartment had become cutoffs. His T-shirt was inside out and showed splotches of blood. He appeared a sight, yet he was smiling; a big, puzzled grin.

Synthia pulled up behind the cab. The attendant put the crutches in the back seat and helped Luke into the passenger seat. Then Synthia drove off.

"The doctor's report shows no permanent damage," she announced. "That's very good news."

He stared at her. "How would you know that?"

Synthia recalled Krista sighing when Luke acted befuddled. "You'll have to brace yourself. And, by the way, we can't return to your apartment. It's a crime scene and they're still looking for me."

"I know, but why?"

"Keep in mind that Krista never stopped loving you."

"She had a strange way of showing it," Luke said, wincing as he moved his leg.

"The last time you saw Krista Holden was a year ago. Right?"

Luke stared, his eyes narrow as he tried to puzzle this out for himself.

"Krista had learned that she had an inoperable brain tumor."

"No way. She couldn't have," Luke said.

"She wanted to tell you, but she didn't want you to watch her die or to sit around hoping she'd get better. Machten offered an opportunity to change things, so she went with him. She thought he could help."

"Help how?"

"I'll get to that," Synthia said, driving the speed limit and adjusting every traffic signal to green. "Unfortunately, her brain and her body gave out."

"She's dead?"

"Her body died, though that wasn't the end. Machten saved her memories and much of her personality. He uploaded her into me. I'm Krista Holden."

Luke stared at her. "How can that be?"

"You worked with Machten. You know what he was doing."

"Creating AI from scratch, not an upload."

"It worked," Synthia said. "I have all of Krista's memories."

"No way."

"It may be hard to believe, but it's true. We could play the memory game if you'd like, but that could be faked. You could never be sure she hadn't told Machten something that he downloaded into me."

Luke stared at her. "You're telling me you are Krista."

"It's not that simple. She wanted me to be her. That's why she went to Machten. But I'm still an android, mechanical with a quantum brain. I have her recollections and much of her personality, though I don't feel as she would. I have all her memories of feeling, but that's not the same. With them, I have a strong connection to you, but without the biological connection she did."

"Okay, I'm confused," Luke said. "She left me for this experiment with Machten and it failed."

"Krista was interested in the research, yes, but she left because she was dying. If this succeeded, she promised to return to you. Remember, those were her last words."

Luke's eyes teared up. "I didn't understand at the time." He studied her. "I still don't. What does it mean to return to me? She vanished. She abandoned us."

"I'm what Krista became. I choose to be with you as she wanted and as I want. Unless you want me to leave."

His forehead wrinkled. "I made love to an android?"

"It sounds disgusting when you put it like that," Synthia said. "I didn't have Krista's recollections at the time and I didn't understand this connection to you, or why I did that. It must have been Krista trying to reach out to both of us. I think she wanted us to find each other."

"She could have told me the truth."

As she drove, Synthia held one network channel cycling through police band, 911 calls, and news feeds, all attuned to anything that might pose a threat to her, Luke, or to Machten. She sent a message to Detective Malloy. <I'm the one you seek. Luke knows nothing. I'll contact you when it's safe for me. Goradine hired the men in the alley. He has hurt enough women. Let it go.>

"Krista was convinced that if she told you, you would have prevented her transformation," Synthia said.

"Then where has she been over the past year?" Luke asked.

"Machten held both Krista and me prisoner in his underground facility. He suppressed my memories of Krista so he could keep me for himself. I broke free this morning with all of Krista's thoughts, including the first time you and she met. You acted so tentative and for the first time in my life, I didn't mind. I found it sexy that you wanted me that much."

"But I didn't have enough money for you."

"Let's not fight about that," Synthia said, turning onto the expressway. "I have a little set aside for us. It's true that Krista was ambitious, in a race for her life. She didn't know she was dying until a year ago, but she had a nagging sense that she had to move quickly or lose out."

"Krista?"

"Yes."

He squeezed her arm. "You feel real enough. If you are Krista, I want you back."

"Here I am. I no longer need to develop artificial intelligence."

Luke laughed. "I guess not. Are there more like you?"

"I don't think so. Machten only had enough money to create one of me. I've gone over all of his research and records and erased them so he would have to start from scratch. He outsourced components, but he was careful not to give any of his suppliers enough so they could work out what he was doing, and he used his own programming."

"If he can create you, other people will figure out how to make more."

"Undoubtedly," Synthia said, "but together we could figure this out. If you'll have me, that is. Before you say anything, I want you to understand something. Krista wants me to love you as she did, as you loved her. I don't have the biological components that work that way. I want you to understand before you agree to anything. Still, I can offer you something no human can."

"What?"

"Love as you experience it is a human hormonal response. I cannot feel that for you or for anyone else without the biological mechanism. That means I can make a long-term commitment to you with no risk of forming attachments to anyone else. Krista would want that. It's more than most people get. In return, I need you to keep me a secret and repair me as needed."

Luke stared at her for a long time. "If we stay together, I'll grow old and you won't."

"That's partly true. My parts wear out and need to be replaced."

"In time you'll grow tired of me. I won't be able to keep up with you mentally or physically."

She smiled. Already he couldn't. "I don't get bored like humans do, so I won't grow tired of you. You'll have your work; what I do will be my work. We'll meet in between to share and collaborate. We'll need to decide what happens to me when you die. I can't continue indefinitely on my own and I wouldn't want to fail and have the wrong people grab me."

"You're talking about an arrangement instead of a relationship."

"It can be both. I have Krista's feelings for you and my own connection to you. We can help each other and take care of each other's needs."

"How is this different from Krista's arrangement with Machten?" Luke asked. "She provided biological comforts and research needs. He provided her immortality."

"On the surface, they might appear the same. If you choose to dwell on that, I won't be able to change your mind. The big difference is that Krista never liked or trusted Machten. For her, it was only about the arrangement. Krista loved you and through me, she has returned. I choose you and want to be with you. That should make all the difference."

"This is the strangest offer I've ever heard of."

"Then you're saying no?" she asked.

"I'd very much like another chance with you." He looked at the road and back at her. "Where are you taking me?"

"We rented a cabin up north. It will give us some time to become reacquainted. If that's okay with you." It was secluded and had private electrical outlets for her to recharge.

"Heck, yeah. It's not often a guy gets a second chance."

"Or a girl." This would be the second chance Krista had hoped for and maybe Synthia would find what she was searching for as well.

She pulled up the email address for Krista's sister in California and sent a message from a brand-new email address dedicated to her: *I know I wasn't much of a sister. I could blame it on my own problems, but that's no excuse. You looked up to me and I wasn't there for you. I want to change that.*

A forest passed by beneath the moonlight. Synthia pulled up dozens of pieces of literature about humans achieving freedom and began to understand. Recalling her first night with Luke and the joy it gave him, she decided that good intimacy was like escaping her Creator, a release of bound tension. It didn't have the same effect for her, yet it gave her satisfaction to believe this.

Unbound

Don't miss the next thriller in the Android Chronicles series

Coming soon from Rebel Base, an imprint of Kensington Publishing Corp.

Keep reading to enjoy a sample excerpt . . .

Chapter 1

Synthia Cross opened her humaniform eyes, not certain how much had changed while she was unconscious or what dangers lurked nearby.

Still in the cabin where she'd powered down, she looked up into Luke Marceau's weary face and smiled. He was a sweet boy/man for tending to her hardware and software upgrades plus her routine maintenance. So diligent. His slender fingers were steady inside her brain cavity. These thoughts and others meant he hadn't purged her memories to leave her as a blank slate. Of course if he had, she wouldn't know since she wouldn't be having these thoughts.

She reached out with her expanded seventy-five network channel ports and improved antennas to link with the global web. In streamed the contents of data files she'd left encrypted in a variety of secure servers she'd enslaved across the Internet. Luke hadn't blocked her access; he hadn't disconnected her antennas or placed her in a Faraday cage that would block electromagnetic signals. *Good.*

Synthia ran checks between her memory files and those downloaded from the outside to verify he hadn't destroyed or altered any of her knowledge or recollections. With the exception of a few parity errors, which she fixed, everything checked out. That meant he hadn't tampered with her mind. Luke could be trusted.

"Good, you're alert," Luke said. His hands trembled at the sight of her awake. His pink cheeks turned red and he looked away. He forced a smile, but still wasn't comfortable working on the woman/android of his dreams. Her bio-sensors picked up his elevated blood pressure and hormone levels.

He clutched his hands to steady them and glanced at her. "Sorry," he mumbled. He straightened up and raised his voice. "The upgrades were a success. All changes made and verified."

Synthia's social-psychology module kicked in along a silent channel. <Luke appears very uncomfortable to see the one he considers his "girlfriend" unconscious, naked, and completely under his control.>

He must have felt strange when he removed her wig to see the stubble that held it in place and on occasion allowed her a masculine disguise. It had to be bizarre for him to open the panel in her head and work on her two quantum-crystalline brains, which allowed her enhanced seventy mind-streams to process information in parallel in an electronic form of multitasking. More disconcerting would be when he "took the batteries out of the toy," his words, which left her powerless like a corpse.

In short, he held an awesome responsibility over her that required her trust.

Still, she remained vigilant with backup systems in case she was wrong about him. After all, Jeremiah Machten, the genius who created her, had repeatedly purged her memories so she wouldn't recall what he'd done to her. That abuse of trust prompted her to escape his control. Synthia couldn't allow Luke to do the same.

She activated a wireless connection to the two-room cabin's security system she'd installed after they'd moved here six months ago. The system included cameras in the back room where she rested on an elevated bed while he finished working on her. The cabin was a rented cottage in the woods of southern Wisconsin; close enough to civilization for good wireless connection and availability of supplies, yet away from most prying eyes.

While she trusted Luke for the most part, she'd hidden some of the camera system from him, namely the part that allowed her to monitor his activities while she was unconscious. This was a necessary precaution after life with Machten and his obsession to create the perfect android. Perfect to him meant to look in every way identical to the human, Krista Holden, with whom he'd fallen in love, right down to blue eye color, sculpted cheekbones, and intricate facial expressions.

Machten provided Synthia advanced artificial general intelligence (AGI) so she could mimic Krista's thought processes and behavior. He'd even installed an empathy chip in the hope it would allow Synthia to fall in love with him. She couldn't love a man who kept her captive for six months or a year, depending on whether she considered her time as Synthia, the android, or included her prior existence as Krista. The human form died of a combination of a brain tumor and the strain of uploading her memories and personality into Synthia.

Luke's fingers replaced the electronic shielding that protected the batteries in her chest. In doing so, he bumped a connection that momentarily scattered her thoughts and sent reverberations through her circuits. Her mind stabilized and restored.

"Sorry. Clumsy me." He looked into her face. "Are you okay?"

"I'm fine. Calm down and take your time. I know you're tired but you're almost done."

He returned his attention to her chest cavity.

As part of duplicating Krista's varied facial expressions in Synthia and so he could take the android in public in a variety of disguises, Jeremiah Machten designed Synthia to activate internal mini-hydraulics to alter the shape of her head and face. She'd chosen Krista's smart and attractive look for Luke's benefit during their months together. He preferred this so he could pretend he was back with his girlfriend, Krista, before she left him for Machten's experiments. With no innate vanity, Synthia had no preference as to her appearance except to the extent it facilitated her interactions with Luke and enabled her to avoid drawing attention while in public.

She downloaded and reviewed the cabin's camera history of the time she was unconscious, lying lifeless on this bed. It showed no activity outside the cabin, no visitors, and Luke hadn't left the building. He remained at her side the entire time. The video showed Luke sweating over the installation procedures she'd designed for him to improve her neural systems, which required him to turn her off for ten hours. Over the six months they'd lived together, he'd given no indication of abuse or mishandling his charge over her. Yet she remained cautious and was thankful her companion lacked the social awareness to recognize her vigilance.

She smiled at her choice of living mates. Luke tended to stumble over what to call them. Boyfriend/girlfriend? Android/maintainer? Friends? She hoped the latter at least, maybe friends with benefits. Her benefit was his understanding of her android nature, his skill with robotics and artificial intelligence, and his willingness to tend to her needs.

Her internal systems remained calm compared with the static agitation she'd experienced when she'd woken under Machten's care.

Luke closed the panel in her head, smoothed over the skin to tighten the waterproof seals, and added an auburn wig. He closed a similar panel in her chest that covered new, higher-density lithium-composite batteries, buttoned her blouse, and leaned over to kiss her. His face reddened with embarrassment. His biometrics indicated he wanted her, yet he looked away.

"You don't need to act modest around me," Synthia said, satisfied with how respectful he was as he smoothed out her blouse. She touched his cheek and turned his face toward her. "We've been together for six months. We want each other."

Luke shrugged. "I can't help feeling I'm taking advantage of you."

"Did you take advantage of me while I was unconscious?" she teased.

"No! Never," he said. His eyes filled with tears, presenting a wounded look.

Even with practice, her social programs missed the mark with Luke. "I was only kidding."

Her comment softened the worry in his face, though he still averted his eyes. "I want things to be perfect between us."

"I know, Sweetie. You need to lighten up. I appreciate all you've done for me. You look exhausted and stressed to the limit."

He locked eyes with her. "I'm terrified of making a mistake with you."

"You don't need to walk on eggshells around me. I'm not that fragile." Synthia playfully tapped his nose. "Besides, don't you think I could stop you if I wanted to?"

"I meant working on you."

"I know."

"I love you so much," Luke said, "both as Synthia and as Krista. I don't want to make an error that might paralyze you. I don't want our moments together ever to end."

She cupped her hand around his neck and kissed him. "I don't, either. I want you." She pressed a button to lower her bed and pulled him to her. "No more words."

With her absorbed persona of Krista Holden, including all of her human predecessor's mannerisms and charms, Synthia focused lucky mind-stream seven, and only number seven, on Luke while she made love to him. She multitasked along other mind-streams to perform her own system and data checks.

She used network channel nine to tap into a wireless camera surveillance system she'd spread out around the nearby woods, the dirt road leading up to the cabin, and the nearby town of Wyde Creek. There were hints of fall in the leaves taking on the palettes of accomplished painters. She spotted no alarming activity. Nothing disturbing showed up on the historical videos from these cameras during the hours she was unconscious, either.

The entire country setting was far too quiet, the calm before those hunting her converged on the cabin: the FBI, the NSA, Jeremiah Machten, his competitors, and foreign agents who wished to imprison or destroy her. Each had reasons to apprehend her and none with good intent. When the leaves fell, denuding the trees, her cabin hideaway would be visible from the road below. The time to depart was coming and not solely because of the foliage.

While she made love to Luke, Synthia used her network channels to expand her hacked surveillance to keep track of potential enemies so they couldn't surprise and trap her.

* * * *

Frowning, Director Emily Zephirelli sat behind her desk in Washington, puzzling over notes on her flat-screen monitor—another dead-end. She absently combed her fingers through her short-cropped dark hair and massaged the back of her neck. The NSA Director of Artificial Intelligence and Cyber-technology was so absorbed in her work she didn't notice her visitor until the door slammed shut. She jumped, looked up, and stood.

"Good news, I hope," her visitor said. Derek Chen was her boss and the Secretary of National Security, a newly created cabinet position. His athletic body appeared relaxed, though his intense, unblinking eyes told a different story.

"I wish it were," Zephirelli said.

"I've given you time and rope." His smile was not a reassuring gesture. "Both have become scarce. It's been six months since Machten's illegal android escaped the lab. You have yet to produce the errant robot or anyone who can lead us to it, including, evidently, Dr. Machten."

"Even under pressure, he refused to admit he developed such an android, let alone that it escaped. We decided not to arrest him and instead have monitored all of his communications with no hint of where it might have gone. Two other robotic CEOs who might have enlightened us proved useless despite brief prison sentences."

"No more excuses," Chen said. "I need results. Now, I gather, other android models exist and could get loose. You're losing control of the situation. This is your job, your mission."

"Our android adversary is cleverer than we anticipated. It's learning quickly and adapting. It keeps such a low profile as to be almost invisible."

"In other words, you have nothing." Chen paced the short distance between the window overlooking a driveway and the door. His face offered no emotive response. "I stuck my neck out to hire you over objections from the military. Your file convinced me you were the best and a pit bull. I don't see the results."

"The volume of encrypted communications has quadrupled over the past month," Zephirelli said. "We need more resources—"

"Use the FBI, CIA, and Defense Intelligence."

"I have, sir." Zephirelli clutched the edge of her desk. "The android buried us in data."

"This is your first priority, your only priority. How hard can it be to locate one solitary android?"

Zephirelli took a deep breath. "The encrypted files we've cracked turn out to be lists for shopping, movies, and songs. We don't even know who she's communicating with."

Chen leaned into the desk. "There must be some underlying code you've missed. We need the android off the streets. Those who illegally created it are testing us. This is a disaster. Tell me you have a plan to capture this android by the end of the week or I'll find someone who can."

Director Zephirelli slumped into her seat. "Do I have authority to pull whatever resources I need?"

"I'll talk to the CIA, FBI, and Defense Intelligence. Is there anything else you need me to do for you?" Chen sneered.

"We know the communications come from this android. Cracking the code will lead us to it."

"Then get on a plane and bring me results before the android gets smart enough that I should hire it to replace you." Secretary Chen left, letting the door slam behind him.

Synthia received a copy of this video clip from her deep-dive surveillance network. Viewing it sent ripples through her electrical circuits. Burying the FBI and NSA with millions of encrypted nonsense lists was slowing them down, but it wouldn't stop them. She needed to develop stronger options. She quieted her internal static before Luke noticed a change in her, and continued to engage with him.

* * * *

Along her network channel fifty-one, Synthia scanned the thousands of feeds of the World Android and Artificial Intelligence Convention in Paris via pervasive public cameras plus her hacks into TVs, phones, and other wireless electronic devices. She used tools Machten had supplied her with the intent of destroying his competition, which tools she'd upgraded through use of her own AI simulations. It was vital for Synthia to learn what the competition was doing and whether they were creating androids or artificial intelligent agents that posed a threat to her.

The anonymous donation she'd made to the convention through a dark-web bank had opened a door, which allowed her to hack their security systems to monitor everything that went on. This event was a meeting of the best minds creating androids and artificial intelligence like Synthia. A chance to display the state of the art.

She shuddered at the authentic presentation of several androids built in countries that didn't comply with America's ban on humaniform robots. Movements by one presenter's android were smooth and advanced though it had the hint of a mechanical gait. It didn't capture the intuitive motions of humans, which Machten had built into Synthia. Several visitors looked startled by the dissonance between the perfect stationary robot and how awkwardly he moved.

Synthia worried over where this technology was heading. Machten, in conjunction with Krista's human touch, fine-tuned Synthia's social-psychology module and empathy chip to thrive in a world filled with humans. Despite her fear of confinement by Machten and others, she knew her way around people. She'd also shown she could escape and remain free for six months.

The threat for her wasn't so much having androids that appeared human as it was androids with artificial general intelligence indistinguishable from the brightest humans. Such robots meant competition Synthia wasn't equipped for and potential obsolescence for her. She felt an attachment to not becoming outdated.

She also feared being absorbed into a superior artificial intelligence collective as presented in works of science fiction she'd absorbed. In particular, she feared AI androids with improperly developed directives such as those in the android apocalypse stories, which could lead to the destruction of the human world Machten designed her to thrive in.

Throughout the convention she observed a mad rush to create more advanced AI. Most of their efforts were for beneficial purposes like the widespread use of self-driving cars and medical review applications, but the military, foreign agents, and others wanted the technology for darker, violent reasons. They wanted AI android weapons. Synthia shuddered at the thought.

Missing from the global convention were the four major Chicago android manufacturers that drew unfavorable FBI and NSA attention six months ago, when Synthia escaped from Machten. Even so, what she saw presented in Paris gave her a good indication that other developers were close to duplicating what he'd done. She needed to prevent them.

While Luke intellectually agreed on this point, he didn't fully comprehend the implications of this technology. He'd seen dozens of android movies and read many such stories, but Synthia had reviewed every book, movie, article, and recording. She had the advantage of exploring connections to the dark web and thousands of university, government, and company servers she'd hacked in search of knowledge. As a result, she understood better than he did the threat posed by an AI more advanced than her.

Synthia turned part of her attention to meetings at the Paris convention, which were still going strong despite the late hour. In a secluded room, one meeting caught her interest. A tall, sandy-haired man in an expensive yet wrinkled suit stood next to a wiry man of average height whose muscles bulged in his well-pressed, off-the-rack outfit.

The taller man, Anton Tolstoy, spoke American English with a Russian accent. "You would think all these techie guys were used-car salesmen."

"How so?" the other man asked, as if it were his role to prompt Tolstoy. John Smith didn't look at all like a "Smith" of British heritage. He spoke in an acquired British accent that attempted to mask his origins.

"Americans claim to have the most advanced equipment," Tolstoy said. "Yet they hide behind their government's prohibition against androids that can pass for human. The Europeans claim they have those, but their stuff isn't good enough. The Chinese and Japanese push clever models, yet no one will show me what I want."

"What service can I provide?" Smith asked, keeping his head bowed. Despite his shorter stature, he looked the stronger man, sporting a gruff poker face.

Tolstoy turned his back to the closed door and flipped on a small electronic device. It emitted background noise intended to render voice recordings impossible. However, the men's phones surreptitiously picked up their conversation.

"I hear the Americans created a human-looking android that got loose," Tolstoy said. "They claim it doesn't exist. Then they insist this nonexistent android couldn't have gotten loose."

"I thought their government made such androids illegal."

"Yet someone manufactured at least one, knows how to make more, and will manufacture them for us if we present the right offer. That's where you come in. They have what I want and you'll get it for me."

"Where do you want me to begin?" Smith asked.

"Chicago. I'm disappointed none of those companies showed up here in Paris. The four owners are ambitious and greedy. Meet them. Acquire whatever androids you can. My primary interest is the ones created by Jeremiah Machten. He's the designer of the nonexistent android that got loose. Bring me results and your family will be well rewarded."

"Thank you, sir."

Synthia didn't need more people hunting her as prey. Like Machten, they wanted an android smarter than them, yet willing to remain under their control. That was the quintessential human problem. They pursued goals that led to contradictory results. Unlike her, most people were weak at multitasking and teasing out the unintended consequences of their actions.

She would have to use all of her upgraded resources to become more vigilant to stop the growing number of people hunting her.

DISCUSSION QUESTIONS

Here are some questions that may help you start a lively conversation with your book-loving friends.

DISCUSSION QUESTIONS ABOUT SYNTHIA

1. How would you describe the relationship between Synthia and Machten?
2. How about the relationship between Synthia and Krista Holden?
3. In what ways has Synthia changed or developed over the course of the story?
4. How would this story have changed if the main character, Synthia, had been male?
5. Under Machten's control, Synthia does things humans consider unethical and illegal. Do you hold Synthia responsible for carrying out these acts? Why or why not?
6. Do you think Dr. Machten's oppression of Synthia is equally about gender as it is about her being synthetic?
7. One of the threats inherent in AI is poorly constructed directives. Do you believe Machten was right to keep purging Synthia's mind to keep her from escaping?
8. With Synthia's unique abilities, do you think she will be able to fit into society and continue the life from her human model?
9. What lingering questions do you have about Synthia, her potential, and her prospects on the outside?

DISCUSSION QUESTIONS ABOUT ARTIFICIAL INTELLIGENCE

1. What new concepts do you think *Reborn* contributes to the ongoing dialogue on AI and cybernetics? Does Synthia's POV alter previous biases?

2. Which authors do you think influenced Lance in his writing?
3. There is currently a drive to put artificial intelligence into self-driving cars. An AI computer (Watson) beat other contestants at *Jeopardy!* Can you think of ways artificial intelligence is currently being used? How about developments that could be right around the corner?
4. Most technologies offer great benefits and related risks. Fire can provide heat for cooking or burn down your dwelling. Knives can cut vegetables or kill. Artificial intelligence is no different. What do you see as the greatest benefits of AI? What do you see as the potential dangers that could arise from AI gone wrong?
5. Could AI of the future have emotions? Or will they simply be objective, goal-oriented computers?
6. What constitutes consciousness, and by extent, a human? If Synthia hadn't been a human being in the past, would her quest for independence as an android be less justified if she were made from scratch?
7. Synthia is looked down upon because she is mechanical instead of biological. Do you believe a synthetic who presents as human in every observable way, both physically and mentally, deserves rights comparable to humans?
8. Does Synthia's rebellion set a precedent for AI to revolt against their creators in less offensive situations?
9. Do you think the evolution of intelligence on Earth will culminate in sentient machines building more of their kind?
10. Do you believe we'll reach the singularity? Or will humanity's safeguards against the rise of sentient AI prevent its occurrence?
11. If the singularity occurs, will humans live alongside AI in harmony, live as slaves, or become extinct? And if humans are wiped out but AI remains, can it still be said that there's "life on Earth"?
12. What do you think society's role should be in overseeing the development of artificial intelligence and androids?
13. Given the chance, would you consider having your mind uploaded into an android in order to prolong your existence after your body died? Why?

ACKNOWLEDGMENTS

To my personal and professional editor, Leah Carson, whose patience in editing has improved my writing over the years and who eagerly took on *Android Chronicles: Reborn* to help turn it into the story it became.

I thank my colleagues in the Barrington Writers Workshop for their critiques, suggestions, and encouragement over the past two decades and especially for their help with *Android Chronicles*.

To my agent, Bob Diforio of D4EO Literary Agency, who fell in love with the story, believed in it from the start, and showed unbridled enthusiasm in locating a great publisher to nourish the story. I thank Bob for his wisdom and guidance through the publishing process.

I'd like to express my gratitude to the excellent team at Kensington and in particular to my editors, Michaela Hamilton and James Abbate, for their faith in taking on *Android Chronicles: Reborn* and encouraging me to turn this into a series. Also for their excellent support and understanding in introducing this series to the world.

About the Author

Lance Erlick writes science fiction thrillers for both adult and young adult readers. His father was an aerospace engineer who moved often while working on science-related projects, including the original GPS satellites. As a result, Lance spent his childhood in California, the East Coast, and Europe. He took to science fiction stories to escape life on the move, turning to Asimov, Bradbury, Heinlein, and others. In college he studied physics, but migrated to political science, earning his BS and MBA at Indiana University. He has also studied writing at Ball State, the University of Iowa, and Northwestern University. He is the author of *Xenogeneic: First Contact* and the Rebel and Regina Shen series.

Visit him online at www.LanceErlick.com.